"I wanted to marry you the moment I saw you."

Diana stumbled, and Lord Brisbane's hand came up under her elbow to steady her. She stared at him. "You jest, surely." She could not believe him, of course, but an irresistible curiosity as to what he would say next stayed her. "You cannot have fallen in love with me, not in such a short time."

"Love at first sight."

Diana blushed. This conversation was the most peculiar she had had with anyone, but somehow her irritation was mixed heavily with a certain exhilaration. . . .

Miss Carlyle's Curricle

Karen Harbaugh

A SIGNET BOOK

SIGNET
Published by New American Library, a division of
Penguin Putnam Inc., 375 Hudson Street,
New York, New York 10014, U.S.A.
Penguin Books Ltd, 27 Wrights Lane,
London W8 5TZ, England
Penguin Books Australia Ltd, Ringwood,
Victoria, Australia
Penguin Books Canada Ltd, 10 Alcorn Avenue,
Toronto, Ontario, Canada M4V 3B2
Penguin Books (N.Z.) Ltd, 182–190 Wairau Road,
Auckland 10, New Zealand

Penguin Books Ltd, Registered Offices:
Harmondsworth, Middlesex, England

First published by Signet, an imprint of New American Library,
a division of Penguin Putnam Inc.

First Printing, June, 1999
10 9 8 7 6 5 4 3 2 1

Printed in the United States of America

ACKNOWLEDGMENTS

I would like to acknowledge Mr. William R. Robbins, curator of the Remington-Alberta Carriage Centre, in Cardiston, Alberta, Canada, for his assistance in finding information regarding specific harness equipment for curricles. I was amazed and pleased to find out about the resources, and the amount of information at this organization, and not the least, the generosity in sending me the information.

I would also like to acknowledge the help of my critique group in figuring out ways to do away with certain unfortunate characters in my book. In particular, I would like to thank Sherrie Holmes, who is the horse expert in our group, and whose breadth of knowledge and devious mind I profoundly appreciate.

Prologue

The horse screamed madly, going wild, and the sickening crash of the curricle's broken wood made Diana Carlyle freeze in horror where she sat on her horse, many yards away.

In the next moment she slipped off her own horse, hitting the ground in a run. She ran to the overturned curricle, reaching for her uncle, who was facedown on the ground. Others came with her—she did not know who, nor cared—and hands came together to turn over his lordship.

"A doctor," she cried. "Someone fetch a doctor, immediately!" She swallowed down bile at the sight of her uncle's bloodied face. "Uncle . . . Uncle Charles . . ." *Please God, let him be well,* she prayed. *He is like a father to me.* The shouts of grooms and spectators roared in her ears, but she ignored them. "Oh, please. Oh, please—you will be well, I know you will be. Please be well."

"Ain't likely, miss," a groom said near her.

She turned fiercely to him. "He *will* be well, you shall see! He only needs a doctor." She felt a touch on her hand, and she turned eagerly back to the man who had cared for her since she had been ten years old, had patched her knees, had taught her to ride and shoot as well as any man.

"Diana?" His voice was a whisper, and he stared at her, but seemed not to see her.

She clasped his hand. "I am here, Uncle."

He gasped, then groaned. "Tell your mother not to worry. I have taken care of her—and you, too."

"Yes, yes, I know, and I have been grateful for it, dear uncle. No one could have done better."

He moved his head, a negative motion. "No . . . no, in the will. You are provided for. The heir . . . not . . . he is . . . Tell Cecelia. . . ." His eyes closed, and the fitful rise and fall of his chest ceased.

"Uncle? Oh, no, please, no!" Diana frantically squeezed his hand, wanting to will her own life force into him. Impossible . . . Surely he was only resting? His hand was already lax in hers. It was not possible. She gazed at her uncle's face, a kind and fatherly face, now seeming to be asleep.

Diana still held his hand and somehow could not let go, for her fear had frozen into incomprehension—how could it be? He had, just moments ago, been all vivid life, laughing as he touched his whip to his horses, as his curricle bowled down the road, swiftly, sure to win the race. She had seen him and had cheered him on. It had been minutes, only minutes ago. She watched for one more breath. One more breath . . .

"Miss—miss, it's done, the good doctor is here—there's nothing more for you to do."

She turned at the voice . . . it was McKinney, the head groom. He had helped her up on her first pony, when she first came to Brisbane House. She stared at him, shaking her head slowly. "The doctor . . . he will make Uncle well, will he not?"

"Ah, miss . . . ah, miss." The groom's face creased in sorrow. "It's best you go to your mother."

She gazed at the doctor, who had lifted Lord Brisbane's hand and felt his wrist, then felt for the pulse at the neck. He shook his head, and a heavy ache pressed into Diana's heart. The doctor gazed back in return, looking grim.

"He . . . he is gone, Miss Carlyle," he said.

"No . . . no." A stubborn part of her did not want to believe him. She turned to the head groom. "The horses, McKinney, should you not be attending them?" Gunshot made her jerk back and drop her uncle's hand.

A tear fell down McKinney's weathered cheek. "There's naught to attend, Miss Diana." The sound of the gunfire and the sight of McKinney's sorrow forced the truth into Diana's mind at last, and she gasped as the dull ache in her heart twisted and turned sharp.

"McKinney's right, Diana."

She rose and turned—it was Sir James, her cousin. She hunched her shoulders against the familiar irritation she felt when he was about, and wished that they were not cousins so that he would have no cause to call her by her Christian name. He looked at her, a small crease between his brows, the rest of his face impassive. "I think your mother would want to hear the news regarding Lord Brisbane from you, rather than a servant."

He was right, and this fact irritated Diana even more. "Of course," she replied, and moved away. She gave a last glance at her uncle, and drew in a shuddering breath. "I will go, immediately."

She ran to her horse, still standing obediently where she left him, though his ears were pricked forward and he shifted his feet uneasily. McKinney helped her up, and she urged the horse to a gallop back to Brisbane House.

Diana worried her lower lip as she left her horse in the stables and hurried up the stairs of Brisbane House. How would Mama react to the news? Surely in her calm, sensible way, although of course she would be sorely grieved, for both of them had been fond of Uncle Charles, her father's brother. Mama had always been strong and full of good sense—she had been Diana's anchor when Diana's father had left them and eventually died, her father who had left them to starve until Uncle Charles had come to their rescue. Mama would know what to say, she would know how to deal with this terrible pain.

"Mama, it's I," Diana said when she knocked on the door of her mother's room, and at her mother's welcome, entered.

"Did your uncle win, Diana?" Mrs. Carlyle said cheerfully. She sat in her comfortable chair near the fire, setting a loop in her tatting. She looked up, then she frowned upon meeting Diana's eyes. "What is the matter, my dear?"

"Mama . . . it is very bad. . . ."

Mrs. Carlyle smiled slightly. "Nothing is as bad as we first think, Diana."

How was she to tell her? She stared, confused, at her mother, uncertain how to breach the assurance her mother always had about her, and not wanting to breach it. "No, listen—it—Uncle Charles—"

Mrs. Carlyle's smile disappeared, and she gazed steadily at Diana. "Yes? What is it?"

"There has been an accident—he was injured—the doctor said—"

Her mother paled. "He is hurt—but surely he will be better."

Diana swallowed and looked away. "No, Mama."

"The doctor cannot tell that in such a short time—"

She raised her eyes and stared at her mother, and her lip trembled. "Yes, Mama, he can."

Silence, then: "He isn't . . . he isn't—"

"Yes, Mama," Diana said, her voice a whisper.

The tatting dropped from Mrs. Carlyle's hands and she gazed around the room, blindly, her face bewildered. "But he cannot—I must see him. The servants—they must fetch cold cloths—he must be injured, only injured, and he could become fevered—"

"No, Mama," Diana said, making her voice louder though her closing throat tried to cut her off. "He—he is gone."

Mrs. Carlyle rose from her chair, the lace and the tatting bobbin falling unheeded to the floor. "Dear God," she said. Her eyes were wide, her face more pale than before, as if she looked at some horror in front of her, and not her own daughter. "I must see him. I shall change my dress and I shall see him, for . . . for it would never do for him to see me in this . . . this. . . ." She took two trembling steps toward the bell rope, lifted her hand to pull it, then collapsed to the floor.

"Mama!" Diana screamed. She ran to her mother's still form and fell to her knees, frantically feeling for a pulse—it was there. She breathed a sigh of relief and rose again to summon a servant. A sudden dizziness swept through her, but she clenched her teeth against it, pulling together all the self-discipline she had learned when she was a child and had felt the dizziness of hunger. She grasped the rope and tugged it.

Sitting down again, Diana carefully lifted her mother's head to her lap, and smoothed away the hair from her forehead. The dizziness had passed, and had turned into an iron wall around her heart. It seemed her life was crumbling, but she could not let it crumble her: her mother needed her, and no tears would help her or those she loved right now. She would cry later, when she had time, when her mother was well enough to put her arms around her and comfort her.

But somehow a line was crossed, a step taken on a journey. Diana took her mother's hand in hers and patted it, and remembered how her mother had done this to her, when she was hurt or sad. Mrs. Carlyle moaned softly, whispering Lord Brisbane's name, her voice sounding lost and lonely.

Diana sat up as straight as she could, while a rising sob lost the battle against the wall she had erected within herself—her numbness was firmly in place now.

A maid entered the room, cried out, and exclaimed, and helped get Mrs. Carlyle undressed and into her bed. Diana instructed the maid to find the doctor and have him come to her mother, then sat by the bed, still holding her mother's hand. When the doctor arrived, quickly, he assured her that Mrs. Carlyle merely needed rest.

Diana sighed and nodded, squeezed her mother's hand one more time, then went downstairs to call upon Mr. Southworthy, the vicar, to arrange the funeral.

Chapter 1

Diana Carlyle rode furiously through the fields and into the woods, her mare's hooves pounding the turf beneath her, pounding as hard as her heart. Cold needles of rain splashed her face, washing away tears of grief. She did not know how else to come to terms with the death of the man who had been, for all practical purposes, her father.

When she reached the wood, she more tumbled than descended from her horse, and leaned, gasping, against the old oak whose large, rambling roots she had often played amongst as a child. She had been happy that her Uncle Charles had brought her and her mother from London and from destitution after her own father had died. Her belly had been full after being empty for so long, and her mother's face had ceased being so pale and wan.

But now she felt an emptiness once again, and her mother's face was again pale and wan, but this time it was caused by a hunger in the heart, left bare and comfortless for the lack of Lord Brisbane's joyful presence.

It had happened so quickly—the accident, the funeral—that Diana felt as if she had gone through it in a disbelieving trance, holding both emotions and reality at bay to keep some semblance of self-control. She had managed to note her mother's bewildered gaze, and had held her hand through the funeral. But when the first shovelful of earth had been thrown upon the coffin, the sound of it had pierced the numbness that had covered her like a muffling shroud, and told her that her beloved uncle was indeed dead—suddenly, violently. She had drawn in a sharp gasp and shook her head in denial, and when the funeral was over, she had walked away as quickly as she could, running the last few steps to the house, and then up the stairs to her bedroom.

She had no comfort in the silence of her room; it reminded her of her first day in Brisbane House, how lonely she had felt in an unfamiliar place, and how her uncle had greeted her with kindness and a gentle pat on her cheek. She wanted to howl her grief, but her gentlewoman's training forbade it.

She had borne the stillness and inactivity for more than a few days—until now. Today, the will would be read, and she could not stand one more reminder of her uncle's death. Her mother's mention of the will had brought on an inner wailing of sorrow, and Diana knew she had to leave before she humiliated herself with an outpouring of tears.

She had run to her room and stripped off her black gown and had pulled on her riding habit, then run into the stables, ordering, in a low, harsh voice, the startled stable boy to saddle her mare. She had had neither voice nor breath for thanks when the job was done; she had hoisted herself astride on the horse, for that was the only way to ride as hard and fast as she wanted, away from death, away from grief.

But here she was, leaning and sobbing against the old oak, for grief had followed her like a Greek Fury, making her want to wail and scream in protest against the snatching away of an important person in her life. She groaned instead, and pounded the bark of the tree with her fists, for the years of discipline she had imposed on herself would not allow the wildness within herself to burst forth as wildly as it wished.

The rain fell. It soaked her riding habit, and soon Diana's sobs ceased. Perhaps because of the rain—the drops falling around her felt almost like the world itself wept, and it was an oddly comforting thought. She still leaned against the tree, sighing and catching her breath from the ride and the weeping, when a sound made her turn quickly around.

It was a man. He held the reins of a fine gray horse, and had walked up behind her, probably while she had leaned her head against the tree trunk. She had not heard him until this moment, perhaps because she had been so caught up in weeping, and because the rush of rain upon the leaves above had covered the sound of his approach. Hastily Diana wiped her cheeks with the back of her hand—a useless gesture, for the rain made them wet again.

"You seem troubled, ma'am. May I be of assistance?" he asked. His voice was low and husky, an intimate sound, and Diana blushed, feeling awkward at being caught in her grief.

She looked up at him. He was so tall that even though she was tall herself, she had to tip back her head. His brows were drawn together in apparent concern, and though she had opened her mouth to tell him to go away, a strong feeling of family likeness made her close her mouth again.

She narrowed her eyes, examining each feature. His hair was black and carefully combed from what she could see just beneath the brim of his beaver hat. It waved only slightly, unlike her own unruly yellow curls—Carlyle curls, her mother often said, for all the Carlyles had curly hair. His face was long and lean, with sharply cut cheekbones, unlike her own heart-shaped one. But perhaps he was related for all that, for the line of his jaw led down to a sharply cleft chin, his lips were fine and sensual, his nose straight and narrow, and he had the characteristic Carlyle eyebrows—thin and just a little slanted at the temples. Was he some relation? She did not remember ever meeting him, and she was certain she had met all of her cousins.

An amused expression flickered in his eyes. "I hope you approve?"

Diana glanced away, feeling her face grow warm, then gazed at him stiffly. "Not if you are trespassing, sir."

"I was asked to come to Brisbane House," the man said. "Lord Brisbane had some business to discuss with me." He smiled slightly. "Gavin Sinclair at your service, ma'am." He made an elegant bow, extending his booted leg at just the proper length from his greatcoat.

Unfortunately, the rain that had accumulated on the curled brim of his hat poured down and splashed upon his fawn pantaloons and into his boot. Diana hastily pressed her hand to her lips, smothering the giggle that threatened to burst out at his grimace. But then she recalled his words, that he wished to see Lord Brisbane, and her laugh died.

He sighed. "This is not a promising introduction, is it? One usually wishes to look one's best when presented to a lady, but I am afraid the weather prevents me from looking as I ought."

"I am not any better," Diana replied. She gestured at her sodden skirts. "Indeed, I must look like a bedraggled cat."

There was a short silence while Mr. Sinclair's gaze went over her. Then his eyes met hers, and she felt a slight shock—she had not expected his eyes to be so very green. None of her cousins had green eyes—they were brown, or hazel, or blue like her own. Mr. Sinclair had large green eyes, fringed with black lashes, but somehow they did not look girlish as they might have. No, they were heavy-lidded, sleepy, as if he had just arisen from bed—nonsense, of course.

As she continued to gaze at him, his eyes did not lose their heavy-lidded look, but became assessing instead, and his smile grew wide. She became uncomfortable—he was very tall, and she was not used to anyone towering over her, much less anyone smiling at her in such a way.

The chill of wet cloth against her skin suddenly made her conscious of how her riding habit must be clinging to her legs. She tried to pull her skirts away, fighting a rising blush. Stupid of her not to think sooner how indecent she must look!

"Not at all like a cat, bedraggled or otherwise, Miss—?" The smile was still on his face, and Diana wanted to remove it, quite forcefully. She disliked anyone looking at her like that.

"Diana Carlyle," she replied. "I live with—my mother at Brisbane House." She had almost said with her uncle; for one moment the memory of the funeral had left her while she talked to Mr. Sinclair.

Diana hunched one shoulder for a moment, a brief, protective gesture against the recent pain. She focused on the words he had just spoken; she felt no better. Perhaps he intended to imply some flattery, but she knew how false that could be. "I suppose you'd best be about your business, though you are too late if you wish to speak to Lord Brisbane," she said brusquely, knowing her voice sounded ill-mannered. She did not care at the moment, and a sudden resentment rose in her at his intrusion into her grief, even though she knew he no doubt meant it kindly. "Both of us will catch our death of cold if we do not find some shelter."

"Too late—?"

The words to tell him of her uncle's death stuck in her throat. She could only shake her head, walking quickly to her mare. She mounted it astride again, ignoring Mr. Sinclair's raised brows. "You may follow me if you wish," she said. "My way is shorter, though perhaps more muddy than the road you were following."

He gazed at her for a moment before he nodded, saying nothing, and mounted his horse as well.

Diana did not look back as she turned her horse toward Brisbane House once again. She relaxed her hold upon the reins, leaned forward in her saddle, and the mare leaped into a gallop across the fields. She wanted to be away from Gavin Sinclair, and his intrusiveness. Her conscience pricked her at the thought. The man had not really been intrusive, though his smile had been—well, she did not know what his smile had been, but she had not liked it. She wished to be alone, and she cared not whether Mr. Sinclair followed her or went by the road he had come upon. Indeed, she would be happy if his stay at Brisbane House was so short that she did not see him—or anyone for that matter.

Mr. Sinclair watched the young woman gallop away from him, but he only followed at a canter, avoiding as much mud as possible. She clearly did not want his company. His smile faded. It was just as well she did not. If all was as he hoped at Brisbane House, then he could go about his business as he wished. If it were not . . . His hand tightened on the reins, and his horse slowed to a walk. Well, he would find out soon enough.

Chapter 2

Diana carefully wiped the mud of the stables from her boots with a rag before she entered the house by a back door, but hesitated before going inside. She knew what she would find: no maids humming as they worked, no footmen whistling merry tunes as they fetched and carried, no smiles to accompany the quick curtsies or bows as she walked down the halls.

The house was silent, only her footsteps made any noise; the servants walked quietly and spoke in hushed whispers. Brisbane House was a house of mourning, after all. Diana shook with the sudden anguish she felt at the thought, and glanced at the black crepe draped almost everywhere. She wanted abruptly to tear it all down. Uncle Charles would have despised such displays.

If he were here, of course. Which he was not. Diana swallowed down the welling sob in her throat. No. She would not cry again. It would be better to think of her and her mother's possible futures. She could not be sure that the new Earl of Brisbane would be as good a man as her Uncle Charles, who saved her and her mother from hunger and want. And, she did not know if her uncle had made any provisions in his will. The will that would be read today, soon, this afternoon.

She went up to her room and changed her clothes, hesitating over the choice of colors. She should, of course, wear black as was proper, but her mind went back to the black already draped over almost everything in the house. No, not black. Brown. She would wear brown—it was dark enough for mourning, and should anyone eye her askance, she would stare them down. Diana smiled grimly, ignoring her maid's questioning look at her choice.

A pang of guilt went through her—she knew her mother would no doubt wear black for the proper length of time and more. She shook her head at herself. She was a selfish wretch, to be sure! She should have seen to her mother, and not have dashed off as she had done. But the pain of loss had seized her suddenly like a white-hot fire, and she had run away in a blind panic.

Dismissing the maid, Diana hurried down the hall to her mother's room. Though she thought her mother ought to be there, she was not sure at first; no response came on her first knock. But then a faint "Yes?" beckoned her, and she opened the door.

Mrs. Carlyle was indeed arrayed in black; the only white she wore was her cap. She sat by the window, looking out at the gray skies that had brightened a little after the earlier downpour. Her eyes lightened when she saw Diana, but her daughter could see the shadows beneath them nevertheless. Mrs. Carlyle said nothing for a moment, only shading her eyes as she looked out of the chamber window, though there was clearly no sunshine.

"It's an odd thing, Diana," she said softly. "Charles should have died in the midst of winter, not in spring." She moved to look at her daughter, and made no noise except for the sighing slip of her dress against the sofa. "Although I suppose the rain is appropriate for this day. He detested rain, you know. I believe he must have been the sunniest man I have ever known." Her lips lifted briefly, but she looked ghost-pale and weary, as if she had not slept at all. A vague uneasiness made Diana look at her mother sharply. Her mother had always had an affection for Lord Brisbane, a sisterly one, Diana had always thought. But now she wondered if there might have been something more. Though she herself mourned her uncle, she had fallen into her bed from an almost depressive fatigue and slept more deeply than usual, and—Diana remembered her mother had eaten little if nothing since Lord Brisbane's death—Diana's appetite had only been a little affected.

Mrs. Carlyle raised her brows. "Is there something amiss?"

Diana shook her head, smiling slightly. "No, Mama, other than worry over you. You have eaten very little since Uncle Charles . . ." Her voice faded for a moment. "Come, Mama, shall we have something to eat? I believe Cook has prepared a roast chicken and sweetmeats." Diana rose, still holding her mother's hand. "We can have it in the library, where it is quite bright and cheerful, and perhaps I can read to you from one of Mrs. Radcliffe's novels."

Mrs. Carlyle shook her head and smiled, gently pulling her hand away. "No, I am not hungry, my dear. Do you go down and eat, and I shall be with you later."

Diana squeezed her hand tightly. "No, Mama. You *must* eat something. Please. Dress yourself in black if you must, but . . . but if you die of starvation, I shall be very angry, for I don't think I can bear it if I lose you and Uncle Charles all in one week."

Mrs. Carlyle looked up at her and gave a reluctant laugh. "In which case, I will most certainly change my dress and come down. I can hardly wish you to become angry at me." She rose from the chair and touched Diana's cheek. "You are a dear—I am truly blessed that you are my daughter."

"Nonsense," Diana said, and smiled widely, and made her voice sound high and nasal. "I am a headstrong girl who will not find a rich husband and save both of us from abject poverty."

"Horrid girl!" Mrs. Carlyle said, emitting another reluctant laugh. "You could not help it that your Aunt Matchett is such a squeeze crab that she would outfit you in only the most drab colors and designs that did not suit your figure. And she did not even bother to try to get you into Almack's even though she was fully capable of it."

"Exactly. If I had been biddable, and less of a large lump of a girl, and less reluctant to leave you, she might have." Diana sobered. "I am sorry, Mama. First my lack of success during a London Season, and now this."

"You are not a lump!" Mrs. Carlyle said indignantly. "Indeed, I almost wish you had not gone to London, if that is the impression you received there. You are not to blame for your uncle's death—what nonsense! And, as to your Season, it's your Aunt Matchett's fault for not showing you off to advantage." She glanced at the clock, then waved at her daughter in a shooing motion. "I think if you are to eat Cook's meal when it is warm, you should go to the library now. I will follow shortly."

Diana met her mother's eyes, then nodded. Mrs. Carlyle wished to be alone. Though Diana was loath to allow it, she understood such needs, for she also valued solitude.

She reached the library at last, a well-lighted room with a warm southern exposure, heavy draperies at the window, and well-padded chairs and sofas—a comfortable place. It was one of her uncle's favorite refuges, for though he was an avid sportsman, he had loved books as well. She caught something, however—a movement, a sound—that made her stop at the threshold before stepping over. Her eyes scanned the room, and her brows drew together in a frown.

Feet. A pair of booted feet stuck out from one side of a sofa. It could be one of her cousins, but it was unlikely, for they always retired to their own rooms when they wished to rest—there was no reason for any of them to rest here. Certainly not one of the servants; the boots were gentlemen's boots, and besides, her mother had trained all the servants strictly. None of them would dare be caught sleeping in the library. Quietly, carefully, Diana walked around the sofa and sat down upon a chair opposite to it, staring at the man.

It was Mr. Sinclair. Her eyes scanned the clothes he wore, and she wrinkled her nose. He must be quite a distant relation—none of the Carlyles were dandies. Even in repose, the man's neckcloth was unrumpled, his fine blue coat was stretched neatly across his shoulders (padded, no doubt), his waistcoat was elaborately embroidered, his fawn trousers hugged admittedly muscular legs—although she had heard some men enhanced them with sawdust—and his boots bore a bright shine that could only have come from some secret polish dandies always claimed they had.

His long, elegant fingers, neatly folded upon his stomach, wore two rings, one an elaborate signet ring, the other quite plain. Diana wrinkled her nose again. Most men she knew—the men she preferred—wore no rings, or if they did, favored only one plain one. If this man was indeed related to the Carlyles—and she supposed he was if his facial features were any indication—he was certainly not like them in manner. Carlyles were robust and hearty men, favoring sport and the countryside, not like this lean, citified creature. She gazed at his highly polished boots again. How he managed to have cleaned them so well after his ride through the rain, she did not know. She cast a quick glance around the sofa—no, there was not even one drop of water on the rugs or the floor, much less the furniture.

"Alas, I still have not met with your approval," said his deep, soft voice, startling her.

Heat flared into Diana's cheeks, and she stood up abruptly, not able to look at him in embarrassment. "Please excuse me—I am not used to finding strangers lounging about in our house."

"Quite understandable," he replied, and rose with an easy grace from the sofa. "The servants had not quite made up my room yet. It seems my letter went astray, and I was not expected today. And I am afraid this sofa was much too tempting—I had a long journey, you see, and had become quite exhausted from it."

She looked up at him, once again impressed by how tall he was. He had to be well over six feet, for she was tall herself, embarrassingly so, she found when she had gone to London. She almost grimaced, remembering how oxlike she had felt in London next to the fashionable sylphs and smaller women. Her Aunt Matchett had tried to corset tightly every part of Diana, but could do nothing about her height, and it had been with considerable relief—in more ways than one—that Diana had come home, thrown off her corsets, and put on her short stays instead. She felt awkward in the presence of this man, but not so very large. Indeed, even without his greatcoat, he looked broader of shoulder than she thought when she first saw him.

He took her hand and bowed over it. "I am pleased to see you again, Miss Carlyle."

His hand was very warm upon hers—she realized suddenly that she wore no gloves, though why she should be conscious of such a thing when she rarely bothered with gloves at home, she did not know. Dismissing the thought of warm hands and the lack of gloves firmly from her mind, she looked into his eyes and found herself staring again. She felt suddenly that he was indeed quite pleased. It embarrassed her—well, he was still holding her hand, for one thing. She pulled away.

"May I ask what your business is, sir?" she asked abruptly. She sounded a little rude, and this flustered her even more. What *was* it about this man that discomposed her so? Perhaps it was that she did not like dandies, and so did not like the thought of him being pleased to meet her. His brows rose, and she was glad that perhaps she had put him off by her manner, though her mother would not have approved.

"I came at the request of Lord Brisbane." He looked at her intently for a moment. "Did he not tell you?"

"I am afraid . . ." Diana paused, tamping down the rising grief. "Lord Brisbane has—he is dead." It was a bald, bleak statement, but better she make herself face the fact now than pretend with sentimental words that it was not so.

A grim look flitted across Mr. Sinclair's face. "So I understand, and I am sorry to hear it. However, my business with him still stands."

For one moment there was silence, and Diana grew aware of an odd tension in the air. She looked at him and then . . . she could not say he changed precisely. The tension between them shifted and dissipated. Mr. Sinclair smiled at her, gave a little sigh, and his eyes caught sight of the mirror above the mantelpiece. He bowed slightly, walked to the mirror, then peered into it and frowned. "How inconvenient it is when one must choose between the set of one's neckcloth and resting to recover from fatigue," he said.

She barely refrained from wrinkling her nose again. "Of course," she said, more politely this time. Her stomach twinged a little, and she remembered that she hadn't requested breakfast yet. "Would you care for any refreshment? I am about to order my break—" She cast a glance at the clock on the mantelpiece. "Well, I suppose it's luncheon."

He turned and smiled widely now. "Yes, please, I would, and it is kind of you to offer."

Heat crept into her cheeks again, and Diana let out an impatient breath—she was blushing again, and she hated it. It was as if a cloak of awkwardness had wrapped itself around her, and once again she felt lumpish and too large, as she had in London. It was the way he looked at her, perhaps, with more attention than she liked. She pulled the bell rope and ordered the maid to bring luncheon—a substantial one, for she could not help thinking such a tall man would eat a great deal, even though he was quite lean.

Another glance at the clock made her wonder if her mother would come down for her meal. She bit back a sigh—she would very much like to go up to her mother, but manners dictated she not leave Mr. Sinclair alone to eat the luncheon she had just ordered, especially since she had already said she wished to have some. She had been abrupt and ungracious as it was.

When the luncheon arrived, Diana noted with a certain envy that Mr. Sinclair did indeed eat a great deal, and very precisely. She smiled slightly. He reminded her of the kitchen cat, Tom Mousekin, a large, sleek animal of impeccable elegance and finicky habits, who picked neatly at the scraps Cook would throw him, but never left any tiny sliver of food behind. That was the word for Mr. Sinclair, perhaps: sleek.

He was so even in his conversation: smooth, urbane, witty. He lounged upon the chair across from her with a dandy's negligent, lazy posture. He seemed to be familiar with most of the tales of the *ton,* or at least the ones she had heard when she had her come-out some years ago, and some others she had not heard—all frivolous, insignificant news. She glanced at him and for a moment her eyes met his. Yet, there was a *watching* manner about him, as if he were trying to search past the social smile she kept pinned on her face. Her polite smile turned wry. He was a cat, indeed, watching potential prey. Well, she was not prey, no mouse to be caught.

"Why are you here, Mr. Sinclair?" she said abruptly. This time she did not blush. Impatience rushed through her, wanting to be done with facades, for she felt suddenly sure that Mr. Sinclair was presenting just that. She had had little patience with pretense when she had been in London, and the relief she had felt in coming home was the relief of discarding the masks that society had placed upon her those torturous few months.

There was a short silence, while Mr. Sinclair continued to gaze at her. Then he straightened in his chair, and though his legs were still casually crossed, she could not feel that the word "frivolous" any longer applied to him. His hands slid to the edge of the arms of the chair and his long fingers tapped out a short rhythm, but his eyes never left her.

"I assume the will is to be read soon?" he asked.

"Yes," Diana replied. "This afternoon, in this room—" She glanced at the clock on the mantelpiece. "In about a quarter of an hour."

He nodded. "I am here for the reading of the will."

"Yet, if I am not mistaken, you did not know of Lord Brisbane's death until today." She frowned. "Do not toy with me, Mr. Sinclair."

He smiled widely. "I see it would be useless to do so." He picked up a cup and drained it of tea. "But it is true. I was contacted some weeks ago by Lord Brisbane regarding his will."

A maid entered the library to clear away the dishes, but Diana forestalled her when she reached for the tea tray and requested more hot water and tea. "More tea?" Diana asked Mr. Sinclair, managing to hide her skepticism. When he nodded, she poured the rest of the tea into his cup, then gestured the maid to take away the pot. "Are you a solicitor, then?"

"No, I am not. His lordship wished to bequeath something to me, and was insistent I come here to discuss it with him."

"Then you *are* related to us." She gazed at him curiously, and wondered why she had not heard of him before.

Mr. Sinclair smiled again. "I suppose I must be."

Diana nodded. "So I thought. You have a look of the Carlyles."

"Do I? I suppose you must have discerned it when you examined me an hour ago."

She winced. "I . . . I was rude, I suppose." She glanced away. "I apologize."

"I did not mind it. Naturally, you were curious," he replied, and his voice was gentle, giving her an excuse. She took the excuse, nodding, and felt relieved.

Diana was about to ask him more questions about his presence, but the door opened, and her mother entered, followed by her cousins, and then her uncle's solicitor, Mr. Barrett.

She had two distant cousins, Sir James Rackbury and Mr. Lionel Southworthy, who looked so very much alike that anyone would think them brothers. But there was a space of fifteen years between them, and they were unlike in nature as a stick from a stone. Sir James Rackbury cast her a smiling glance from his dark eyes, then his humor fled as he caught sight of Mr. Sinclair. Sir James's brows rose as he looked at Diana again—perhaps he wondered at this intrusion from a stranger. Certainly she did!

Mr. Southworthy gazed at Mr. Sinclair curiously, as if in recognition—and there, she was right to see a family resemblance for it was clear to her that the vicar did. She introduced Mr. Sinclair to them, and the vicar stared even harder, his face seeming to pale. But he was a studious man, more often than not within doors with his books, and so was naturally fair-skinned. She smiled at them, then sat down again.

Diana shifted uneasily in her chair. She had liked Sir James when she first met him—he had arrived at Brisbane House a year ago after long journeys elsewhere, and he was very much a Corinthian. She approved of this far more than Mr. Southworthy's occasional pious censure of her fondness for sport. She supposed Mr. Southworthy could not help it; he was the vicar, after all. Perhaps a vicar must disapprove of anything that might seem a threat to a virtuous woman, since the vulnerability of women to wickedness always seemed to be the point of the various religious tracts he gave her.

Sir James, however . . . she squashed her feelings of discomfort. He was an amiable fellow, to be sure, and most ladies in the area seemed very much to find his intense vitality attractive. Further, it was silly to judge a man by the way he handled a horse. Sir James was a superb sportsman overall; it was not his fault if he could not handle horses as easily as she did. Indeed, even Vicar Southworthy was a better horseman, though Diana would never tell either man so, since her mother had said it was not at all politic to mention it to them.

Diana allowed herself a small, rueful smile. Her mother once said that Diana judged people too harshly on their competence in sport, and it was true. She had tried very hard to rein in her judgments, but her sojourn in London during the Season had only reinforced her beliefs about people's natures: that sporting people were much less prone to present a false face to society than those addicted to fashion. But Mrs. Carlyle was right, and Diana tried her best not to be so prejudiced.

It was with a good grace, then, that she took yet another tract from Mr. Southworthy, and nodded to Sir. James. The vicar flicked another curious glance at the newcomer, but Mr. Sinclair did nothing but smile and nod as they passed him.

Mr. Barrett went to the large table that had been set earlier near the library windows. The solicitor looked uneasy, and Diana felt a little sorry for him; he was a small, neat man, perhaps uncomfortable with what must be the most emotional and upsetting part of his duties. He took out a white pocket-handkerchief, and carefully polished his spectacles before putting them on his nose again, then drew out some papers from a small leather case. Slowly he spread them out, sighed, then looked at the black-clad company before him.

"I regret I must be present at such a sad occasion," he began, then cleared his throat. "But Lord Brisbane was meticulous and careful in all his estate matters, and of course it is my duty as his solicitor to carry out his wishes to the last detail." He ran a hand over the papers—a nervous gesture. "Unpleasant. Most unpleasant," he muttered. "I shall go through the smaller bequests first, and then we shall proceed to the, er, more important ones."

It took a long time. Diana was glad that she had ordered more tea, otherwise she would have fallen asleep at the tediousness of it all. She glanced at her mother, clearly abstracted and not paying attention to Mr. Barrett's droning voice, and then at Mr. Sinclair. She could not tell if his sleepy look was his natural expression, or if he felt indeed as drowsy as she. Sir James's usual intensity had an overlay of boredom, while Mr. Southworthy gazed dutifully at Mr. Barrett.

The solicitor cleared his throat, catching Diana's attention once again. "And to my niece, Miss Diana Carlyle, the best sportswoman I have had the good fortune to know, I bequeath my racing curricle, for I know she will take care of it to the best of her abilities."

Diana's hand shook, spilling tea from the cup she held. She put down the cup, blindly, almost upsetting it, before Mr. Sinclair gently took it from her hand and set it in the saucer. "The curricle?" she asked.

"Yes, Miss Carlyle." The solicitor looked at her sympathetically. "It is to do with as you wish."

She stood suddenly, the sensation of her wringing hands the only thing that kept her from total numbness. "Is it not wrecked? I had thought—since my uncle—" Her throat closed, and she could only stare at the solicitor, unable to speak, her legs shaking.

Mr. Barrett gazed at her kindly. "No, Miss Carlyle, it has only some slight damage to the body, and the wheel and axle need some repair, but it can be mended in a very short time. I understand it is an unusual vehicle—"

"Unusual? It is a scandal that such a vehicle be given to a young lady!" Mr. Southworthy cried. "A perch phaeton, at best, but a curricle?" His lips pursed together in disapproval. "Especially when the vehicle was the cause of such a tragedy."

"What—I don't—A scandal?" Diana's numbness faded to bewildered pain as her gaze fell on Mr. Southworthy. The pain quickly gave rise to anger. "A scandal that my uncle has done me the honor of giving me his curricle? That the best sportsman in this county believed me to be worthy of it?"

"With all respect due to Lord Brisbane," Sir James said, "I believe the speed at which he was going in the curricle and some unfortunate rut in the road caused his accident. An excellent whip, his lordship, but even excellence can fall before mischance." There was an edge to his tone, as if he believed Lord Brisbane's judgment to be faulty, or his abilities less than excellent.

Diana turned to Sir James and her hands turned into fists, and her voice rose. "Whatever you might think of Lord Brisbane or his abilities, I am honored—*greatly* honored—to have received this gift."

"Diana!" her mother's voice was sharp with reproof.

"I won't—*won't*—have them saying anything against Uncle Charles, Mama! Anything!" Diana cried passionately.

"Diana!" her mother said again, frowning.

Diana felt her hand taken gently and she turned to find Mr. Sinclair standing near her and nodding sympathetically. "You must admit, Miss Carlyle, that it is a most unusual bequest. It is not many young ladies who are judged capable of driving a curricle, and even more unusual is the thought of a young lady owning one. Obviously your uncle knew differently. However, you cannot expect such a bequest not to startle anyone. Indeed, am I mistaken in thinking you, too, were surprised?"

Diana stared at him for a moment, caught by the look of understanding and command in his eyes. A glance at her mother made her feel ashamed at her loss of control. She shook her head slowly, her face heating. "No, you are right, Mr. Sinclair. I was not expecting it. I have been overset—I was fond of my uncle." She turned to her mother. "I am sorry, Mama. My outburst was inexcusable." She cast an embarrassed glance at Mr. Bartlett. "Please, sir, do go on. My apologies for the interruption."

The solicitor nodded kindly. "Understandable, Miss Carlyle. This is a grievous time, to be sure." He looked over his spectacles at Sir James and Mr. Southworthy, both of whom seemed to be looking elsewhere.

Diana looked at Mr. Sinclair gratefully. "Thank you, sir," she murmured.

"It was nothing, I assure you," he replied. "It must be difficult for both yourself and your mother."

Her mother—shame overcame Diana, for in her outburst she had not thought of her mother, only of herself. She cast an apologetic look at Mrs. Carlyle across the room, and saw her mother nod in acceptance, then saw her smile slightly as she looked from Diana to Mr. Sinclair. Diana became conscious of his hand still holding hers, and she pulled away, sitting hastily on her chair.

Mr. Bartlett cleared his throat again and adjusted the spectacles on his nose. He peered at the papers before him. "There is an additional bequest, Miss Carlyle, one I am sure shows your uncle's concern for your welfare." The solicitor smiled encouragingly at her. "It says, 'I also bequeath to Miss Diana Carlyle a stipend in the amount of seventy-five pounds per annum, and a dowry of an additional twenty thousand pounds per annum upon her marriage to the next Earl of Brisbane."

"What?!" Diana stared at Mr. Bartlett, amazement and horror hitting her at once. "But he said—I cannot—this is preposterous! How could he think—oh, no. Oh, dear heaven." The bequest was an incredible fortune, but the conditions felt like a prison. She groaned and briefly covered her face before bringing her hands down, clenched, into her lap.

Mr. Bartlett looked more uncomfortable than ever. "I am sure he meant it for the best, Miss Carlyle. He did mention the

London Season you had, and how, er, none of the gentlemen seemed to be to your taste. I suppose he wished to secure your future before he departed this world."

She thought back to the words her uncle had spoken to her before he died, that he would provide for her. She had not thought on it until now, for she had always depended on her uncle to know what was best for her; had he not come to her and her mother's rescue so many years ago? She had never protested his directives before—having a governess instead of going off to school, for example, or learning how to polish tack and curry a horse, even though such things were normally left for servants; she had generally found his orders sensible if not always pleasant. She had expected she would have nothing to protest now, either.

But this! She cast a quick glance at Sir James and felt a little ill when he grinned at her. She thought of the stipend she'd been bequeathed—it would be enough to keep her in clothes if she were frugal enough and stayed at Brisbane House—but the dowry amounted to a fortune. It was very clear Uncle Charles wished her to marry and be the next Countess of Brisbane. He had been like a father to her . . . and she supposed this was the best way he could think of to give her the title, since he had no children of his own. She groaned again. She would refuse to marry, that was all there was to it. Glancing at Sir James, she saw his amused expression and she clenched her hands tighter—it was better than giving her tongue free rein to say what was on her mind.

Uncle Charles had provided for her mother as well, for Mrs. Carlyle also received a stipend of seven hundred pounds per annum, and a provision should she marry again as well. Neither bequest was a fortune, except for Diana's dowry. However, her and her mother's combined income was perhaps enough for them to live comfortably, if modestly. Indeed, Diana thought, casting another quick glance at Sir James, she would prefer to forego the fortune, for though she was sure that her uncle had meant well, she did not think Sir James would make a satisfactory husband, despite his popularity with the ladies. Indeed, it was precisely that popularity that would keep him from being an ideal husband. Attractive or not, she had no faith in the idea that a rake could make a good one, for old habits died hard. A fortune was not worth a lifetime of misery. And though Sir James was known to be a successful gamester of extraordinary luck, she did not believe such luck typically lasted a lifetime.

"And finally," Mr. Bennett read, " 'I hereby bequeath to my heir, Gavin Sinclair, the grandson of my eldest aunt Mrs. Elizabeth Sinclair, she who was born Lady Elizabeth Carlyle, daughter of the Fifth Earl of Brisbane—' "

"What?" Sir James rose swiftly from his chair, staring hard at the solicitor. "Who is this Gavin Sinclair? *I* have never heard of him before!"

Mr. Bennett looked at the man over his spectacles. "Mr. Gavin Sinclair," he said patiently, "as the grandson of the late Mrs. Sinclair is the next Earl of Brisbane, since the title goes to 'heirs male whatsoever.' Unusual, I know, but the first earl was not known to have been particularly, er, prolific, and King Charles II wished to bestow a great honor upon him and his family for the great deal of work he did to help restore the King to the throne." He frowned as he looked at each one of them. "Did not his lordship mention this to you?"

"So that's what he wanted to see me about," Mr. Sinclair said softly, looking sleepier than ever and sinking deeper into the sofa cushions. "Well, well."

Chapter 3

Diana turned and stared at Mr. Sinclair, who continued to lean back in his chair and regard Mr. Bennett with the same lazy expression he had worn throughout the reading of the will. Mr. Sinclair the heir, and not Sir James? She glanced at her mother, but Mrs. Carlyle only looked at her calmly before she turned her interested gaze to Mr. Bennett.

"No, he did not inform us," Mr. Southworthy said, his face looking pinched, almost ill. "This is most irregular."

"A pity," Mr. Bennett replied. "However, his lordship was not one, usually, to reveal his intentions or his reasons to anyone regarding his estate."

"A pity, indeed," Sir James drawled. He turned to Mr. Sinclair. "Cousin, my congratulations."

Mr. Sinclair inclined his head. "And to you, cousin, my condolences."

Sir James laughed lightly. "One does not care to be choused out of an inheritance, to be sure. But I am a gamester, Mr. Sinclair, and am familiar with the risks of play."

"But this *is* an inheritance," Mr. Sinclair said gently.

For a moment Diana thought Sir James had cast him a sharp look, but it was gone, and she was sure she had imagined it, for Sir James merely shrugged.

"All life is a game, sir, and has its risks," he said.

"Of course you are right," Mr. Sinclair replied genially. "Then, too, you are next in line, are you not? Who knows what card fate will turn, after all."

"You are a gamester, then, too?" Sir James asked.

Mr. Sinclair shuddered. "No, indeed I am not. I don't care to take risks with games of chance."

Sir James smiled slightly, and if his expression held a little contempt, Diana could not blame him. Mr. Sinclair was clearly a fashionable fribble, slothful to the point of not even caring to put anything to the risk. Slothful at best—perhaps even afraid, although she would not hand out such a judgment as to call him coward unless she saw clear evidence of it.

But if Mr. Sinclair noticed Sir James's contempt, he showed no sign of it. He merely sank further into the chair cushions, and his expression became more sleepy than ever as Mr. Bennett finished the reading of the will.

The door to Mrs. Carlyle's dressing room burst open, and Diana hurried in. "Mama, you *must* tell me—did you know that Mr. Sinclair is Uncle Charles's heir?"

Mrs. Carlyle sat on a chair near the window, her workbasket of tatting threads open beside her. She gazed at her daughter and raised an eyebrow disapprovingly. "I don't think I said you could enter, my dear."

Diana gave her mother a mischievous glance and sat on a chair near her. "I know, but you would have let me regardless, because you did see how curious I was, and I *know* you know something about the bequests, so of course you must have expected I would hound you until I found out."

"Terrible girl! Where you learned your manners, I do not know." But Mrs. Carlyle did not hide her smile when she looked down at the lace she was tatting on her lap. "Oh, very well, then! I knew there was a possibility that Sir James was not."

"Did Uncle Charles tell you?"

Sorrow passed over her mother's face, then she shook her head and made another loop with the tatting bobbin. "Not precisely. I knew there was a possibility that Elizabeth Sinclair's grandson was alive, but Charles did not know for certain. It was only in the last year or so that your uncle thought he had located him."

"Thought?"

Mrs. Carlyle frowned slightly. "I had always believed your uncle should have investigated further a long time ago—I told him he should, ever since his wife died many years ago. I suppose he felt too . . . lost to have thought of it." She pressed her hand upon Diana's. "Charles did love Emily very dearly, and never, never blamed her for their lack of children. Not like—" Her voice faded and tears formed in her eyes. She brushed them away with the back of her hand, then gratefully took the handkerchief Diana gave her. Diana bit her lip—she well knew that had she been male, she would have been Uncle Charles's heir, and it was something she remembered her father saying to her before he died. But she was not, and so the line would continue through the descendants of her great-aunt, Elizabeth Sinclair.

"He was a good man, love," her mother continued. "He should have married again, but I think he did not have the . . . the heart to do so." She bent her head to her tatting again, concentrating on a number of stitches and loops before she looked up again. "But I suppose my urging made him try to find his heir at last."

Diana gazed at her mother, uneasiness filling her. Her mother looked at her calmly, tired and worn with grief, but there was nothing else in Mrs. Carlyle's expression to explain the uneasiness. Diana gave herself a mental shake. Well, life had been uneasy and unsettling altogether—what else could she expect when someone so well liked as her uncle had just passed away?

"I am surprised Mr. Southworthy did not know of it," Diana remarked.

Mrs. Carlyle smiled slightly. "You know how your uncle did not care to discuss his matters until they were dealt with. For all anyone knew, Mr. Sinclair was dead. Your great-aunt did not get along with the rest of our family, for she made a love-match with a gentleman far below her in rank, and your great-great-grandfather would not speak to her. There had been some mention of her son—or was it the current Mr. Sinclair himself?—being lost at sea. It clearly must have been the elder Mr. Sinclair." She looked out the window for a moment. "I suppose no one thought to follow the course of their lives, since there had always been a direct male heir until now."

"Poor Sir James! I think he must have been sorely disappointed to find he had not inherited," Diana said. "But he comported himself well, I believe, considering the surprise."

Mrs. Carlyle gave her a sharp look. "He is to be commended on his behavior, I suppose, for I am sure he was quite dismayed—he has been living on the expectation for years."

"I do not see how he could have been," Diana said. "He is a very good gamester and he has won wagers hand over fist for ages. They say he cannot lose."

"Is that so?" Her mother raised her brows. "And where did you hear this? In the stables?"

"You must know that I could never have heard it from Aunt Matchett." Diana grinned.

"Hmph. However, I am sure you listened to all the gossip in London when you were there, for I have commanded McKinney *not* to tell you stable gossip."

"Yes, and the stableboys are more forthcoming than McKinney."

Mrs. Carlyle burst out laughing. "Odious girl!"

"Well, Mama, I had nothing to do *but* listen to gossip in London, I assure you! It is the most tedious place in the world aside from the plays and the music."

Her mother shook her head, smiling wryly, clearly not about to argue the point, and continued her tatting. Diana gave her a sidewise look, frowning.

"Mama, did you also know that Uncle Charles wished me to marry Mr. Sinclair?" she asked abruptly.

Mrs. Carlyle sighed before looking up from her lacework. "I did know he considered you as close as a daughter, and had told me many times he wished you had been his son, so you could inherit the title. I suppose this was the closest he could come to do just that."

"But Mr. Sinclair, a stranger . . ."

The corners of her mother's lips turned upward for a moment. "Nothing says he must remain a stranger, and for all we know he might not be averse to the idea."

"Oh, Mama, do be serious! You *must* see how utterly impossible this is!"

"Your uncle did not think so."

"With all due respect to Uncle Charles, I have recently determined he was either not in his right mind, or he was surely far more fallible than either of us gave him credit for."

"Diana!" Mrs. Carlyle said reprovingly.

"Very well, he was in his right mind, but *very* fallible in that he did not foresee my justifiable consternation at finding he had arranged a marriage for me without even consulting me."

Her mother glanced at her and shifted uncomfortably in her seat. "I did tell him that you might object—"

"Ha! So he *did* tell you!" Diana leaned forward in her chair. "Why did you not—"

Mrs. Carlyle held up her hand. "I wanted to tell you, but he pledged me to silence. I felt I had to keep his confidence, my dear. You know your uncle always had his reasons—very good ones—for his decisions. I trusted he had a good reason this time, as well."

"Perhaps he did, but would it have been too much for him to reveal it to either of us?" Diana said bitterly. "I tell you, I shall not marry Mr. Sinclair—he is nothing but a fribble!"

"You say that as if it were some grave sin, Diana," her mother said reprovingly. "It is not. You do not know the man at all, so you cannot know what virtues he has—"

"Or has not," Diana said swiftly.

"Pshaw!" Mrs. Carlyle said, her voice impatient. "You have only just met the man; you judge too quickly."

Diana gazed at her mother for a long moment, while the older woman bent her head over her lacework. "Why do you wish me to marry this man, Mama?"

Mrs. Carlyle raised her eyes to her daughter's, gazing at her earnestly. "You will be safe, my love."

"Safe? What do I have to fear?"

"Poverty. The chance that you will no longer be welcome at Brisbane House at some time, should the next Earl of Brisbane marry another. The chance that you will marry an irresponsible man, a wastrel."

Diana stared at her mother. It had briefly occurred to her they might have their own place to stay, but now the idea had been spoken, it shook her to her bones to think she might no longer live in this house. "But . . . but how do I know this Mr. Sinclair is not a wastrel as well?"

"Your uncle would not have put him in his will if he thought he was," Mrs. Carlyle said confidently. "He thought it best you marry the next earl, which is why the stipend he bequeathed you is so small, and the dowry such a fortune."

Diana swallowed down the tight feeling in her throat, but it did no good: she felt as if her life were slowly being squeezed from her, or at least the freedom to which she was so accustomed. She did not wish to wed a stranger. But there was one hope, however, and she smiled grimly.

"What my uncle did not foresee was Mr. Sinclair could easily refuse to marry me. He seems to be well off and may not need my dowry to run the estate, despite the pittance bequeathed to him."

Mrs. Carlyle's expression was for a moment uncertain, but she shook her head. "I am sure your uncle has accounted for it."

Diana gazed at her mother, wondering how she could be so certain . . . perhaps her mother had always relied this heavily on Uncle Charles's opinions and decisions, and Diana had not, until now, seen it. Certainly, she had had absolute trust in her uncle's decisions—until now, now that it was so contrary to her wishes. She watched her mother set yet another loop in her tatting, a quick and sure movement, her head bent over her work. She could not see her mother's face or the expression on it. Diana felt suddenly that perhaps her mother did not want her to see. Anger rose in her—it was no use talking to her mother, for it was clear that she would tell her nothing . . . for now.

Diana gazed in silence out the window while she tried to quell her anger. It was still cloudy, but had not rained for a few hours. Perhaps she could go out on her horse again, or in a carriage. . . .

Her thoughts came immediately to the curricle she had inherited, and she shuddered. It was hers now. She had driven it before . . . before her uncle died, and he had told her that she was the best whip he had ever seen. He had been proud of her, and she had wished then that he had been her father. It could not be, however, but there was one thing she could do: have the curricle repaired and drive it as he had taught her. It mattered not that it was unusual for a woman to drive such a vehicle. Her uncle had given it to her, and he had meant her to drive it.

She stood up abruptly. "Mama, I am going down to the stables to look at the curricle."

Mrs. Carlyle looked up from her work, her eyes widening. "Is this wise?"

Diana gazed at her quizzically. "I am not afraid, Mama. There is nothing it can do to me, after all."

"But it needs repair . . ."

Diana smiled slightly. "Of course I'll not drive it! I am merely going to look at it. Perhaps I shall talk to McKinney about the repairs it needs."

Mrs. Carlyle looked worried. "I do not know what seized Charles to bequeath it to you. It is not proper or safe."

Diana rolled her eyes. "Oh, Mama! How is it you don't question Uncle's judgment where my marriage is concerned, but you question this? You know I have driven it any number of times. And what do you think will happen to me in the stables? That the carriage will somehow fall upon me? It can do nothing while it is sitting there in the stables, I assure you!"

Her mother still looked worried, and Diana took her hands and pressed them. "What, do you think Uncle Charles might be haunting it in some way? I would welcome seeing him again, I believe."

Mrs. Carlyle smiled slightly. "As would I, for I am sure if he were a ghost he would be caring for us still. No . . . I am a silly woman to be sure. It must be as you say. Do go, then, and see what you can find out from McKinney."

Diana turned to leave, but her mother's hand stayed her. "Did you see where Mr. Sinclair went before we left the library?"

"No, why?"

"We cannot be sure he will let us stay here at Brisbane House, you know, and I think it best to find out whether he means for us to stay or go."

"So soon?" Diana asked. Her mother merely looked at her gravely and said nothing, and Diana knew it was necessary. "I . . . I don't remember. I suppose he might be in his room—certainly he looked as if he might fall asleep where he sat during the reading of the will."

Her mother nodded. "I will find him and ask."

"Will you need me, do you think?"

Mrs. Carlyle smiled. "No, it is not necessary. Do go to see the curricle. Mr. Sinclair seems a kind gentleman, perhaps enough to house us while we find a place to settle, at least."

Diana nodded slowly, and with a kiss on her mother's cheek, proceeded down to the stables.

When Diana reached the stables, she saw that they had a new stablehand. She smiled at him briefly before saying, "Where is Bob Staples?"

The thin, awkward youth smiled shyly and took off his hat, ducking his head. " 'E got ill, miss, did Bob. Started squeaking about 'is blinkers, and McKinney sent 'im 'ome, and Bob sent me to take 'is place—I'm 'is cousin, miss, beggin' yer pardon."

"His eyes?" Diana frowned. "I am sorry to hear it—is a doctor seeing to him? I hope it is not serious."

The stablehand rubbed his forehead in thought. "I dunno, miss. But me aunt 'as got summat to fix it."

Diana fished in her pocket for some coins and pressed them into the youth's hand. "Here—please give this to your aunt, in case Bob needs to see a doctor. Bob's a good young man, and I would like to have him return." The youth's face fell, and she continued hastily: "Though I'm sure you'll do good work and prove yourself capable—" She paused, for she realized she did not know his name.

"Nate, miss, Nate Staples," he said.

"Nate, then. I am sure the new Lord Brisbane will need more servants, and if you show yourself to be a hard worker, I can recommend you," she said, recklessly committing Mr. Sinclair's—she bit her lip—the new earl's resources to the upkeep of the stables. But she had continued supervising them as she had when her uncle was alive, and the earl must know of it by now. However, he had said nothing to stop her.

Nate's face brightened and he bobbed his head in a respectful bow. "I'd be grateful if you could, thank you, miss."

Diana smiled, then proceeded into the carriage house just behind the stables.

The curricle sat propped up and leaning to the side, a little like a boat that had been tossed ashore against rocks after a storm. The fine wood of the carriage body was marred from the overturning that day of the accident; she could see the clawlike scars where it had been dragged for a short distance after it fell.

Fell . . . She closed her eyes, blocking out the sight of the damage, but it only brought horror-tinged images of how the horse had gone wild, and how the carriage had overturned—slowly, it seemed in her memory, though she knew it must have been too quick to let her uncle jump free.

Tentatively, she put her hand out as if the curricle were a wild creature with fur and teeth. Silly, of course. She pressed her hand firmly on it. The wood was smooth and cool to the touch, rough where it had been scored by the rocks in the road. It is just a curricle, Diana thought, a carriage. Not a deadly monster ready with gaping jaws to tear and destroy. Her mother clearly felt as if it were, and for that reason would not go near the carriage house, at least for now.

Diana could understand her mother's feelings; the accident

had torn a hole in the fabric of their lives and it was not a thing so easily stitched up. But she had other memories: memories of her uncle handing her the reins, and how nervous she had been, yet happy and proud that he had such confidence in her; the first tentative lurch of the carriage; and finally after several practice drives, the thrill of increasing speed over the newly macadamed road.

She could not look upon the curricle with horror when she also remembered so much joy. Her uncle had felt confident enough in her abilities to bequeath it to her. She would have it repaired immediately, perhaps try it out a few times to make sure it drove as well as it used to, and out of respect for her mother's grief, sell it. Perhaps, if she and her mother could still stay at Brisbane House, she could use the money to buy a less expensive and more sedate carriage. A gig, for example. She grimaced at the thought of "sedate" then grinned. A high-perch phaeton, perhaps. Not as sporting as a curricle, but certainly not sedate, and certainly quite fashionable. There! That should keep her family from criticizing, and she could turn her thoughts to other matters.

Such as the very annoying and embarrassing stipulation in the will regarding her *possible* marriage to Mr. Sinclair—or rather, Lord Brisbane. She thought of the man who wore the title, and it sat ill on her tongue. Such a frivolous man could not be worthy of it, or at least not as worthy of it as her uncle had been.

"Miss Carlyle—"

Diana jumped, then gasped as she quickly turned, for her hand caught hard on a large splinter of broken wood. It hurt, even with the strong kid riding glove she wore, and she cradled it in her other hand.

It was Mr. Sinclair—Lord Brisbane. He raised his brows. "You have injured yourself . . . because I have startled you, I am sure." He took her hand and bowed over it, but did not release it. "May I look at it?"

"You are not a physician," Diana said, then gasped again at the pain as she tried to pull away.

"True, but I know something of injuries and of healing." A grim look settled about his mouth for a moment, and Diana wondered how he had come to know of such things. She relaxed and allowed her hand to remain in his.

He took off his gloves, then slowly, carefully, her glove, his head bent a little, his eyes concentrating on her hand. Diana glanced at him, glad he was not looking at her, for she felt . . . a strange unease, a shiver that should have made her want to pull away from him, but did not. If he had looked at her she did not know what he would have seen on her face—embarrassment, perhaps, but not exactly that. She pressed her lips together firmly—how silly she was!

The earl turned over her hand and pressed it gently, then looked at her questioningly. "Does it hurt?" he asked.

"A little."

He slid his thumb a bit, a caressing movement, catching on her skin; his thumb seemed slightly callused. He pressed down, a little harder.

"Ah!"

"It hurts there, then." He took her hand between his, rubbing lightly. "Bruised, I believe, but not badly." His rubbing became more firm, and Diana could not help staring at how the long, elegant fingers of one hand smoothed over the palm of hers, while his other cradled the back of her hand like an egg in a nest. The strokes of his fingers were hypnotic, moving over the hollow of her palm, up and around the pads just at the base of her fingers and her thumb. She closed her eyes, letting out a slight breath, her hand relaxing, limp, at last.

"Is that better?"

Her eyes shot open. "Yes, of course—that is, yes," she stammered. He still held her hand; she quickly pulled it away.

He smiled widely, then grew somber, but she could not help thinking he was smiling still, somehow. She felt heat rise in her face and she turned away to the curricle. "Thank you," she said, remembering her manners.

"You are welcome," Lord Brisbane replied. He tapped the curricle with a finger. "It must have been a magnificent carriage. I can see, here, how it was joined." He ran his fingers over a seam of the carriage body, and Diana thought of how those fingers had moved over the palm of her hand. "This is very fine workmanship."

She drew in a resolute breath and let it out, determined to banish the odd, unsettled sensation that had seized her. "Yes," she replied. "My uncle always went to the finest carriage makers in London. To buy anything less, he believed, was a false economy. A carriage made with the best workmanship and parts will last at least twice as long as one of the inferior make—" Her breath caught. Except for this one, she thought.

"Except for this one," he said quietly, and her eyes flew to his, startled that his words had echoed her thoughts. His expression was kind and held, she thought, a measure of pity.

She did not want his pity. She lifted her chin and said, "This shall last as long as a new one, for I intend to have it repaired."

Lord Brisbane nodded. "It is not badly damaged, true, and I am sure once it is back to its fine form it will bring in a pretty penny."

This was precisely what Diana had intended to do, but somehow it irritated her to have *him* say it. It was *hers,* her uncle had given it to her, and it was the only thing she had of him except for memories. She would not even have a home, only if this Lord Brisbane so decreed. Rebellion rose: the curricle was *hers* and *she* would say what would be done with it, not him.

She smiled grimly. "I shall repair it—and then *drive* it."

Lord Brisbane's brows rose, in skepticism, she thought. "I believe that is not wise."

Diana looked him in the eyes, her chin tilting a fraction higher. "I am very experienced in driving it, believe me. My uncle taught me, and he was confident in my abilities."

"And yet," Lord Brisbane said gently, "he met his end with this carriage."

"Are you saying my uncle had his accident because *he* was at fault?" Diana demanded. His lordship merely gazed at her, his eyes half closed, looking down his nose at her as if again in skepticism. It infuriated her. "His lordship was a superior horseman and whip. He belonged to the Four-in-Hand Club. No one, *no one,* can say he could not handle his horses."

"And yet, this time, he did not."

"I do not expect you to understand such things," she said, looking him up and down, barely able to conceal her anger, and squashing down a growing dread. "Perhaps there was some fault with the carriage, the way it was made, that did not appear until that moment. I don't know, but whatever it was, I intend to have it repaired. But it was *not* Uncle Charles's fault."

"If your uncle was such a good driver, how was it that he did not notice anything awry from the outset?"

"If there was anything awry with the carriage he most certainly would have noticed it, and if not he, then McKinney, our head groom."

"But the groom noticed nothing as well?"

"No."

Lord Brisbane ran his hand over a curve of the carriage in a contemplative manner. He glanced at her. "I understand this McKinney has been in your uncle's employ for many years." It was a statement, but with just a hint of a question in it.

Diana frowned. She had heard of landlords who, upon inheriting an estate, proceeded to rid themselves of all the old servants and replace them with their own handpicked ones. It was a stupid practice, inefficient, and bound to cause ill will in the surrounding neighborhood. "If you are thinking of blaming McKinney for the accident or of discharging him from his post, I would advise against it. The man has been employed here since my uncle was a very young man, and his service has been loyal and faultless. Indeed, he felt most deeply regarding the accident and proffered his resignation, which I refused to consider."

"You?"

Diana blushed lightly; it was not her place to accept or decline a servant's employment unless it was her own, personal, servant. "McKinney was distraught, and Uncle Charles had said more than a few times that my word was as good as his when it came to the stables," she said stiffly. "If you must know, I directed him to Sir James, thinking he would be the heir."

"Ah."

That was all he said, an unassuming sound, but it made her very conscious that she had presumed, and presumed wrongly. "Sir James will not have discharged him, I am sure," she said.

"Mmm hmm," he said, gazing at her thoughtfully.

Diana shifted her feet uncomfortably. "I am sure McKinney is about somewhere. You may speak to him yourself."

"Is he?"

"But of course. I saw him—" She stopped and realized she had not seen McKinney lately. "Surely Sir James did not . . ."

"There may be some other explanation for why McKinney is not here," Lord Brisbane said.

Diana made herself look at him, but she could not hold his gaze long, for remorse hit her hard. "I have presumed a great deal," she said. "And I was wrong to do so. I . . . I apologize."

"Yes," he replied, but there was no censure in his voice. She felt a finger under her chin and she stared at him. He smiled slightly. "Come, cousin, it is no tragedy. Let us be frank: I well know that your uncle's wish that we wed was unexpected, and highly unusual. Would it be less awkward for you to know that I had no knowledge of it? I met your uncle only a year ago, when he first found me, and because of business our subsequent meetings were infrequent. Had I known of the conditions, I would have protested, of course. I am not certain why he decided we should suit, but he did, and made it nearly impossible for you not to comply."

"Mama said it was perhaps the closest he could come to giving me the estate . . . he thought of me as a daughter, almost a son, I think." His hand left her chin, and she looked down at her hands, then up at the earl again. "Then, too, perhaps he thought it the best way to take care of me and my mother."

"I wonder, then, that he did not give you a larger annuity."

She shook her head. "Uncle Charles was never one to reveal

his reasons, and we had never real cause to ask, for our lives had always run smoothly while he was with us. I am sure everyone on the estate thought so."

"Which makes me seem very much the interloper, I see," Lord Brisbane said, smiling wryly. "Making it even more difficult to see me as a prospective husband and heir to the estate."

Diana felt definitely guilty now, but made herself look directly at him. "Yes, that is true, and I am sorry for it. My uncle was held in highest esteem by everyone; it would be difficult to accept the presence of any heir, but to have a complete stranger makes it even more difficult."

"Held in esteem by everyone? He had no enemies? No detractors?" Lord Brisbane shook his head and put on a morose expression. "I have a great deal to live up to, indeed. Most certainly I shall fail, and the estates will fall to ruin."

Diana cast him a suspicious look, then laughed reluctantly. "You need not try to pull the wool over my eyes, my lord. I suspect you are quite capable of managing this estate, and it is no doubt one reason my uncle saw fit to want you to marry me."

He raised his brows in question. "And how do you know?"

"I am honest enough to admit you are more perceptive than I had given you credit for. You talked of business—I suppose you were not precisely an idle man, for your hands are not as smooth as I suppose a dandy's might be. Since your clothes are of a fine cut, I imagine your business endeavors were successful. I suspect you were in trade; you seem to be familiar with the making of carriages, or at least woodworking of some kind. Then you mention you were familiar with illnesses and healing." She smiled slightly. "I imagine you must be engaged in some sort of merchant shipping. Such a business would at once give a man the opportunity for making a fortune"—she gestured at his Bath superfine coat—"thus enabling him to buy whatever he wishes in clothes, and give him the opportunities to learn of ships and their construction. The illnesses and healing—one would have to be more self-reliant regarding these things if one had to travel to foreign lands."

"Well, well." Lord Brisbane rocked back on his heels, then smiled widely. "I congratulate you, cousin; you are correct on all points. *Very* perceptive. I see it would not do to underestimate you."

Diana grinned. "You are correct, my lord, it would not. Be warned!"

"I am grateful for the warning. You are a formidable woman, to be sure. It is a good thing I had not the intention of asking you to marry me; I had a distinct feeling it would displease you." His voice was solemn, but she thought she saw his lips turn up for a moment.

"*Very* wise of you not to wish to propose to me, for you would be living under the sign of the cat's foot, and no man could wish a marriage like that." She shrugged off the feeling of discontent. She had never had a proposal before, why shouldn't she have one now, even if it had been dictated by Uncle Charles? She turned to leave the carriage house and Lord Brisbane moved in step with her.

"Now there, cousin, your perception has failed you." He gave her a small, crooked smile. "I wanted to marry you the moment I saw you, and have no fear at all of being henpecked."

Chapter 4

Diana stumbled, and Lord Brisbane's hand came up under her elbow to steady her. She stared at him. "You jest, surely."

"No, alas, I do not." His smile widened, and his normally sleepy look had fled, replaced by sparkling mischief instead.

"You *are* jesting, and trifling with me," Diana said, and marched toward the house. "Do not, for I dislike it, and as you said, I am a formidable woman, and could make more trouble for you than you could like." She could not believe him, of course, but she did not repel him with her words as she could have; an irresistible curiosity as to what he would say next stayed her.

"Behold me trembling," Lord Brisbane said, his long legs easily keeping up with her.

"Oh, you are odious!" She eyed him sternly. "You cannot have fallen in love with me, not in such a short time."

"Love at first sight."

Diana blushed. "Nonsense! There is no such thing."

Lord Brisbane sighed. "So I thought, myself. But there you were, rain-soaked and beautiful, and I was instantly lost."

"Lost on the road, not in any other wise," she retorted. "You are making fun of me, for none of that can be true."

"Of course it is true. You were definitely rain-soaked."

"Oh, and you are in the habit of falling in love with rain-soaked women, is that it?"

"Not at all," Lord Brisbane said. "However, if a woman is beautiful, it would certainly be an incentive."

She frowned. "Now I know you are hoaxing me. I am not at all beautiful. I am too tall for that."

"Not for me."

Diana looked up at him—obviously this was true. "Well . . . well, then, I am not fashionable."

"Fashion does not make for beauty."

"Quite the contrary," she said. "I have had my Season in London, and know that it's your fashionable sylph who is much feted. Fashion does indeed dictate what is beautiful." She wrinkled her nose. "I am not sylphlike; therefore I am not beautiful."

He cocked his head and looked at her. "No one has ever admitted admiring you?"

She rolled her eyes. "No, of course not."

"More fool they." He shot a quick, laughing glance at her. "No doubt they were intimidated by your formidableness."

"I am not—" She stopped and closed her mouth, belatedly remembering that she had indeed agreed she was formidable. She gave him a sour look. "Believe me, I was as meek as my Aunt Matchett could make me."

"Impossible," he replied. "Nothing could subdue those magnificently flashing and scornful eyes—are they gray or blue? Blue, I believe."

"They are pale blue," Diana said firmly. "And they neither flash nor are they scornful."

"No? They seem to be, now."

She let out an exasperated breath. "Only because you are the most provoking man imaginable."

Lord Brisbane shook his head mournfully. "Worse and worse. First I am odious and now I am provoking. A very good thing I decided not to propose to you; you would have refused me immediately and I would have been cast into abject despair."

"I doubt it," Diana replied, banishing a slight feeling of discontent. "Count yourself fortunate: I am persuaded you would not wish to marry a woman you hardly know, and I would much rather live on a pittance than marry a complete stranger."

His lordship's expression lightened. "How gratifying to find you are not mercenary and not looking to marry a fortune or a title. Should I ever take it in my head to propose to you, I shall do so in happy confidence that your acceptance would come from your heart."

"And if I were to decline?"

"There would be nothing for it but I must put a period to my existence," Lord Brisbane said cheerfully.

Diana stopped, then turned to stare at him, her hands on her hips. "My lord, I think you must be the strangest man I have ever met."

He appeared to consider her words seriously, then shook his head. "Since your sojourn in London was so short and you have grown up in the country most of your life, I cannot think your experience of men to be very great at all." He smiled. "I am quite normal, truly."

He had an answer for everything it seemed, but Diana's annoyance with him was weak at best. She smiled slightly. This conversation was indeed the most peculiar she had ever had with anyone, but somehow her irritation was mixed heavily with a certain exhilaration. She had never traded quick and spirited words with a man before; her conversations in London had always been awkwardly constrained or excruciatingly polite. Indeed, she noted in surprise, the awkwardness she had felt when she first met this new Lord Brisbane had disappeared.

"You are smiling, I see," he said. "But I assure you, no one has ever accused me of being odd."

"Really?" Diana could not help chuckling. "I am surprised, my lord." She continued walking to the house.

He frowned suddenly, falling into step beside her. "Now *that* is a problem—I am not at all used to being called 'my lord.' It makes me feel quite strange, and is no doubt an explanation for my behavior—if, as you say, it *is* strange."

Diana gave a snort of laughter, only half suppressed when she pressed her hand over her mouth.

"Indeed," he continued, "every time I hear it, I am hard-pressed not to turn around and look for someone much older and more dignified than I." He smiled as suddenly as he had frowned and said, "However much I might seem strange to you, in the interests of not being as much of a stranger, I would be honored if you could call me Gavin, cousin."

She was silent for a moment while he opened the door of the house for her. She felt a little uncomfortable, but he was a cousin, however distantly related, and she felt she should make up for her earlier presumption. She nodded and stepped through the doorway. "Very well . . . Gavin. And you may call me Diana."

He gazed at her intently for a moment then smiled. "Diana it is, then. Thank you." And he entered the house behind her.

They had not gone but two steps into the hall when a door opened at the top of the stairs and Mrs. Carlyle appeared.

"There you are!" she exclaimed upon seeing them, and descended the stairs. "I have been searching for you, Mr. Sinc—that is, Lord Brisbane."

Diana grimaced. "I am sorry, Mama, I forgot that you wished to speak to him—I met him at the carriage house. I should have requested he speak to you immediately."

Mrs. Carlyle nodded, then hesitated before saying, "My lord . . ."

The earl smiled as he bowed over her hand. "Please, Mrs. Carlyle, the title sits ill on me. I would be pleased if you could call me Gavin."

Mrs. Carlyle smiled then continued. "Gavin, then. I have been meaning to ask you . . . it is very awkward, for we have no real claim upon you. But if you would be so kind as to let my daughter and me stay for perhaps a month or two, at least until we can find another place to stay, before we leave—"

Gavin's brows rose. "Leave? Must you? I have been looking forward to your showing me how to go on, for I know none of the servants, as I am sure you must. Indeed, I am a lazy fellow, and would prefer to have as little to do with the running of the household as possible. I was hoping you—and your daughter—would stay and act the hostess for me until such time I acquire a wife." He glanced quickly at Diana, then returned his gaze to Mrs. Carlyle.

Mrs. Carlyle looked, puzzled, from Diana's heated face to Lord Brisbane, then said, "Are you looking about you for a wife, then?"

He grinned. "Not particularly, for I believe I have found one that I would like very well, but the set of her mind is such that it will be a while before she can even begin to see me as a prospective husband." Diana shot him a fulminating look, and wished very much to box his ears.

"Well, you are an earl now, with property, so perhaps that might help persuade her."

"Alas, no, I have found that such things have little value for the lady. I believe character is of more importance to her."

"I suppose it is well that she looks for virtue in a husband rather than property," Mrs. Carlyle replied, "but she must not be very practical if your changed estate is not a consideration." She paused, looking at Gavin uncertainly. "However, if you are sure you wish Diana and me to stay here until you are married, I shall be happy to act as your hostess meanwhile."

"Perhaps even beyond that," Gavin replied.

Mrs. Carlyle smiled wryly. "I doubt that, my lord, unless you intend to comply with the will and ask Diana to marry you, to which—and I mean no offense, sir—she may not agree, being a headstrong young lady."

Diana could stand it no longer. "I have already told Gavin that I am reluctant to comply with that part of the will and am content to live with the portion already given me, rather than marry a complete stranger," she said in a suffocated voice. "We really do not need to discuss it further."

Mrs. Carlyle smiled slightly, and Diana realized that she had used Lord Brisbane's Christian name without thinking. He was, therefore, not as much of a stranger as before.

Diana groaned. "Oh, for heaven's sake. This is not a time to think of marriages or that silly condition in the will, and I swear I shall run away to a . . . a convent if you mention anything even close to this subject."

"Indeed, yes," Lord Brisbane replied somberly. "Very inappropriate, so soon after such a terrible loss to the family."

Mrs. Carlyle sighed sadly. "Indeed, and you are right to say so, my lord, for though I am sure my brother-in-law would have disliked all this sad ceremony, it would not be proper to do anything less than the best for him. We shall observe the proper length of time for mourning, and then we shall think of marriages. Meanwhile . . ." She cast Diana an arch look. "Meanwhile, it would be quite appropriate to invite our neighbors to a few dinners or quiet entertainments, so that you may look about you for a prospective wife—and do I assume from your words that you are open to having a wife?"

Diana gritted her teeth.

"Indeed I am, Mrs. Carlyle," his lordship said. "At the very least, it is my duty."

"Very proper." She nodded approvingly. "Well, then, I shall do my best to introduce you to all the good families of our acquaintance."

"Thank you," he said gravely.

"And I," Diana said in as sweet a voice as her vexed temper could summon, "shall make sure every mother of every eligible young lady in this county knows you are looking for a wife. Just think of the hordes and hordes of ladies who will come calling once they know the position of countess is open."

"Diana!" Mrs. Carlyle remonstrated.

But Lord Brisbane merely smiled pleasantly. "I shall be very grateful, of course."

Diana gazed at him suspiciously. There was, she thought, just a bit of a challenge in his voice. Very well! He had said she was a formidable woman. He would see how right he was.

Lord Brisbane said nothing more of his feelings for her in the succeeding days, and Diana became annoyed at herself for wondering if he would again. Not that she wished him to mention them again; she was not in love with him, so it did not matter. He teased by innuendo, however, gazing at her whenever anyone spoke the words "heart" or "sentiment" or any other word of that sort. It gave her the distinct feeling that he would broach the subject again sometime in the future.

To be honest, she thought it would be pleasant to hear it again, particularly because she had never heard anything remotely close to a proposal from any man. It was a novelty, that was it.

She was not in any way falling in love with him or even fond of him—impossible! They had nothing in common, for he was still a dandy and quite citified, arising late in the morning as was the custom in the city, rather than earlier as was the custom here. His valet, a thin whippet of a man, seemed to disdain the other servants, who were quite in awe of him. It was rumored that he shined his master's boots with a secretly made bootblack, and that Lord Brisbane would spend at least an hour in front of the mirror perfecting the folds of his neckcloth.

Diana had no use for such vanity and frivolity. Indeed, she had more serious things on her mind: no one had seen McKinney after the day of the accident. She had searched, had asked around the local villages about him, but no one seemed to know what had happened to the head groom. He had a few friends in the village, but they had not seen him; perhaps he had returned to family in Ireland, they said.

It was possible, but Diana did not think that he would have left without taking his leave of her. He had taught her to ride her first horse, and had given her good advice about training them as she grew from child to young woman; indeed, she had come to see him more as a friend than a servant.

She could not ask Sir James, since he had gone to London, not long after the funeral, which frustrated her. If McKinney had gone to Sir James and offered his resignation, then Sir James would have been able to tell her whether he had accepted the resignation or not.

Not even the stablehands knew what had happened to the groom, which seemed exceedingly odd, for McKinney had prided himself in running a tightly organized stable, and never went on holiday without making sure all duties were accounted for. Indeed, he ran the place so well and so unobtrusively that it was no wonder she had not noticed his absence immediately, for the place ran just as smoothly without him. Under his instruction, the other grooms knew exactly what to do, and when. Lord Brisbane seemed satisfied with their service and said the groom just under McKinney—Joe Baggins—was a promising young man and could fill McKinney's shoes just as well. Since Diana knew Joe had a will of iron and could run the stables efficiently with just a word or two in his gentle voice, she could not protest this appointment. But she felt hurt, no different than if a dear friend had turned his back on her without a word of explanation.

It was with relief, then, that Diana walked to the stables one day to find Sir James riding in. She was dressed in her habit, ready to go out for a morning ride on her gelding, Lightning. She gazed at Sir James's mare, a showy piece and well-muscled, but a nervous beast. She wondered if the horse would be less nervous if Sir James had not been riding it. She winced as he came to a stop, the reins pulling just a little too hard on the mare's mouth.

Sit straighter, and not like a sack of potatoes, she wanted to say to him, *and don't be so ham-handed,* but she had promised her mother that she would not judge people by their seat on a horse, and knew that it would be rude, besides. But really, the man had one of the worst hands and seats she'd ever seen. She put a smile on her face, however, and greeted him, and he gave a brief bow over her hand after he dismounted.

His gaze flickered over her hands, and he smiled sardonically. "Well, I see you are not married yet."

"Of course I am not," she said, irritated. "There is no reason why I should be."

"He couldn't come up to scratch, eh?"

She opened her mouth, then shut it again, wanting badly to tell him that Lord Brisbane had said he had fallen in love with her. But she was sure the earl was jesting, and she knew Sir James would mention it in company and set everyone to chattering. Sir James had a way of casually letting drop interesting bits of gossip, sometimes to fuel some bet or other he had made, but sometimes just to stir rumors and bring attention on himself. If she told him, he would mention it, and that might move Lord Brisbane to propose marriage out of honor, and she did not want to be put in such an uncomfortable position.

"That is none of your business," she said, knowing her reply would make him think that the earl had not one inclination to propose. Once more, she would have failed to get herself a husband and failed to keep herself and her mother from being hangers-on to the new earl. She burned with humiliation, but kept her face serene and shrugged. "And there are more important things than that at the moment." She hesitated, then said, "Have you seen McKinney, our head groom? I have not seen him since the day of the accident. He had given me his resignation, and I referred him to you, thinking you would be Uncle Charles's heir." *But then, you are not the heir,* she thought, and almost smiled to see irritation flash over Sir James's face.

He stared at her for a moment before saying, "No, he did not come to see me, cousin. I have not seen him since . . . I think it was the day the will was read." A small crease formed between his eyebrows, but the rest of his face remained impassive. "Unfortunate," he continued, "for I wished to speak to him myself." Sir James took the reins of the horse and led it toward the stables.

Diana looked at her cousin questioningly. "Is there something amiss?"

"Only a few questions about the accident. I have no great confidence in the stability of that curricle." His taut smile was a warning. "It would be best to sell it after it's repaired. Or burn it, tethers and all, if the sight of it might cause you pain."

"I am not as weak as that," Diana said, and lifted her chin. "I had thought of selling it, but I mean to have it repaired and drive it."

He gazed at her in silence for a moment, then his smile turned indulgent. "I wonder if you should."

"If you mean that there is something wrong with the curricle, then the problem should be fixed when it is repaired."

"And if that is not the problem?"

"Are you suggesting that I cannot drive it?" Diana demanded. "I assure you, I have driven it any number of times before the accident. I have never had a problem with it before."

"*I,* however, have not seen you drive it without your uncle accompanying you."

"That is because you did not visit Brisbane House regularly, and so missed those occasions I drove it alone."

"That may be," Sir James replied, "but that was before the accident." He smiled skeptically. "Technique makes up more than half one's driving skill, but confidence makes for the rest. I'm willing to wager your confidence has been severely shaken after seeing your uncle—ah, forgive me. It is a delicate subject, is it not? One that most ladies would prefer not to discuss."

Or have been present to see, Diana mentally finished for him. She gazed at his bored expression, and realized what it was that always irritated her about Sir James. It was that dismissive air he wore whenever he spoke to her, as if her thoughts and words were trivial and her opinion of no consequence. It made her feel diminished, and she did not like it. Perhaps it was why she disliked London so, confined not only by the tight corsets her Aunt Matchett forced upon her, but by the circumscribed set of subjects her aunt had decided were fit for a lady to converse upon, and what events and functions a lady was allowed to attend.

"Few *people* care to discuss such things, true," she said carefully, not wanting to be put at a disadvantage. "However, such grievous incidents do happen, and it serves no one well to ignore the fact."

"Even so, a lady of *delicate* sensibilities would have avoided the situation altogether," he said.

There, it was out, he had said it at last—apparently she had no delicacy at all. Sir James clearly felt the realm of carriages and carriage races to be beyond the scope of understanding of women. She could have understood his reluctance to believe in her skill if he had not seen her drive, as Lord Brisbane—Gavin—had not. But Sir James had seen her drive, and it did not convince him. It made angry heat rush to her face, and she held her tongue between her teeth to keep from spitting out the hasty words that built up behind them.

"I am glad I was there, Sir James," she said evenly, when she could. "At least I can rest easy at night, knowing, however little I or anyone else could have done, that I could at least give my uncle some comfort before he died."

"I suppose it is useful to be strong-minded," Sir James replied, looking her up and down, and his tone made Diana feel as if it was vulgar to be so strong.

Formidable. Suddenly she remembered her conversation with Lord Brisbane; there had been admiration in his voice when he had said the word. Her anger fled, and she smiled, feeling quite cheerful. "Yes, it is very useful. It would have served no one well if I had had the vapors or had gone into strong hysterics."

"Indeed," Sir James said, and looked away, obviously bored.

But Diana did not take offense at his manner. In fact she felt unexpectedly lighthearted. Why should she care what Sir James thought of her? Her own mother had not kept her from attending the race, for though Mrs. Carlyle herself did not like such things, she did not think it improper. If her mother—a gentle lady of good conscience and decorum—did not think it amiss for her to be present at her uncle's race, who was Sir James to criticize? Indeed, there were more important things to attend to at the moment—such as the location of the head groom.

"But this triviality has sidetracked me," she said. "If you do not know where McKinney is, then perhaps he approached Lord Brisbane with his resignation." She frowned, and they stepped into the stable.

Sir James turned a slightly more interested gaze upon her. "You discussed it between yourselves?" He gestured to a stableboy who took the mare from him.

"Lord Brisbane brought McKinney's absence to my attention, in fact," she said, turning to the stall that held her own horse. Lightning raised his head at her voice and nickered softly, making Diana smile.

"Indeed, our conversation almost followed the one between you and me—" *Except that it had a quite different ending, to be sure!* Diana thought, and reached into the stall with a bit of dried apple. The gelding sniffed it and delicately took it between its lips. Diana patted the horse and shook her head ruefully. "But he did not say whether McKinney approached him at all. . . ." She realized that Lord Brisbane had not mentioned it directly; she had only assumed it from what he had said.

"A word of warning, cousin."

She turned to look questioningly at Sir James and raised her brows at his grim expression.

"His lordship is not all what he seems," he said.

She smiled slightly. "Oh, I know that. He is not as lazy as he makes himself out to be."

"Far from it," Sir James replied. "Have you not wondered why it was that you have never heard of Mr. Sinclair until now? Do you know anything of his background or where he came from?"

Diana gazed at him, startled. "Well, I know he has been in trade . . ." she said slowly. Did she know? She had guessed it from Lord Brisbane's conversation, and he had said she was very perceptive. He had not, really, confirmed it.

"A common merchant," Sir James said. "More or less." There was a bit of a sneer in his voice. "Possibly less—a nobody."

Anger shot through her, quick and hot. "Oh, my," she said sweetly. "Do I hear regret? Even envy? How inconvenient for you that Gavin appeared to oust you from your inheritance." Her voice turned hard. "You would do well not to spread rumors regarding Lord Brisbane. It cannot do your consequence any good, for everyone shall know you have been expecting to inherit, and what a comedown that will be for you!"

Black fury in Sir James's eyes made Diana take a sudden step back, rustling the hay at her feet, and her horse moved uneasily in its stall. Then the expression was gone, and a thin smile appeared instead. " 'Gavin,' is it? Well, well. I see where your interests lie. What a nice performance you gave at the library. I was almost fooled. But you are no different from any other woman."

Diana gritted her teeth. "We are cousins, and he has permission to call me by my Christian name just as you do for the same reason—*James.*"

"But you jump so quickly to his defense, my dear," Sir James said, mimicking her earlier sweet tone of voice. "And what, really, do you know of him? I, on the other hand, have spent a good deal of time investigating his past while I was in London."

She stared at him, at once curious and yet reluctant to take the bait. She shrugged. "My uncle had every confidence in his solicitor. If Bartlett found no fault with the present Lord Brisbane, I am sure no one else should."

"You are still convinced of your uncle's infallibility, are you? And yet you protested the conditions of your dowry at the reading of the will . . . or was that a pretense?"

She stared into Sir James's dark eyes, feeling caught, as if she were a fly whose wings he had pinned to a board. "Uncle Charles meant it for the best. That it is not my conception of what is best for me does not erase his concern—his very great concern—for my welfare," she said at last. She moved to her horse, patting its neck comfortingly.

He smiled then, and shrugged. "A politic answer. I think you'll see, however, that the truth regarding the present Lord Brisbane is not in his favor."

"What do you mean?"

"I shall not tell you, for you are obviously enamored of him."

Diana gave him a level gaze. "You are quite mistaken."

Sir James shrugged again. "I advise you to stay away from Lord Brisbane. At best he is nothing but a useless man-milliner, caring for nothing but his clothes. At worst—" He smiled. "Much worse." He turned and proceeded out of the stables, but turned slightly, glancing over his shoulder at her. "By the way, I would advise you to get yourself another horse—your gelding is much too difficult to handle."

"Only for you," she shot back. She grinned fiercely as he gave her another black look and strode away from her to the house.

One of the undergrooms saddled Lightning for her. True, the gelding would normally not be seen as a lady's mount, but few ladies were as tall as she. And true, even her uncle had questioned her choice of a horse. But she had known the moment she had set eyes on the wild-eyed bay colt that this one was hers. And so it was: the bay obeyed only her, and had come willingly to her as she whispered to it and fed it from her own hand. She was the one who trained it as it grew larger and stronger.

Her smile grew wider. The stablehands had once told her Sir James had tried to ride Lightning at one time and the gelding had thrown him. Sour grapes was behind the man's anger, and resentment that he had not been the heir to the Brisbane title or estates.

She shrugged mentally as she mounted the horse, gentling it with soft words as it pretended to startle at the familiar gate it always passed. With the next game of chance he won, Sir James would soon forget his disgruntlement. He always did, whatever his temper may have been at some setback. This tantrum of his—for that was what it was—would end soon, she was sure.

Chapter 5

As Diana spurred her horse out into the stableyard and into a gallop when she reached the fields, she shook off thoughts of Sir James and what he had implied about Lord Brisbane. The morning was too beautiful to waste on uneasy speculation. That was all it was, speculation. Unless she applied to her uncle's solicitor and asked difficult and awkward questions—and there was no real reason for her to ask them—all she could do was question Lord Brisbane or those who knew him.

Nearing a small copse of trees, she sat back a little in the saddle, once she was quite a way from the house, easing her horse into a trot and then a walk. She closed her eyes for a moment, letting a cool breeze brush her face and her hair. The sun shone brightly, and she regretted that she had decided to wear her black riding habit instead of her lighter weight blue. The dress was very warm, and perspiration prickled at the nape of her neck. She had worn it because she was still in mourning, but if she had come out earlier in the day, she could have worn the cooler riding dress and no one would have been the wiser.

She glanced around her—there was no one about. It would do no harm to unpin the jockey-bonnet and let her hair loose down her back. Quickly, she took it off, then unpinned and untied her hair. She would hang her bonnet on a branch to fetch before she returned home. Her hair would become tangled, but the breeze would run through it and cool her quite a bit, and she could run her fingers through it to untangle it before binding it up again.

The air wafting through her hair was glorious. She ran her fingers through it, massaging her scalp a little, and shook her head, and the length of it fell down over her shoulders to her waist. There, now! She would become sadly brown without her bonnet to shade her face, but it was not as if her skin were perfectly white, after all. It was something her Aunt Matchett used to complain about all the time in London, and had made her put lemon slices all over her face every evening to lighten it. The lemons had made her skin no more pale than it was now, and she was glad to have ceased such nonsense once she returned home.

"Now we shall have a good gallop," she said to Lightning, and the horse nervously flicked its ears back for a moment. "Oh, don't be so finicky, silly! You have galloped when I have had my hair down before, and you have done just fine. Now, let's go!"

She nudged her horse forward, leaning over his neck, urging him on faster and faster. Diana grinned widely as the ground passed quickly under her, her hair flying behind her, fluttering at her back like wings. No one did this in the city without someone crying scandal; it was only here, at home, she could ride and be free. Surely there was nothing as wonderful as this, the power and grace of the horse beneath her, the soaring speed as Lightning leaped over small brooks and shrubbery.

They reached the edge of the estate and Diana slowed her horse, then turned back. She would not go home immediately, but take another way through the woods. The heat was rising, and both she and the horse could cool down in the shade, then rest by the pond there. Then they would have another good gallop, and both of them could return home eager for a midday meal.

The shade beneath the trees was indeed cool, just right after the heated ride. Diana rode Lightning to a stump and carefully dismounted onto it. Still holding the reins, she gazed speculatively at the bay horse. She had trained him to stay in place if she loosely tied or even only draped the reins over a bush or a low tree limb, and for the most part the horse obediently stayed where he was. But every once in a while, he would be in a mischievous mood, and after an experimental tug at the reins would find them loose enough to know that he was not tied to anything at all, and off he would go. Horses were not particularly intelligent animals, but Lightning was an exception to the rule and was for that reason often more contrary than most and a little more difficult to train.

Well, there was nothing like consistency to remind an animal of its training. This time she would tie the reins firmly and the horse would know that he was not free to go anywhere.

"You *will* stay," she said sternly as she tied the reins to a low branch. "See, I have put you near the pond if you want to drink, and there is plenty of grass to crop, too." The horse eyed her skeptically, lipped the knot on the branch as if in defiance, then lowered his head to the grass and began to eat.

Diana walked to an old oak, then sat on one of its large roots. A scattering of primroses grew around it, and she picked one, twirling the stem back and forth between her fingers in a contemplative way. She thought of what Sir James had said; she could not help wondering about Lord Brisbane, about his background. She had not asked him . . . there never arose the opportunity, or it never appeared to be the right moment. Dinner conversation tended to dwell upon general subjects, and upon the war abroad, or taken up in telling Lord Brisbane about the tenants and the nature of the property.

But no personal exchanges were ever made. Mourning made everyone keep their distance for fear of some unintentional hurt. Even Sir James and Mr. Southworthy kept to themselves, not mentioning the accident or the late earl.

Except for the current Lord Brisbane. His manner was still lazy, his eyes still heavy-lidded, but he listened and commented in his quiet voice, and somehow Mama would laugh at something he said, and Diana found herself talking of her life and her uncle.

It was like that last evening. When the ladies and gentlemen went into the drawing room after dinner, the vicar conversed upon the state of the war, in which he was highly interested, but soon afterward retreated into reading some religious works. Sir James engaged Lord Brisbane in a short discussion of upcoming prizefights and races, but soon left to partake of a cigar out-of-doors.

She had been playing a few tunes on the pianoforte all the while, not really wanting conversation, and watched Lord Brisbane wander over to the windows and look out at the sunset in the distance. He had been impeccably dressed in a black jacket with pale yellow knee breeches and a cream-colored embroidered waistcoat. His shirt points were higher than the rest of the gentlemen's, but not as high as she had seen some dandies wear.

He had moved to her mother, who was stitching some tatting she had made to a collar. The earl made some comment, and Mama had laughed and blushed, shaking her head slightly. She had made a shooing motion, and he had grinned, and turned toward Diana.

He had stood, watching her play for a while, then forestalled her when she reached to turn the sheet of music. He turned it instead, and she nodded her thanks to him. She finished the piece—it was a Mozart divertimento—and he clapped his hands. "You play very well," he said.

"Thank you, my lord," she said. "But I beg to differ. I have heard better musicians than I in London."

"I said you play very well, but not like a *professional* musician."

"Now I know your proclamation of love was false," Diana sighed mock-dolefully, for she did not take offense at obvious truth. "I thought if one were in love, one loved everything about the beloved." It was a daring thing for her to say—but something prompted her to say it, and for some reason she did not think Lord Brisbane would mind. Besides, they were far enough away from everyone else so that she would not be overheard.

"Well, I have heard that love is blind, but I have never heard that it was tone-deaf," he replied.

She had begun a sonata, but laughed and stumbled in mid-phrase. "Oh, now look at what you have done! I shall have to start over again, and will sound like the veriest beginner."

He grinned. "No, not like a beginner. You do play very well. Did your mother teach you?"

"Yes, and then Uncle Charles bought this pianoforte and paid for a music master in addition to a governess. So you see, I have been brought up a lady." If the last few words were said with more than usual emphasis, she could not help it. Sometimes her Aunt Matchett's voice echoed in her ears, criticizing everything she did. After a month in London, the sound of it had given her a stomachache.

"That must have been dull," he replied.

She looked up at him in surprise. "Why do you say so?"

"Aside from the music, I have often thought the education of young ladies to be tedious in the extreme: dancing, stitching, nothing beyond basic reading, writing, and arithmetic, barely any geography, and perhaps a smattering of Italian, enough to sound affected and cause acute pain to any Italian within hearing distance."

Diana choked, almost touched the wrong key, and hastily corrected herself. Luckily, the music was a *largo* piece, slow enough to cover her hesitation. "If you must know," she said, managing only barely to hold back a laugh, "I was bored with all of it, except geography, and that subject made me frustrated, for my governess could never tell me what the countries were really like, nor did she think it proper for me to procure books that would." She sighed. "How I wish I could have had a boy's education. I could have gone on a Grand Tour, and learned Latin and Greek, and learned enough Italian to"—she gave him a sidelong glance—"to learn fencing."

Lord Brisbane nodded. "I understand the best fencers are Italian."

"You are an odd man, indeed, my lord."

The earl started, and looked behind him. "My lord . . . ? Ah, you mean me."

Diana laughed. "Very well—Gavin. Yes, very odd."

"How so?"

"I have not been able to shock you—so far—with any of my notions." The sonata ended, and she rested her hands on her lap.

"Do you mean there is something shocking about you? I am all ears." He leaned forward expectantly.

"I would have thought what I have told you already was shocking enough. Certainly most everyone of my acquaintance has thought so," Diana said primly, again suppressing a laugh.

"As did your uncle?"

She looked down at her hands for a moment, then met his gaze squarely. "I owe my uncle a great deal. If it had not been for him, my mother and I would have starved. I was not his heir—he had no real obligation to care for us, except that we were his younger brother's family."

Lord Brisbane had nodded gravely, and his eyes had been understanding. "That is enough to gain anyone's loyalty. Was it difficult?"

"Yes," she had said, and had told him of the cold and hunger she remembered, and how her mother had grown so thin and pale. She had even told him how the servants had found her father on a cold winter's morning at the steps of their house, dead from drowning in the gutter because he had been in such a drunken stupor he had not the wit nor the will to rise when he had fallen. She had stopped, suddenly, alarmed at what she had told him, something she had not even discussed with her mother. But Lord Brisbane had only nodded, and had gently directed the conversation elsewhere, much to her relief.

How had he done it? Diana wondered, plucking another primrose and twirling it between her fingers. A breeze wafting through the woods lifted the hair from her face, and she closed her eyes, feeling the warm sun and cool air alternating across her skin. She sighed. She was not one to give confidences, but she had told Lord Brisbane—Gavin—almost her whole life story. She shook her head, puzzled. He was an odd man, indeed. She had never encountered anyone who . . . who *listened.*

That was it. Whatever his manner or the subject that might

arise, he always seemed to listen, carefully, as if noting down every word she said. She drew in her legs and put her arms around them, resting her chin on her knees. His attentiveness was pleasant . . . flattering, in fact. It made her feel as if what she said mattered to him.

Her stomach growled and she sighed again, rising from the tree root on which she had been sitting. She should go home and have some breakfast—she looked at the sky—rather, luncheon, and—She stopped, as she looked for her horse near the pond.

Her horse. Her horse was gone.

The image of the bay nibbling the knot she had tied on the reins rose from her memory and she groaned. Yes, Lightning was an exceptionally smart horse—so much so that he had apparently learned how to untie simple knots. She had been so immersed in pondering over the nature of Lord Brisbane that she had not even noticed her horse had loosed himself from the branch and wandered off, no doubt back to the stables for some grain or hay.

She would have to walk back, and in fact have to take the roundabout way, because she had left her jockey-bonnet on a tree some distance away. She gazed at the smooth cool pond nearby. Well, her horse had returned to the stables before her in the past; the servants would not come looking for her for a while. It could not hurt to stay here a little before she left. She picked up a rock and threw it at the pond, watching it splash in a very satisfying manner. It had been a long time since she had skipped rocks across water . . . could she still do it?

She had only thrown her fifth rock before she heard a thunder of hooves in the distance. She turned and watched a horseman galloping toward her through the gap in the woods—he was a good horseman, she noted. He came nearer, and to her surprise it was Lord Brisbane.

His eyes had lost their habitual sleepy look, his jaw was set, and his lips were tightly pressed together. He looked grim, as if expecting to face some dire trial. Diana smiled as his eyes found her in the dim light of the woods, but her smile faded as he continued to look grim, even furious. He dismounted, then took her by her shoulders.

"Where were you? Why did you not come back immediately? Are you hurt? And why were you careering about the place without a groom?" His voice was low and harsh.

She stared at him, bewildered at his words, and then, slowly, anger sparked and grew.

"I have always gone about the estate by myself and have never come to harm. Indeed, if you had asked the grooms, they would have told you that I often come here, that I have never been thrown by my horse, and he has in the past escaped from me to return to the stables by himself." She tried to pull away from him, but he held her firm. "And no, I am not hurt, as you can clearly see."

"Excuse me for my concern," he said sarcastically. "I merely saw you crossing the fields at an insane speed, your hair flying behind you, and found your bonnet snagged upon a branch. Shortly after you entered this wood, I saw your horse galloping back without you, and you nowhere in sight. Of *course* I should have assumed you were perfectly well and uninjured."

For a moment his words stopped her, for she could see how someone unused to her ways would think she might have met with some mishap. But there was still little cause for him to react so vehemently. She made herself shrug.

"You have no reason to concern yourself with me. I am not your ward, only a distant relation, and a hanger-on at that."

"Is that what you believe I think of you? Someone unwanted?" His brows drew together, his hands loosened their grip on her shoulders, but one hand came up and cupped her chin. "You don't know the danger—I thought I had lost you, Diana." His thumb ran softly against her jaw and his fingers moved across her cheek to her loosened hair.

His touch made her let out a long breath, and she stared at him. "Danger? There is no danger. Lost me? How can you have lost me when you have never . . . I have not . . ." Her voice faded as she looked into his eyes and saw a terrible yearning there, as if he were poor and starving, and she a treasure just beyond his grasp. She felt as if he were someone else, not the dandy full of quips and jokes, not the man who—she thought—had not much concern for things above his neckcloth or boots. Was Sir James right, that there was something in Gavin's background of which she should beware? She had seen this small part of him before, but she had not bothered to question it or wonder much.

She felt his fingers stroke the back of her neck, and she knew she should step away. She should, perhaps, even be afraid. But she felt no fear, and continued to stare at him, wondering now what was behind those heavy-lidded eyes that watched her, and the soothing voice that coaxed confidences from her.

He continued to stare at her, his eyes moving from hers to her lips and back again. "Danger . . . of course there is. I am in danger of loving you too much, Diana."

She took a quick breath, not able to look away. *He is not jesting,* she thought. *He is serious.* An odd, shimmering heat rose in her belly, and she trembled.

"If I were to kiss you, what would you say?"

"I . . . I don't know—that is, I should say—I—"

For the first time, he did not listen, but put his lips on hers. *They are soft,* she thought, then: *I should be afraid.* But her hands only clutched the lapels of his coat, for her knees felt weak. His mouth moved over her lips, gently, then firmly, as if he were tasting them. One of his hands gently caressed the back of her neck. She closed her eyes, thinking of his long, elegant fingers and how they had moved over her skin when he had held her hand that day in the carriage house, and how they were now moving over her shoulder to her back then down to her waist, holding her hard against him. He shifted away from her, his lips leaving hers, and she made an involuntary, protesting sound.

A half laugh, half sigh came from him, and he kissed her again, and this time her hands moved from his chest to his face, touching his cheek hesitantly. His skin was smooth, and then less so as her hand moved to his chin.

His hands abruptly caught her wrists, and he moved away from her. Diana opened her eyes, her heart hammering. He gazed at her, his smile wry. "Now this, my dear, is quite shocking. You should not let men kiss you, particularly when you do not know them well."

A blush heated her face, and she tried to pull away, but he still held her. He was strong—stronger than she thought a dandy of lazy habits should be. "You see," he said, "though you think it is none of my business where and when you ride, it is, very much. You are under my protection, and if I say so, you shall have a groom with you at all times when you ride." He smiled wickedly. "Unless, of course, you are with me."

She did not know whether to slap him, be relieved that he had returned to his usual levity, or try to convince him that she did not go about kissing men. She stared at him, unable to say a word. Finally, she shook her head. "I don't think I shall wish to be with you."

"No? You will have to convince me better than you have done for the last few minutes."

Embarrassment caught her, and she glared at him. "For your information, I have never been kissed by a man. How should I have—have known how to act?" *But you know you shouldn't have let him kiss you,* said a nasty little voice inside her that sounded very much like her Aunt Matchett. *You could have stopped him.* Her stomach began to hurt. "And besides, I see no reason why I should go about with you or anyone else. I always inform the servants when I am going out. I have never come to harm before, so I should not now or in the future."

His smile faded, and the twinkle in his eye disappeared. "You are a soothsayer, are you? Tell me, how do you know you will not come to harm in the future? As formidable as you are"—the twinkle in his eyes returned—"you, indeed no one, is proof against accident or hurt."

She felt suddenly as if the walls of her life were collapsing in on her. She had not returned to Brisbane House from London to be hemmed in and tied down by senseless rules. If she could not roam the world as she had always wished, she could at least roam the estate at will.

"It has never happened before, there is no reason why it should now," Diana repeated stubbornly. "I have always been careful, and my horse, for all that he pretends to be, is not at all skittish."

Lord Brisbane sighed, then suddenly sat on the stump she had used earlier as a step down from her horse. He pressed his hands over his eyes and groaned. "If only I had not fallen in love with a stubborn, willful woman."

"More fool you for doing so," she said brusquely, not sure whether she wanted to laugh or scream, for she at once wanted his arms around her again and wanted to run away. Lord Brisbane unsettled her, and made her want to shore up the walls inside of her that she had created after her uncle died, so that his words would not settle in her heart.

He lifted his head and an angry glint entered his eyes. "So I am beginning to think. Very well, then." He rose and when she stepped away, took her arms in his hands, and held her tight when she tried to struggle from him. "Listen to me, Diana. Listen!"

She stopped, then watched him warily.

"You are an intelligent woman, but your passions run away with you, I think." He smiled ruefully. "As have mine. No matter. I only want you to listen, and not run away." Diana nodded slowly, and he sighed again.

"Think now," he said, slowly, as if choosing his words with care. "Have you ever wondered if your uncle's death was purely an accident?"

Chapter 6

Diana gazed at him, dread and denial seeping into her, and slowly shook her head. "You must be mad. Of course it was an accident; I saw it myself," she said. She tried to step away from him. "Let me go!"

The earl groaned. "Diana, you said you would listen." She stilled herself, watching him warily. "I will let you go, but you must listen. Please."

"Very well," she said reluctantly.

He released her and she walked away slowly, and he moved backward, his hands raised on either side of him as if in surrender, or to show that he would not touch her again. He sat once more on the stump, and rested his hands on his knees, while she sat upon the oak root. He looked at her in a considering manner, and he frowned, as if wondering how he would frame his words. Finally, he smiled.

"You are a wild one, as your uncle said you were. He said I would like you, and in that he was right."

Diana relaxed a little. "Did he say that? I suppose he was right about me being a little wild. He did not think London would suit me, though my mother insisted I have a Season there." She hesitated. "I am sorry about my outburst. I should have waited."

Lord Brisbane grimaced. "Well, I was at fault. My behavior was not exemplary." He gave her a speculative glance. "Any other woman would have slapped me."

Diana felt heat rise in her face. "I rightfully should have, but, well . . ." She could not help the small smile that crept upon her lips. "It was my very first kiss, and I was curious. There, I admit it, and no doubt you are very shocked."

"No," he replied, grinning. "That is usually the way first kisses happen, I believe."

"But most people would not say or understand such things, I am sure."

"Yes, but I am not most people," he replied.

She laughed, then grew sober. "That is all very well, but I think we need to get back to the matter at hand—my uncle's death."

"I was hoping to avoid that for a bit. Kisses are much more enjoyable to talk about, I believe."

"No doubt," she said tartly. "But you have requested that I sit and listen to you. Here I am, and so you might as well begin."

He sighed. "Ah, well." He hesitated, then said, "Your uncle sent for me about a year ago; at that time, I had some idea we were related, but distantly, and . . . let us just say my family had not any contact with his for many, many years. I had thought he wished to see me for a matter of business, for I have a good reputation in my line of work—"

"And that is?"

He grinned. "A vulgar thing. I have worked for business insurers—Lloyd's for one—to make sure the claims against their policies are not false."

Diana raised her brows. "I would think a gentleman's word would be enough."

"Yes, but not all businessmen are gentlemen, and even some gentlemen think businessmen do not deserve their word of honor." His expression changed, and grew somber. "Sometimes a man, foolish in his business decisions, can grow quite desperate and make a false claim on his property's insurance, hoping to regain some of his fortune." His voice drifted off, and he gazed at the pond before him, silent.

"Was . . . was my uncle one such?" Diana asked. He blinked and looked at her for a moment. "What? Oh, no, he wasn't. Your uncle had a good solicitor of impeccable reputation in

Bartlett, and your uncle made sound business decisions." He frowned. "He wanted me to investigate some . . . odd happenings. Or so he said. He also mentioned his will, and that he wished to discuss it with me at some time in the future, but beyond that, he said nothing. I met him several times regarding the investigation he wished me to conduct, but I could not start it before I was done with some others. I had finished my last assignment the day before I came to Brisbane House to meet your uncle. Unfortunately, word had not reached me that he had met with an . . . accident before I left London." He glanced up at the sun peeping from between the tree branches and he rose. "Come, shall we continue this conversation on our way home? I daresay you shall want your luncheon soon."

Diana did not really want to leave, for she had been drawn in by his deep, soft voice and had been all rapt attention, and was about to say no. But her stomach growled at that moment, and she winced in embarrassment. "Yes, I think I shall."

He laughed. "Good. I am fairly gut-foundered myself." He rose and went to her, then took her hand, bowing over it.

"How vulgar of you to say so," she said, chuckling. They walked to his horse, and he helped her upon it.

"And how vulgar of you to understand what I just said."

Her chuckle turned to a laugh. "Now you see my uncle was very right; I am quite wild and have willingly listened to and learned stable talk." The horse moved forward.

"There, I see we do have something in common: You have learned vulgar stable talk, and I have learned the vulgar tongue of the docks." He snapped his fingers as if an idea had suddenly come upon him. "I have it! Let us teach each other what we know, and then we shall practice it in company, and see how many people we can either shock or confuse. When we are out of mourning, we shall invite all those people who tried to confine you to tedious society talk, and horrify them so they never come near Brisbane House again."

She laughed again and shook her head. "Oh, no, for then who shall see your magnificent waistcoats and wonderfully tied neckcloths? You dandies need an audience, after all."

"You are right," Lord Brisbane answered, considering the problem. "Public displays of vulgarity will never do. I see we shall have to be vulgar . . . in private." He gave her a wicked glance, and she blushed.

"Nonsense . . . and you have gone off the subject again."

"How persistent and perceptive you are," he said, with a crooked smile. "Well, then: I had asked a few questions of common acquaintances concerning the matter your uncle wanted me to investigate. However, by the time I was able to meet your uncle again, it was too late." He sighed. "I had thought his concerns had not much basis, but now after his death . . . now I think they most certainly do."

"Then . . . then you don't think his death was an accident? But I was there! It was not from carelessness on his part, to be sure, but one of the horses went wild—perhaps there was a problem with the curricle."

Lord Brisbane shook his head. "I doubt there was anything wrong with the carriage," he said. "Your uncle bought it about a year ago, am I correct? And you rode and drove in it during that time?"

Diana nodded.

"And in all that time you did not have any trouble with the horses or the curricle? No accidents?"

"No, none . . ." she said slowly. Surely it could not be true! She deliberately pushed aside the pain and grief as she thought of the accident again, examining the incident in her mind as best she could remember.

"Then how can a perfectly good, new carriage suddenly have a fault in it that caused the horses to panic?" he asked.

"Perhaps it had some flaw that did not surface until the race."

"That is a possibility, but unlikely; the workmanship is very fine, with great attention to detail. I would be surprised if your uncle did not inspect it himself before he bought it. Certainly the rest of the carriages in the carriage house are the best I have seen anywhere, of very high quality. I think it very strange that your uncle would stint on this one carriage."

"He never stinted on his carriages," Diana cried. "Never! He always said it would not be safe—and yes, I know, a curricle is often seen as a dangerous vehicle, but that is precisely why Uncle Charles took such pains with the quality of his purchases. Indeed, he had this one made to order. . . ." Diana realized what she was saying, and stopped. She gazed at Lord Brisbane, dread rising in her again.

"No . . . not the carriage. But perhaps one of the horses," she continued desperately, not wanting to think that anyone could have wanted to hurt her uncle. "Perhaps there was something wrong with one of the horses. Indeed, one and then the other went wild, right in the middle of the race. If it was not the curricle, then perhaps some other problem—a burr under the pads on the back of one of the horses." She knew the idea was unlikely as soon as she said it, but she wanted to find some excuse, any excuse, to keep her uncle's passing an accident, not anything so horrible as— The walls around her heart trembled, and her hands turned into fists, trying to keep herself calm.

Lord Brisbane shook his head. "No, a burr would have been felt immediately, and your uncle—indeed, any of your grooms—would have seen it and removed it from the outset."

"Well, then, perhaps some insect stung the horse," she said.

"Now that is possible," he replied. "However, you yourself have wondered where your head groom is, and have said that he would not leave his post without letting you know that he was leaving. Do you not think that is the least bit curious?"

"Well, yes, of course, which is why I have been asking about him in the village."

"Yes, so I have heard," he said. "I would be careful about the kinds of questions you ask regarding McKinney."

"Why so?"

He looked at her somberly. "They could be . . . unfortunate. And, considering that your uncle has had near-accidents in the recent past, I cannot help thinking that McKinney's disappearance so soon after this one is not a coincidence."

Diana stared at him. "Other accidents? But when did—"

The earl merely looked at her.

"Of course," she groaned, anger rising at her uncle. "It would not be something he would tell us." She gazed at him. "Does Bartlett know?"

"Yes," he said. "But he can do nothing. There is no solid proof, nor do we have any real suspect."

"Then how can you say it is not an accident?"

"Because your uncle's last letter to me said he knew who it was, but characteristically, he did not say who."

Diana frowned. "But that does not make sense. If Uncle Charles knew who it was, then why did he decide to do something as risky as a curricle race? Surely such an event would be a tempting opportunity for someone bent on—on—"

"Murder," Lord Brisbane said bluntly. "From what I can tell, your uncle is the sort to tempt fate just so he could find out for himself who it might be."

"But I cannot think who might want to kill him! He was a good man."

They had come to the stables at last, and the earl led the horse to the door. "Good men have been killed when it served the purposes of the killer," he said. He lifted his hand up to her to help her down from the horse. "You may list any one of the seven deadly sins and that would be motive enough."

Diana took his hand and placed her other hand on his shoulder as she slid off the horse. His hand went to her waist to steady her, and their position was not that different from when he had started to kiss her in the woods. She looked at him, and he smiled slightly, probably guessing what she was thinking.

"I do not see how it could apply to any of our acquaintances, for surely my uncle's goodness would make them think twice before they did him harm," she said hastily and stepped away from him.

Lord Brisbane's smile grew larger before he called for a stablehand to take away the horse.

"Lightning's got his oats," the stableboy said to Diana, and she nodded, assured that her horse was well.

The earl turned to her and tucked her hand in the crook of his arm, escorting her toward the house.

"And here I thought you a perceptive woman," he continued and glanced at her. His smile turned sympathetic. "In reality, you would see it yourself, but am I correct in believing perhaps you do not wish to think of all this . . . unpleasantness? It is difficult enough when a beloved member of the family dies, but to think that his life was deliberately cut short makes it much worse. Even nightmarish."

A sigh escaped her, and she felt as if the lid on a tightly closed pot inside of her were suddenly lifted, easing the pressure within. "It has been difficult lately," she admitted. "Sometimes I do not *want* to think at all, which is not at all like me."

"No, I imagine you think a great deal," Lord Brisbane replied. "Indeed, I am regretting I have told you any of this. It is not a burden I would wish on anyone, much less a lady."

Diana withdrew her hand from his arm. "I am not so weak-minded as that," she said firmly. "In fact, I am glad you told me, for I am beginning to detest not being told things, especially if it's deemed to be in my best interests." She crossed her arms in front of her. "*Especially* if it is in my best interests."

The earl grinned. "I understand completely. I myself have a deeply ingrained dislike of being uninformed. I wonder, however, if I have rushed my fences, so to speak."

"Why do you say that?"

"For one thing, I have declared my sentiments toward you much too early."

"Oh?" Diana said in an ironic voice.

He grinned, then sobered. "For another, I should have kept my investigation to myself until I have had more evidence. You have raised some good objections, and all I have is your uncle's word that he suspected someone was trying to kill him in the last few months."

Diana drew in a deep breath. "If my uncle said it, then it was so. He was never one to imagine ghosts or goblins, but had a great deal of common sense."

Lord Brisbane nodded. "So I believe as well. However, it is always good to have it confirmed, biased though it is."

"Biased!"

"Yes," he replied. "It is natural for dependents to think highly of a generous and benevolent benefactor."

"An opinion he deserved," she said swiftly.

"Of course. But it can blind one to the realities of a man's character, and in this case it is best to think as objectively of him—and everyone around him—as possible."

"Everyone? Do you mean to say that any acquaintance, near or far, might be suspect?"

"Yes. Particularly near."

Uneasiness washed over her. "But that might mean anyone—the vicar, Sir James, any of the grooms, my mother, myself—"

"Yes," he said again.

"Then why did you tell me all this? For all you know, I might have done the deed."

He stopped, and she became still next to him as she watched his face turn grim. "Of course, you might have," he said slowly. "However, the chances against it are strong. You were not in London when the other accidents occurred, and it would have taken knowledge of his daily habits for anyone to have perpetrated them. You could have hired someone to do it, of course. Your motive? You could have thought you were due some large bequest, and wished to get it. Or perhaps you knew of the requirement that you marry the next earl, and wished to see yourself a countess."

Diana whirled away from him, clenching her teeth against the nausea that filled her throat. "How *dare* you think such things of me!" she cried at last. "He was like a father to me! I would never, *never*—"

"Stop!" he commanded, and the word halted her in her steps. She did not turn around, however, but stood there, trembling from anger and a strange despair at what he had said of her.

He walked around in front of her and gazed at her sternly.

"Hot at hand, indeed," he said. Then his expression relaxed, and though his lips did not smile, there was a twinkle in his eyes. "Think, my dear. I did not say you were like that. Your face shows too much, and you blush too easily to hide a lie. I don't know of anyone who can blush on command."

Her face grew hot, for she did try to control herself, but it seemed she was not very good at it.

"There, you see? You are blushing now."

She gave a reluctant laugh. "Very well . . . you are right. And I am sorry for my outburst." She turned back to the house and he fell in step beside her. "You are a very needling man, you know. Or, not needling, but you have a way of hitting truths, even unpleasant possibilities, about one."

He grimaced. "Yes, I do, don't I? Graceless is what I am, and I am sorry for it. You deserve better consideration than that." He opened the door of the house and stepped aside for her to enter first.

She gazed at him, and suddenly knew she would not like him any other way. "No," she said. "I would prefer the truth, however badly I may react to it." She hesitated. "My life has become . . . unsteady. I do not know what to expect from one day to the next, really. But the truth is immovable and sure. I would much prefer to know the truth." She took in a deep breath, searching for something within herself, something she could hold on to. "That is all I have right now to depend on, I believe."

Lord Brisbane took her hand in his and raised it to his lips. "No, you have more . . . but it is a good start."

She gazed at him, and felt suddenly a little lighter, and with a small smile, gave his hand a grateful squeeze, and stepped into the house.

Chapter 7

After a fortnight had passed, Mrs. Carlyle suddenly announced, during a short silence at dinner, that they should go to Lady Jardien's supper and musicale.

"Already?" Diana asked. "It is but two weeks since . . . it has only been two weeks." The earl said nothing, taking a bite out of a lobster patty instead; his expression was mildly interested and questioning as he looked at Mrs. Carlyle. Diana was glad they were the only ones dining that evening—the vicar sometimes took his dinner with them, particularly on Sundays, and would probably have protested. This time he was attending to some business at home, however. Sir James, as well, was away, probably at some inn near some cockfight or other.

Mrs. Carlyle was silent for a moment, as if inwardly drawing herself together. Then she smiled a little, saying, "A fortnight since your uncle died. Yes." A mischievous expression grew in her eyes. "But he would never have wanted us to become hermits, and you must admit, it would be beyond cruel not to satisfy our neighbors' curiosity about the new Lord Brisbane."

It was true; there was not one day that a neighbor or acquaintance had not called upon the earl to offer their condolences, to introduce him- or herself, and to eye the black-creped walls of Brisbane House and the new earl with curiosity and speculation.

Diana bit her lip; she herself had received some speculative looks, and she was certain at least some word of her uncle's bequest had been spread about. But she made sure to have an air of indifference about her when anyone mentioned the new earl to her, or at best a polite acknowledgment of his generosity at letting her mother and herself remain at Brisbane House.

"Are you sure, Mama, that we should?" Diana asked. "I would not like our neighbors to think we would stint on any proper observances."

Mama looked at her in surprise, and Diana winced, thinking perhaps her words were uncharacteristic: she had not ever given the impression she was overly concerned about the proprieties. Then her mother smiled, reaching over to pat her hand.

"You are right to be concerned, and I know you wish only the best with regard to your uncle. But going to a musicale, with no dancing, is perfectly proper, and we shall still be wearing mourning of course. I know your uncle would have wished it." With a last pat on Diana's hand, her mother returned to her meal. "I am happy, also, that you have become more thoughtful of society's ways." It was a gentle reproof; though her mother never kept Diana from riding as fast or where she wished on the property, she did not like it when Diana had returned so wantonly disheveled, especially in the company of a gentleman.

Diana moved uneasily in her chair, and catching Lord Brisbane's quick grin, felt a flash of irritation. He probably guessed it was not from a sense of propriety that she did not want to go out into society quite yet, but rather from uneasiness once she went out at last. He seemed not at all moved by it; but she knew local society's curiosity would hardly affect him. No one would care to hint broadly at or question the Earl of Brisbane. But no one would feel such restraint around her, and she would have to fend off the questions as best as she could. Which was, alas, not easy for her.

There was, also, the question of McKinney, the head groom. She had asked questions sometime ago, and then had stopped at Lord Brisbane's suggestion, for she had found no information about him at all. Then, too, she had seen echoing questions in people's eyes, and realized that they, too, wondered about it, especially so close to the last earl's death. She flicked a glance at the current earl. He had been quite right.

The earl was silent for a moment, then said, "Perhaps it would not be amiss to go to—what is her name? Lady Jardien?" Mrs. Carlyle nodded. "Lady Jardien's musicale. As you say, it would be good for me to come to know my neighbors." He smiled. "And it would hardly do to have them expire from curiosity."

Mrs. Carlyle smiled in return. "It is in about three weeks, time enough for us to procure appropriate evening wear." She turned to Diana. "We can go to Miss Marling's in the village and look at the dresses she has, and perhaps we can make up something in those styles."

Diana nodded. "You will look marvelous, as you always do, Mama," she said, barely keeping herself from grimacing. She did not particularly like the styles Miss Marling had in her dress shop—they were in fashion, but far too frilly and fussy for her taste. She smiled at her mother fondly, if a little weakly, not quite sure how to reply otherwise. The shop's gowns suited her mother's petite and delicate frame very well, making her look as if she were a fairy queen rising out of a mist of lace and frills. Diana looked down at her plate, pushing some green beans about on it. But Miss Marling's designs only made her look—well, she did not care to think about it. She shuddered. Mama loved her so much that she could not be convinced that her daughter looked anything but lovely in whatever she wore.

"If it would not be too presumptuous," Lord Brisbane said, with a slight hesitation, "I understand there are more than a few recent magazines at the bookseller's depicting the latest styles from London. Perhaps you would like to select something from them for Miss Marling to make?"

She glanced up from her plate and caught Gavin—Lord Brisbane's—knowing gaze. The man was too perceptive. But it was out of the question; both her and her mothers' stipends together would not cover the cost of any sort of London-designed gown. They would have to save what they had over the course of many months to afford it; three weeks were hardly enough time.

"Oh, no!" Mrs. Carlyle exclaimed, though she smiled with gratitude at the earl. "No, there is no need for that. We shall do very well, I am sure."

Lord Brisbane frowned slightly. "As you wish," he said, and turned the conversation to another subject. Diana gazed at him, watching how the set of his chin nevertheless became more firm, and felt somehow that this was not the end of the matter. She shrugged. It did not matter. She had enough on her mind as it was.

For instance, she wanted, badly, to disprove Lord Brisbane's contention that her uncle had been murdered. But she could not deny that McKinney's disappearance so soon afterward made it very suspicious. The idea that McKinney had done the deed had come to her—who would not think it? But it made her feel ill—she could remember, clearly, McKinney's stern but kind face when he had put her up on her first horse, and how his hands had been gentle on hers when he had placed her fingers on the reins. He had never argued with her uncle that she could remember; the groom had always considered her uncle's requests with respect, and admired his horsemanship. Indeed, McKinney had entered enthusiastically into the many breeding and stable projects her uncle had proposed. She could not see what could cause the head groom to suddenly wish to—kill his employer. She swallowed down the taste of bile at the thought. But she had to try to be objective; certainly McKinney had access to all the horses and all the equipment and could easily have done something to cause the accident.

She gazed at Lord Brisbane, who was listening to her mother and eating in that precise way of his. He was still a puzzle. She had talked to him from time to time, but he revealed little of himself, hardly anything at all, and would turn the conversation to something else before she realized what he had done. Usually it was with a provocative word, said with such levity that she was not sure whether he meant it or not. It kept her off balance, and she was not sure if she cared for it, especially since her life had lost much of its balance already.

And yet . . . a part of her *did* like his levity and the way he hinted at or outright stated his admiration for her. She half despised herself for liking it; she had had so little praise from a marriageable gentleman that she could not help wanting more of it from him. Not that she wished to marry Lord Brisbane, of course! She hardly knew him, and the kiss he had taken—yes, taken, come to think of it—she had allowed only out of curiosity and because it had been so sudden.

Then, too, she realized, she did like him. She watched him say something jokingly to her mother, and how her mother laughed, and Diana felt grateful. Her mother had been pale and listless for the weeks after Uncle's death, and she was still so every once in a while when she thought Diana was not watching. But Gavin—Lord Brisbane—could make Mama laugh occasionally in her old way, and not reluctantly. Uncle Charles's death had been a terrible shock to Mama and she had grown so thin that her clothes had hung upon her and she had looked more ethereal than ever. But this evening, Mama did not pick at her food as usual, but ate a decent amount, even though it was not as much as she had in the past.

There was a brief silence, before Gavin cleared his throat, and looked apologetically at them. "I hope you do not mind—I had intended to ask you, but forgot, I'm afraid—but I have invited a friend of mine to stay for a while. He is a good fellow—Mr. Edwin Goldworthy—and someone I have long known."

Mrs. Carlyle shook her head and smiled. "My lord, you never have to ask! You are the earl now, and this is your home. You may invite whomever you wish."

He grinned. "Ah, yes. I forget, you know, for I am not at all used to it."

"You are quite doing well," Diana said. "Our tenants have already spoken well of you, and that is a good start." She smiled at him. He *would* make a good landlord—perhaps not as good or in the same way as her uncle, but a good one nevertheless.

He gazed at her, and his smile faded a little while his eyes held a question in them. Diana looked away, remembering his funning declarations of love and the occasional kisses he took when she was not expecting them, and could feel her face growing warm. *That* kind of question she did not feel she could answer, and would not. She glanced up to catch her mother's complacent and smug expression, and felt a welcome irritation banish the embarrassment.

"Well, then, when can we expect him?" Mrs. Carlyle asked, turning to Lord Brisbane.

"In a little more than a fortnight—ah! A problem: he will be here perhaps a day before the musicale. I should not wish to leave behind a guest."

"You need not worry," Diana said. "The invitation no doubt says 'Lord Brisbane and guests' so you may bring him, I am sure." Lord Brisbane looked relieved, and Diana gazed at him curiously. Here was another puzzle: he was a cultured man, widely traveled and widely read. He had good address and good taste in clothes—or at least, as good as any dandy might, and she had to admit, he was not all that extreme in his tastes. Not only that, but he had an excellent seat on a horse. Yet, there were the little things he seemed not to be aware of: not knowing or assuming that he might invite whatever guest he pleased to such an event, and his unease with the title. The latter she could understand, but coupled with the former—a thing most people of good society understood—it seemed odd.

No doubt his upbringing was odd, but there it was again: she knew little of it; he spoke of it only obliquely. Sir James had mentioned something about Gavin being from the merchant class—or worse. Perhaps the earl was ashamed of his upbringing, and so did not wish to speak of it. He was, however, of a noble family, and that was nothing to be ashamed of. Then, too, Diana thought ruefully, his upbringing could not be any more impoverished than hers had been before her uncle had brought her and her mother up from near starvation.

She returned her gaze to him, and when he looked at her this time and smiled, she did not look away, but smiled as well. Her heart warmed to him a little; perhaps they could be friends. If it were true that he had had a difficult childhood, it was something she could understand and that they had in common. She, too, knew what it was to be poor, and more. She turned her mind to Lord Brisbane's past rather than her own past fears.

And whatever his past misfortunes, it seemed not to have damaged what must surely be a native kindness, however odd he was at times. To see that, she only had to reflect upon his concern when they had first met, and his successful efforts in cheering her mother from time to time.

Perhaps her mother was right. Oh, not that Diana should wed him. But perhaps she should be a little more kind to him, as he had been kind to her mother and herself, and try to know him better. They could be friends, and certainly that would be a comfortable thing. She had, she reflected suddenly, no friend in whom she felt comfortable confiding, though others often confided in her. It had not bothered her much before, for she had been wholly occupied with her uncle's concerns about the estate and the stables. Then, too, she knew too well how much she'd been pitied for not having found a beau in London, and knew such things were much talked about in ladies' circles. Their arch and condescending pity hurt, so she had, therefore, avoided them as much as possible. Gentlemen, too, tended to stare at her, which she disliked. She looked at Gavin again, and decided that she would, indeed, try to be his friend.

Thus Diana managed, almost completely, to ignore her mother's knowing and very smug expression when dinner was done. And when Lord Brisbane asked if Diana would care to walk about the gardens, she was able to reply without the slightest awkwardness, exactly as a person might who was bent on forming a very platonic friendship with another.

As soon as they left the house, Diana was glad that she had agreed to walk with Gavin. It was a warm and beautiful evening, the sun still well above the horizon, and the rosebuds were beginning to bloom at last. A few lilies had begun to nudge their way above the ground, and more primroses lined the pathways than earlier in the month. She did not protest or pull away when the earl tucked her hand in the crook of his arm; she reminded herself that she would try to be a friend to him, and allowed herself to be comfortable.

She could almost feel that she was no different from any other lady; she was certainly shorter than Gavin. As a result, she did not feel as if she were such a large lump of a creature, and certainly not as awkward.

"Let us go to the maze—have you ever been there?" she asked.

He looked at her quizzically, then said, "No. I've seen it from my chamber window, but have not gone near it."

"It was sadly neglected when we first came here, and terribly overgrown," Diana said. "But Mama has quite the green thumb, and she ordered it shaped back to its original form. I often liked to try it when I was a child, but I am afraid I never did discover the key to it or find the middle."

"Did not your uncle tell you?"

"No, and it was the most irritating thing! Nor will the servants." She nodded at the entrance of it, an arching rectangular hole in a tall wall of shrubbery just at the level of the top of her head. "He would not, and always said I must discern it for myself. I had always to call for help, which is why I always inform a servant I am entering it before I do."

Lord Brisbane paused and considered the entrance in a thoughtful manner. "I am not entirely sure it would do anything for the dignity of my title if I were to call out my distress at being lost in a maze."

Diana laughed. "No, I suppose it would not, but I have called out every time I have entered it, so no one would think it unusual of *me*. I shall do it, and your dignity shall be intact."

His expression cleared. "How grateful I am that you are willing to sacrifice your dignity for mine."

"You are a silly creature, to be sure!" She shook her head. "Now why is it that I suspect that you truly care nothing for your dignity?" She placed her hand on his arm—she felt more comfortable now doing it. It even felt pleasant.

"Of course I would care," he replied. "A dandy never looks about him for help—it would mean he would have to move his head around this way and that, and it would not only disturb his shirt points, but ruin the crease of his neckcloth."

She chuckled. "You know, I also suspect you are not as dedicated to your clothes as you would make yourself out to be. Indeed, there are at least two instances in which you allowed them to be less than perfect."

"My dear, you pain me," he said, putting his hand over his heart. "How could I let anything of Weston's tailoring be treated with less than the best of care?"

"But you did." They turned a right corner, then were faced with two choices of paths. "Since this is your first time in the maze, you may choose the direction in which we will go."

"Ah, so I will be at fault when we are lost, is that it?"

She smiled widely. "Of course. A just payment for having me call for help to preserve your dignity."

He laughed, then nodded to the right path. "Let us go through that one." They stepped through the arched threshold of leaves, and he glanced at her. "Well, then, tell me, when have I been any less than impeccably dressed?"

"When we first met, you were riding in the rain. You bowed, if you remember, and your hat dripped water in your boot."

"Ah, well, I was overcome by the sight of you. I knew not what I was doing."

"I am surprised you did not detest me after you found your boot ruined."

He smiled warmly at her. "It was worth it. I would ruin half a million pairs of boots for you."

His words disconcerted her, but she would not give in to any sort of silly feelings. "Only half a million?" she teased.

"I am not *that* wealthy," he said. "Besides, I would want to spend the rest of my fortune on *you,* of course."

"Beware of such offers, my lord!" she said. "I might ask for terrible extravagances, and then you would be in the basket."

They came to another choice of pathways, and after a slight hesitation, the earl chose the left one. "Such as?"

Diana knew he had inherited almost no money when he became earl, not enough to run the estate and certainly not enough for luxuries. It was only a little more than what she had been bequeathed if she did not marry. Yet, he displayed no worry over it—did he think she would marry him eventually? Certainly if they did, their combined inheritance would be a very great one—but she pushed that thought aside. She cast about in her mind for an outrageous extravagance.

"I have it: a very large and grand mansion."

"Well, you would have one immediately in Brisbane House if I proposed to you and you accepted." His smile grew warmer.

Again she felt disconcerted, but remembered the "ifs" in his reply, and staved off the oddly depressed feeling that had seeped into her. She made herself smile in return. "I am afraid that is not enough. We must have another, oh, in Scotland. A castle, in fact."

He considered this. "I am persuaded you would not like it. Castles are very drafty, and it is very cold in Scotland."

Diana gazed at him. "You have been in Scotland, then?"

"Yes."

She waited for a moment, but he said nothing more, and impatience flashed through her. "Oh, you are impossible!"

He raised his brows. "How so?"

"For a man who seems to be very good at conversation and at drawing out other people, you are not at all forthcoming about yourself." They came upon another path and Lord Brisbane led her directly down it.

"My life is not at all that interesting, believe me," he said, but his voice became distant, and his face somber.

"Perhaps that is for me to judge," she replied. "I, for one, think that anyone who has traveled much must have very interesting tales to tell."

Lord Brisbane smiled slightly. "My tales are mostly full of seasickness and scratching out an existence where I could, believe me. Quite tedious." He made another turn, and the maze suddenly opened up to a clearing.

"Ohhh," she breathed, and looked about her with delight.

The middle of the maze contained a small garden, with a marble pond. In the midst of it was a statue of a flying horse, a Pegasus, also made of marble; its wings were spread wide, and its hooves pawed the air. The mouth was open, and sprayed forth water that sprinkled around it in a circle. The water fell with a light, laughing, burbling noise as it hit the pond's surface. It was warmer within the maze than outside, so the rosebushes at each corner of the garden had flowers fully open. Their scent colored the air around them, and the red and pink of the buds against the deep green of the shrubbery were in vivid contrast to each other. Primroses lined the walks, between which were patches of soft green grass, and brown-eyed pansies nodded their heads at the edge of the pond.

"Oh, my!" she said. "Oh, my! I cannot believe it—I am here! After so many years. And it is so beautiful—much more than I had ever dreamed. Why did not my uncle tell me how to come here?"

A marble bench sat near the water, and the earl led her to it. She did not sit immediately, however; sheer delight at being, finally, in the middle of the maze had seized her, and it rose in a bubble of laughter in her chest. She closed her eyes and swung herself around, arms outstretched. The laugh burst out at last, and then she sat down next to Lord Brisbane.

"A prize is that much more beautiful when it is long in achieving," Lord Brisbane said.

She turned to look at him, and his expression caught her breath: he gazed at her as if she were the prize of which he spoke. "Why do you say that?" she asked.

"Because it is true," he said simply.

Diana shook her head slowly. "No . . . I mean, why do you say that and look at me . . . like that." She did not know how to put it into words—the expression in his eyes made her heart beat faster and made her tremble, as if she felt a little afraid.

He raised his brows. "Like what?"

"Like—oh, I don't know!" She turned on the bench and gazed at the pond, and shuffled her feet restlessly on the gravel beneath her. Bending, she picked up a pebble and tossed it into the pond. It made no more noise or disturbance than the splashes of water already falling into it. "As if . . . as if I were not too tall or too plump or my skin too brown. As if my hair were not yellow, or my eyes too pale a blue. As if I did not stride like a man, or ride too fast or too wildly."

He took her hand gently, looked tenderly into her eyes and bent so close to her she trembled again—was he going to kiss her? But then Diana felt something heavy drop into her hand.

"Try this," he said softly, his voice floating to her ear in the most romantic tones she had ever heard. "A large rock will make a much more satisfying splash than a pebble."

She stared at him, and the next breath she took spurted out in a laugh. The next one she tried to suppress with her hand, but it burst through her fingers, and the next she did not even try to repress. "Oh! Oh, y-you—!" She gasped and laughed again, helplessly. "You are—are t-terrible!"

His face took on a morose expression. "I was only trying to be of help."

Diana doubled over, pressing her hands to her mouth, but it only made her laughter turn to shrieks. "Oh, ohhh! How could you—oh, I swear I almost thought you were—and then the rock—"

"Well, I was, but I thought throwing the rock might be more satisfying to you," he said, grinning.

She stared at him, wide-eyed, her lips still trembling with laughter. "Oh, no—that is, it would be satisfying, but it is not to say—I mean—" She stopped, and she could feel her face becoming more warm than it was already from laughing.

He shook his head. "You are a strange young lady, to be sure! I have never met a woman who rated her looks so low."

"I have it on good authority that I am as fashionable as a milkmaid." She shrugged. "Coarse and awkward. I heard it many times in London."

"From whom?"

"My Aunt Matchett, and then it was picked up by those around her." The words still stung, even as she said them. She looked away from him. "No one would dance with me at the end of my Season, for fear that I would step on their toes, and being as big as I am, no doubt I would have injured them quite severely."

Her arm was suddenly seized, and she stared at Lord Brisbane's abruptly stormy face. "Stand up."

"What—?"

"I said, stand up."

She stood, and stared at his neckcloth, suddenly not able to meet his eyes.

"Now, look at me."

She did not, not right away, and his hand came under her chin, forcing it up. Her eyes met his at last, reluctantly, and he gazed at her with a blazing intensity—she did not know if it was anger, or something else.

"You have to look *up* at me, do you not?"

She nodded, slowly.

"Therefore you are not tall, not to me."

"But—"

He put his hand over her mouth. "Hush! Listen, for once." His hand moved gently away from her lips and caressed her cheek. "Your skin is not brown, but golden. It shines as if it were gilded. Your hair—" He plucked at the pins that held it in place, and it fell to her waist as he threaded his fingers through it. "Your hair is not yellow, but the color of the sun, almost blinding in its brilliance. Your eyes are not pale blue, but the color of the summer sky."

Her breath came quickly as she stared at him. "Please—" she whispered, and a light trembling shook her. "I'm not—"

"No, say nothing." Lord Brisbane's voice was softer now, but just as commanding. "Listen." His hand moved to cup her chin, gently this time. "Your lips are the color of new roses, and sweeter than Spanish sherry." He bent and touched them with his own, briefly, and she could not help making a little sound, a sigh that seemed to come up from deep inside. "Big?" His hands slid to her waist, and he gave a laugh, sounding breathless. "My hands can almost go around your waist."

She could not stop looking into his eyes; they froze her to the spot—no, not frozen, for she felt too warm now, as if she had been running. "Only the front of my waist. And your—your hands are very large." Her voice came out, also breathless, a whisper.

He laughed again, a husky sound. "How convenient, since you insist on emphasizing how big you are. Just think how well they can hold you."

It was all she could think of, the way his hands caressed her waist and drew her close, the way his fingers massaged the small of her back. Or no, there were his lips as well, the way they hovered over hers, not quite touching her mouth as he gazed into her eyes. She could feel his breath flow over her hips, a prelude to his touch. A laughing wild look flashed in his eyes, and his hand pushed up her chin so that her lips reached his at last.

She moaned—she could not help it. It came up from the pit of her belly, from the depths of her heart. She grasped his shoulders, and tiptoed so that she could press her mouth against his. His hands—his hands moved from her waist to her hips, pressing her close to him, and a heat rose from there, tingling outward to her skin.

He moved his mouth a little from hers. "Open them, Diana," he whispered. He kissed her again, licking slightly the corners of her mouth. Tentatively, she parted her lips, and his were upon them again, kissing her deeply, pulling her closer than ever.

A movement, a tug, and she found herself sitting on his lap upon the bench, gasping, for his lips had left hers and had kissed a trail from her chin to her shoulder. She closed her eyes, feeling drugged and dizzy, and tightened her grasp on his shoulders.

"You make me feel wild, Diana," he said, his words hot upon the soft skin of her throat. "God help me, I have never wanted a woman as much as I want you."

She could say nothing, caught up in the sound of his voice, the feel of his breath upon her skin, the touch of his fingers moving slowly upward from her waist to the side of her breast. Her own breath caught, then started again, fitfully, and she tried to swallow down the trembling that coursed through her. "Please—" she said, her voice barely a whisper. "Please . . ." She did not know what she asked; it was the only word she could seem to say.

He stilled, his forehead resting in the crook of her neck, then slowly he raised his head to look at her. "I should ask you to marry me."

Ask me, cried a voice inside her. *Ask me.* The sensual fog slowly lifted from her mind, and she answered herself, *No, I hardly know him.*

He sighed, shaking his head. He rose, half lifting her as he did, and then letting her slide down until her feet reached the ground.

"Why?" she blurted.

He grinned suddenly, and the sight of it twisted her heart. "I don't think you would accept. And . . ." His grin turned wry. "I don't think I deserve you."

Diana moved a little away from him, anger and frustration lancing quickly through her. "Should I not be the one to determine that?" she said. "I have already determined we could be friends—" He shot her a surprised look. "Yes, friends. You have virtues I look for in a friend: certainly one of them is kindness. I have seen how you work to make my mother laugh—and I am grateful, for her spirits have lightened, and she has begun to eat more than she has been. I have been worried about her, you see, and she won't listen to me when I try to make her eat more." She touched his sleeve, lightly. "I am grateful."

"I—you are welcome," he said, suddenly seeming at a loss for words.

"Indeed, I agreed to this walk to learn more about you—" She broke off, a blush heating her face, thinking of what they had just been doing. "Not—not that!"

Lord Brisbane smiled slightly. "No? I thought you were curious."

"I—I was," she said honestly. "But I wished to know *you* better. I believe I know what all the kissing was about."

His smile turned quizzical. "Do you?"

Diana nodded. "I have heard it from the stablehands when they thought I was not about and listening. It hasn't anything to do with love, but with pleasure, and I know enough that it would not do to go very far into it, or else it will be like what the stallions do to the mares, and I shall begin to breed." Diana made herself look at him, even though her face still felt warm. "I may be as wild as my uncle said I was, but I know enough not to cause such a scandal." It was difficult to think of how humans might go about it, but the idea had occurred to her that it might be somewhat similar. She knew it was not something she should even be mentioning to him, but however much she did not care for society's conventions, she was not willing to bear a child out of wedlock. She did not know, she realized, what he truly wanted of her, whether he wished to dally with her or marry her in earnest. He had said, over and over again, that he wished to marry her, but refused to propose. What was she to make of that?

She watched him warily—was he angry at her?—as his face grew suddenly red, and his lips pressed tightly together.

And then he threw back his head and roared with laughter. She frowned, wondering what he thought was so funny.

"Ah, Diana—" He wiped the tears from his eyes, then looked at her, and burst out laughing again. "Oh, God, only you, only you. If the thought of breeding stallions and mares isn't enough to put off kisses, I don't know what is." He held out his hand. "Come, my dear, let's be friends." He glanced at the dimming sky. "If you are so concerned about scandal, then we should not stay here very long. And I promise you, I will keep scandal away from you as best I can." She took his hand, he brought hers to his lips, and they walked out of the middle of the maze.

It only took a few minutes before Diana realized that Lord Brisbane had not faltered once in turning this way and that in the maze, and they were out before she had a chance to remember she was to call out to the servants for help. She gazed at him accusingly.

"You knew the key to the maze all along!" She pulled her hand from his arm. Oh, how irritating he was! He could have told her at the very beginning!

He gave her an apologetic look. "Well, yes. It is one of the things that goes along with being the Earl of Brisbane. I found it immediately among the estate papers."

"Oh! See if I ever go into the maze with you again!" She stamped her foot on the grass, and moved away from him.

"Wait, Diana—"

She stopped, but did not turn around. Footsteps sounded behind her and then he came around and gazed at her solemnly—almost. There was a twinkle in his eyes, and she tried very hard not to respond to it. "Diana, I took you there because I thought you would like it."

There was a wistful note in his voice, and she could not help relenting. "Oh . . . very well. I did like it," she admitted.

"I am glad," he said simply, but his gaze fell on her lips.

"That does not mean I shall allow you to kiss me if we do go again into the middle of the maze," she said.

"I understand," he replied. "I will only kiss you if you allow it."

Diana stared at him, frustrated. How was she to answer that? She hadn't thought she would allow such things each time, but they had happened nevertheless. "I do not want any scandal about the two of us," she said firmly.

"I promise you, our kisses will not cause any scandal," he said promptly.

She let out a little growl—it seemed no matter what she said, it came around to kissing again.

"You are impossible!" she said, and gave him a burning look. His only response was a chuckle, and Diana felt she could do nothing but cross her arms before her and keep herself from looking back at him all the way to the house.

But when she finally stepped into her room, she realized she had not got him to tell her anything about himself at all. How odious he was! Diana thought, and tried not to think of how she had thought quite otherwise when they were in the maze.

Chapter 8

A large coach-and-four rumbled up to the front of Brisbane House two days before Lady Jardien's musicale. It was a very fine one, a bit overwrought with decoration, Diana thought as she looked out of her chamber window, but very well-made nevertheless. It made her think of what Lord Brisbane had said of the workmanship of coaches and she knew at once the man who stepped down from the coach must be Mr. Edwin Goldworthy.

She hurried downstairs, telling a passing maid to send her mother to the drawing room and for a servant to bring refreshments. Only a few minutes passed after she entered the room before the butler opened the door, and Mr. Goldworthy was announced.

Diana liked him immediately. He was a large, burly man, with apple cheeks, a snub nose, and merry eyes. He was perhaps almost fifty; his graying hair was neatly arranged, as was his neckcloth. Though he dressed plainly, his clothes were well-tailored, if a little old-fashioned.

"I am pleased to meet you, Mr. Goldworthy," she said, holding out her hand. "I am Diana Carlyle, the late earl's niece. I have ordered refreshment. I hope you do not mind that I have taken the liberty of assuming you would like some after traveling so far."

"Aye, I would at that, thank you, miss," he said, smiling gratefully as he bowed over her hand. "For it's a trifle sharpset I am, and as you see, there's quite a bit of me to keep up." He looked about the drawing room, his brows raised. "Well, it's a fine bit of property Gavin has got himself, I must say." Diana gestured him to a chair, but he grimaced and shook his head. "Nay, I'm still in my travel-dirt, I'm afraid, and would dirty the furniture."

She smiled at him. "You need not worry; I have come in very dusty from outdoors many times myself, and so my mother has made sure to cover the furniture well." She gestured at the embroidered cloths pinned to the chairs and sofa.

Mr. Goldworthy hesitated, eyed with distrust a chair that looked much too delicate for him, then sat in a sturdy armchair with a deep sigh. He was silent for a moment, then looked at her keenly. "Well, you're the young lady Gavin—I suppose I should be calling him 'his lordship' now—has been telling me about."

"Has he?" Diana said as indifferently as she could, and gave a surprised smile so that there would be no doubt there was nothing between herself and the earl.

"Not that he's said *much*—he's a closemouthed lad, for all his chatter."

"So I have noticed."

Mr. Goldworthy nodded knowingly. "A grand strappin' wench, he said, one who'll have none of him." He leaned forward confidentially. "But I'll tell you, lass, he's a good 'un, and you'll not wish for a better man in a scrape." He chuckled. "Aye, and I'm betting you'll be more than a handful for him, and good for you, Miss Carlyle, for a milk-and-water miss could never bear his fits and starts. I'll wager you'll set him straight."

Diana opened her mouth and shut it, unable to decide whether to laugh or be offended. But she looked at the man's guileless eyes and cheerful smile, and found herself chuckling in return. "To be sure, I am not at all a milk-and-water miss, but I'll not marry him. For one thing, he hasn't proposed."

Mr. Goldworthy rocked back in his chair and his blue eyes widened. "Well, and I never thought the lad backward, for he always did have a way with the—" An alarmed look flashed across his face. "Eh, never mind that!"

Unease mixed with amusement made Diana's smile turn wry. But it occurred to her that she might get the best of Lord Brisbane after all, for she perceived Mr. Goldworthy to be unusually garrulous. A maid entered with tea and biscuits, and after Diana poured, she waved the maid away.

"So, Mr. Goldworthy," Diana said, and smiled brightly, "have you known Lord Brisbane long?"

His anxious look fled, and he smiled widely. "That I have, miss, since he was a lad—fifteen, if I remember."

But Mr. Goldworthy said no more, for the door opened once again, and he rose from his chair as her mother entered, and behind her, Lord Brisbane. The earl grinned and held out his hand. "Well, Mr. Goldworthy, I see you have arrived in fine shape."

"Eh, Gavin my boy—er, my lord—it does my heart good to see you." The man shook his hand warmly.

Lord Brisbane grimaced. "Not you, too. I swear if I hear you 'milording' me I'll go into an apoplexy. I'm not used to it, Ned, and I don't know if I'll ever be."

Mr. Goldworthy nodded his head wisely. "Well, it's a thing you'll have to get used to, and soon, for you've got a right good business here on this property. You wear the title along with the business, I'm thinking." He glanced at Mrs. Carlyle, who stood next to the earl.

"Ah, I have been remiss," Lord Brisbane said apologetically. "May I present Mrs. Cecelia Carlyle? She is Miss Carlyle's mother, and the widow of the late earl's brother. Mrs. Carlyle, Mr. Edwin Goldworthy."

Mr. Goldworthy sighed deeply as he bowed over Mrs. Carlyle's hand. "A great pleasure to meet you, ma'am." He smiled at her. "A great pleasure, indeed."

Mrs. Carlyle smiled in return, and Diana was surprised to see a light flush appear in her mother's cheeks. "I thank you, sir," replied Mrs. Carlyle. "I see my daughter has been entertaining you—do you wish for more refreshment?"

"Nay, it's enough, thank you ma'am. I'll need to see how the servants are unloading my trunks—" He turned to Lord

Brisbane. "Which reminds me, my boy, I've fetched the boxes from Madame—"

"You're a devilish rattle, Ned!" Lord Brisbane interrupted, frowning. "I tend to forget it when I'm away from you, but now that you're here, I'm sure I'll not tell you anything of importance for the whole of your stay."

Mr. Goldworthy grinned, nudged the earl with an elbow, and winked at Diana and her mother again. "Never you mind him, ladies. Gavin pretends to have a poker up his—er, back, but he's always been an openhanded chap, though you'd never hear him say so." He gazed at the earl fondly. "Good as a son, he's been to me, give you my word!"

Lord Brisbane rolled his eyes, and Diana bit her lower lip to suppress a giggle at his discomfort. She must definitely make a better acquaintance with Mr. Goldworthy. He was a font of information, and had no hesitation putting the earl to the blush. She watched the earl talk to his friend and her mother, and was content to observe. How amusing it would be to have Mr. Goldworthy about! Yes, if Lord Brisbane would not reveal anything about himself, Mr. Goldworthy certainly might. In fact, Diana thought, she would make sure he did.

Somehow, though Diana meant to talk to Mr. Goldworthy at some time between his arrival and Lady Jardien's musicale, she rarely saw him except at dinner. Indeed, she rarely saw Lord Brisbane, either. Both of them had much business to discuss, apparently; Mr. Goldworthy was clearly some sort of merchant seaman, and Lord Brisbane clearly had an interest in his business, and from their conversation, it seemed that the earl had even worked for Mr. Goldworthy at one point. But she could get no other information from either of them; Lord Brisbane was as uninformative as ever, and Mr. Goldworthy only laughed and referred her to his friend whenever she asked questions.

Frustrated, she turned her thoughts to the work she was supervising at the stables, and inevitably thought of McKinney. There was still no sign of him, no word, and Diana could not help thinking that he had encountered some mishap. She hoped whatever it was, he was in good hands, and that he would return soon, or send some word about his condition. He would not have gone so suddenly without taking leave of her, or at least of the earl.

The clock chimed on the mantelpiece of her chamber fireplace; she had perhaps half an hour before she must begin to dress for the upcoming musicale. Despite the fact that Diana had gone to Lady Jardien's house before, she did not care for parties and she could not help feeling a stupid anxiety about it. She would be stared at, and she hated it, for it made her feel like some freak of nature—awkward, even afraid. It would make her feel more confined than she did now.

She glanced out her chamber window—the sky was becoming dim—and she rang for her maid so as to begin dressing. She sighed impatiently, wishing she had more freedom, as much as any man might.

It was not that she rode about the estate any less, but that Lord Brisbane insisted she take a groom with her. She had not complied the first time, leaving before a groom could set out with her, but the uncomfortable look in the servant's eyes when he did catch up with her and his apologetic determination to stay by her side made her realize that she was not going to escape.

She protested, but only a little. The earl was concerned for her safety, and coupled with McKinney's disappearance, even she could see there might be good reason for his concern. Going to a musicale was not the same as riding a horse, of course, but it was going *elsewhere* and that at least was something.

A light knock at the door announced the maid, who entered at Diana's "Come in" with a dress draped over her arms. Diana frowned.

"I do not recall asking for this dress, Annie—indeed, I do not think it is my dress at all, for I have never seen it before."

The maid smiled shyly. "His lordship asked that you be given it, miss—a present. He's given one to your mother as well. It's straight from London, too." She tenderly laid it on the bed, spreading out the skirts and smoothing out any wrinkles.

Diana stared at it, uncertain. She had never seen a dress like it. It was very beautiful, clearly an evening gown, but no one could say that to wear it would be disrespectful to Uncle Charles, for it was black, and very well suited to mourning. She shook her head. "No, I do not think I should wear it—it could not be proper for me to accept such a gift from Lord Brisbane."

The maid looked disappointed. "I'm that sorry, Miss Diana. 'Twould have looked right pretty on you, I'm sure."

Another knock sounded on the door, and Diana's mother entered in a rush, her eyes sparkling. "Oh, my dear, did he give you one, also? He is too, too generous!"

Diana gazed questioningly at her mother. "I am not sure we should accept them, Mama. Is it proper to accept such a gift from an unmarried gentleman?"

Mrs. Carlyle's brows rose in surprise. "Well, I am glad you are thinking of the proprieties, Diana." She worried her lower lip for a while in thought. "You may be right, for he *is* a distant relation . . . perhaps it would not do, though how kind of him to think of us!"

"Indeed, Mama," Diana said, and could not help looking with some wistfulness at the dress laid out on her bed.

Her mother sighed, and turned to the maid. "Annie, do bring out the dress that we made from one of Miss Marling's designs." The girl nodded, and went to the wardrobe with reluctant steps.

When Diana was finally dressed for the evening, her mother nodded in a satisfied manner, but Diana barely kept herself from grimacing. The black frills at her shoulders made her look a yard wide, as did the white bows just under her bosom. It made her glad she had worn the stays that made her bustline smaller; she would have looked like a milch cow without them. The hem was lined with batting—the latest style, she had heard from Miss Marling herself—and stood out away from her feet. She looked for all the world as if she were some highly decorated and black-creped funeral bell.

"How pretty you look," Mama said, and patted her daughter's cheek. Diana smiled weakly. "Now, I shall put on my dress, and then we shall be ready, with at least half an hour to spare."

Diana nodded, and when her mother left, she gazed at the dress Lord Brisbane had given her and sighed. It was beautiful, with puffed sleeves so tiny they hardly deserved to be called sleeves. The only relief from the severity of its cut was from the gold net overskirt and the gold bands along the bodice and the hem. But what could she do? She had felt distinctly uncomfortable thinking of her conversation in the maze, and how she had teased Lord Brisbane about asking for extravagances, and how he had said he would spend his fortune upon her. It had all been teasing, and yet here was this lovely dress, a thing a lady did not accept from a gentleman. She could not accept it, and had taken refuge in propriety. She sighed. How ironic it was that she now found propriety so convenient, where she had thought it very inconvenient before Gavin Sinclair arrived.

Her mother called to her at last, and Diana descended the stairs, hoping she could put on a pelisse before Lord Brisbane saw her. Her hope died a-borning, however, for he was standing at the foot of the steps, impeccably dressed in black, his neckcloth a pure white, and his black knee breeches with one crease. He looked up at her, transferred his gaze to her mother, and frowned.

"Did you not receive the dresses I sent to you?" he said abruptly.

Her mother stopped, and looked confused. "I did, my lord, but—"

He smiled at her. "Not 'my lord.' 'Gavin,' if you please."

She looked more flustered than ever. "Gavin, then. Well, we did receive the dresses, but we cannot accept them, I'm afraid."

A sad, wistful look crossed his face. "You do not like them, then?"

"Oh, no, no!" Mrs. Carlyle said hastily. "They are lovely, to be sure! So beautiful." She sighed longingly. "Indeed, I wish we could wear them, for I cannot help thinking they would suit us perfectly."

"Do they not fit, then?" he asked. "I asked your maid for one of your old dresses and sent them straightaway to Madame LaSalle's on Bond Street to pattern from."

Madame LaSalle's! Even Diana knew that the woman was one of the best modistes in London, and made her clothes with precision and style. She watched her mother's eyes widen and heard her draw in a long, melancholy breath.

"Ohhh . . ." Indecision flickered over Mrs. Carlyle's face, then she shook her head. "No, we did not try them on—"

Lord Brisbane's face took on an aggrieved expression, and Mrs. Carlyle began to look guilty in response. "You did not try them on." He sighed mournfully. "I see." Her mother looked more guilty than ever.

Diana gazed at him sharply. A glance in her direction showed a distinct twinkle in his eyes. She lifted her chin. "I am afraid it is not proper to accept such gifts as these from an unmarried gentleman, my lord."

He smiled pleasantly at her. " 'Gavin,' please."

She gritted her teeth. "Gavin."

He pursed his lips thoughtfully, then turned to her mother. "Is this true? Even if the gentleman is a relative, though distant?"

"Well—" her mother began to say.

"A distant relative who is grateful he has a hostess—indeed, two hostesses—and wishes them to be well rewarded for their work." He looked at Mrs. Carlyle earnestly. "Indeed, I do not know how I would manage without your supervision in this household. It is you who approves the dinner menu, and makes sure the housekeeper does all she should, is it not?"

"Yes, it is," Mrs. Carlyle replied. "But it is in return for giving us a home—"

The earl raised his chin and looked down his nose at her, the picture of offended hauteur. "Are you saying that I am not conscious of my duties to the Carlyle family? That I would throw defenseless females—*ladies* who are related to *me*—out into the cold unless they become my household drudges?"

Mrs. Carlyle looked alarmed. "No, no, I would never say such a thing!"

"Then you must see that I am very grateful for what you have done for me, and am only expressing my gratitude." He smiled cheerfully at her. "Certainly you can see I cannot have you dressed in anything but the best?"

"Oh, no, of course not," Mrs. Carlyle said, looking at once anxious and bewildered.

"Besides, it would never do for his consequence," Diana snapped. Oh, how cleverly he managed to twist her mother around his finger! But she would not give in, no, she would not.

"Diana!" her mother said in a scandalized voice. "How could you?"

The earl sighed. "I see it now. She does not even wish to try it on—no doubt she believes my taste is execrable, or perhaps she thinks me overbearing."

Mrs. Carlyle shook her head. "No, my lord. She *will* try it on. Then we shall see." She turned to Diana. "Come, my dear. You cannot be so rude as to refuse to try on the dress, can you?" A pleading look entered her mother's eyes, and Diana felt helpless before it. She knew it would give her mother great pleasure to wear such a fine dress, and to see her daughter try on hers. Indeed, it was probably many, many years since her mother had worn such a gown, if it was anything like the one the earl had given Diana. It was a London dress, one only ladies of very high *ton* would wear, the height of fashion. A stab of guilt went through her, and she nodded reluctantly.

"Very well, Mama, I shall try it on."

Her mother sighed in relief. "Come then, hurry. We have not much time." She almost ran up the stairs, and summoned a passing chambermaid to help her, while she requested Annie to help Diana dress.

Annie beamed with enthusiasm when she found she was to put the black-and-gold dress on Diana, and hastily shook it out and unbuttoned the frilly one that her mistress wore. Diana grimaced when the maid said, "You'll have to wear other stays, miss, not these. They'd show above the bodice, you see." She shrugged, and the maid pulled out another, less confining set of stays. If she was lucky, the color and line of the dress would deemphasize the unfortunate shape of her body.

Fifteen minutes later, Diana looked into the mirror and her heart plummeted to her stomach. "Oh, no," she whispered.

Her maid gazed at her, clearly puzzled. "What is wrong, Miss Diana?"

"I—I—cannot wear this!" She tried to swallow down a panicked nervousness and failed.

It was not Diana Carlyle she was staring at in the mirror, but some other woman—queenly, majestic. Her maid had redressed her hair in a severe knot at the back of her head, with long curling strands streaming down below her shoulders to complement the style of the dress. She had thought the gown would be fairly plain, even austere, and it was, compared to the frilly dress she had worn before. But the waistline was a little lower than the other—she remembered there seemed to be an emerging fashion for a lower waistline than before—and hugged her very closely. The sleeves were little nothings of puffed black silk gauze bordered with gold piping; her arms, if it were not for her gloves, would almost be bare. But the gold net overskirt gave it an exotic Byzantine look, and the bodice—

Diana closed her eyes and groaned. The bodice was also of many-layered black silk gauze and on anyone else it would have been modest. But the gold band that lined the top of it barely restrained the expanse of flesh that almost overflowed the edge. She could not even bind her bosom as she often did, for it would make the bodice too loose and reveal more than it should.

A knock sounded at the door, and alarm flashed through her. "Don't—!" But her mother entered before she could say more.

Her eyes widened. "Oh, Diana!" she breathed. "Oh, my dear, dear girl! How beautiful you look—so fashionable!" She waved the maid away. "Annie, do go down and tell his lordship that we will be down soon." The maid curtsied and left.

Diana closed her eyes in embarrassment, and put her hands over her chest. "Mama, do you have a fichu? A gold one, perhaps?"

Mrs. Carlyle looked puzzled. "Whatever for? You look perfectly well—beautiful, as I said."

"Mama, you always say that. But surely you realize I cannot go out in—in this!"

Her mother looked her up and down, looking more puzzled than ever. "The dress is perfect for you—I see now that frills and large bows are completely wrong for you, and I only wish I had known it earlier. I have never seen you look better, truly."

"Thank you, Mama, but I am *not* going out in this dress," Diana said through gritted teeth. "It is indecent."

Mrs. Carlyle looked her over again. "Nonsense. It is black, perfect for mourning. The bodice is no different than mine, no higher or lower. Indeed, I believe you were hiding yourself behind all those frills and bows of Miss Marling's."

Diana held her tongue, forbearing to point out that Miss Marling's designs were all that they had in the village to date, and she herself had never insisted on the bows—Miss Marling had. She gazed, a little resentfully she admitted, at her mother's dress: a lovely confection of airy black and lavender ruffles with pearls glinting amongst them with fugitive light. True, her bodice was just as low as Diana's, but her mother's delicate form did not overflow it as did hers. Instead, Mama looked like a fairy princess emerging out of twilight mist.

Diana sighed. Her mother would not be convinced, she knew. But she would not leave this room wearing this Byzantine queen's gown. She looked her mother in the eye.

"Mama, I am going to wear the other dress."

Mrs. Carlyle looked startled, then a martial light grew in her eyes. "No, my dear, you are not. You look lovely, and you *will* go to Lady Jardien's musicale in this dress."

"Mama, please—"

"No!" Mrs. Carlyle eyed her sternly. "No, Diana. I do not know what has come over you. Truly I do not. All these outbursts, and swinging from extreme missishness to hoydenish behavior." She sighed, and her face grew sad. "I suppose it is for lack of masculine guidance in your life. If only your father had not died, or if Charles—"

Anger flared. "No it is not, Mama! We can do very well without masculine *guidance*. Did it really do us any good when Father left us to starve? And when Uncle Charles died—we are only hangers-on, after all—"

Her mother jerked as if struck, then paled, and immediately Diana's anger disappeared, replaced by deep remorse. "Oh, Mama, I am sorry! So sorry. I didn't mean—please forgive me." She turned away, covering her face with her hands in shame. "I have been so—I don't know! I had felt so safe when Uncle Charles—when he was with us, and I never had to think of anything, just riding and driving carriages, reading, music, and doing as I wished. But now—I cannot feel comfortable being so obliged to Lord Brisbane." She felt her mother's arm come around her in a hug and looked up to see her smile.

"Oh, my dear girl. I understand how difficult it can be to feel so—I felt that way when your uncle first came for us. That is why I continue to keep house as I did when your uncle was alive. Lord Brisbane—Gavin—is a kind, generous man, and we should be thankful. And do you not still oversee the stables? I do not think Gavin has said you should not, and in fact has left it all to you to manage, especially now that McKinney is missing. I believe Gavin must rate your judgment and abilities quite high in these matters, do you not think?"

Diana gazed at her mother and realized she was quite right. Lord Brisbane had said nothing to countermand any of her orders to the grooms and neither had he asked her to discontinue her uncle's projects in the stables. Diana had gone on as she had before her uncle had died, supervising the building of an addition to the stables, and the breeding of cattle. She had thrown herself into the work, wanting, somehow, to keep her uncle alive in this way, not even thinking of how unusual it might be for her to supervise it.

"I . . . I suppose you are right," Diana said slowly. She gave a reluctant smile. "Either that, or he knows how stubborn I can be and is afraid of getting in my way."

Her mother laughed. "Perhaps so, and if so, think how wise a man he must be to know it." She touched Diana's cheek fondly. "Surely it could not hurt to please such a man in this one thing?"

Diana thought of how unusual Lord Brisbane was, and nodded. He was infuriating sometimes, frustrating, and annoyingly closemouthed about himself, but nothing she had done so far shocked him, or so he said. He had only agreed with her, laughed, or kissed—Diana stopped the thought, and grew conscious of her dress again.

She drew in a breath and let it out. "You are right, Mama. There is no need for me to be missish." Indeed, she would pretend she was dressed as usual, perhaps in her riding dress. She never felt anxious or exposed in her riding habit, but in control of herself and of everything around her. Clothes were just that—clothes. No more, no less. There was no reason why she should feel any different in this gown than in anything else.

And yet, when she descended the stairs once again, she could not help seeing Lord Brisbane's habitual sleepy look disappear to be replaced by widened eyes. He bowed over her hand when she approached him, and she heard a distinct sigh leave him, then saw an odd regret appear in his eyes as he rose and gazed at her.

For all her determination not to be missish, she felt a blush enter her cheeks, and she made herself look away. "Shall we go?" she asked. There was silence for a moment, and she fiddled with a fold in her skirt as a footman brought her pelisse and put it upon her shoulders. She wondered if the gentlemen guests would stare at her as Gavin did, and she almost turned back up the stairs.

"Yes. Yes, of course," came Lord Brisbane's voice. Diana looked up at him at last—he was still looking at her—and she turned to her mother. "Mama, I believe you should go before me."

Her mother looked suddenly indecisive. "Oh—oh, dear. I have forgotten my reticule." She gazed at Lord Brisbane. "Do go ahead with Diana into the coach—I shall be with you presently, only a moment." She turned and hurried up the stairs again.

Lord Brisbane took Diana's hand and placed it on his arm. "I do believe your mother wishes to leave us alone," he said as they walked away from the stairs down the great hall. "Now, I wonder why?"

Diana suppressed her nervousness and gave him a sour look. "She has an odd idea that my uncle's will is perfect in every way."

"A wise woman, your mother," he replied calmly. "I have thought so from the start."

"A *fond* mother, to be sure," Diana replied firmly. She remembered her words to her mother in her room, and remorse touched her again. "More fond than I deserve, surely."

The footmen opened the double doors and they walked down the steps to the waiting coach. Lord Brisbane held her hand as she stepped into it, then entered himself, sitting opposite her.

The coach was the largest in the carriage house, but the sunset's light hardly penetrated the interior, and the carriage lamps just at the windows only highlighted brief surfaces—a cheek, a brow, the glint of whatever shiny surface might be within. It was a close and intimate space, but Diana looked at the earl, his face partly in shadow, and he seemed more of a stranger than ever. He was, in a way, reserved, she thought, always deflecting conversation away from discussions of his life. How odd that was in a man who seemed at times lazy and at other times outright chatty.

The light shifted from Lord Brisbane's cheek to his chin—he was looking at her askance. "Your mother thinks differently. And . . . I think you have been in the habit of taking care of her, have you not?"

She gave him a sharp glance; he was right, she realized. She had tried to take care of her mother ever since she was very young. "We take care of each other, my lord." That was true, too. Her mother would do anything for Diana; she had always felt strong and secure in this knowledge. It was her rock, her anchor. "She is a strong-hearted woman. And I—" She gave a short laugh. "I have always been physically strong. Hence my London nickname, 'the Milkmaid.' "

His hand was warm through her glove when it took hers and brought it to his lips. "You do not look like a milkmaid now."

No, she did not, but his words made her feel a little frightened. She lifted her chin. "No, I suppose I do not. In this gown, I look like a mosaic from an ancient ruin."

He laughed and released her hand. "I hadn't thought of it that way, but surely you must admit it is far more grand than a milkmaid."

"I do not think it is a good thing to be grand." She remembered how she had towered over many of the men in London, and how she felt she had to crouch and slump to fit in some way. A memory from before her arrival at Brisbane House stirred: it had not been good for her to look older than her years, either. It could cause trouble and even hurt.

"But of course it is," Lord Brisbane said, and his face moved so that it was completely in shadow. "When you are grand, you are free to do anything you wish, and people will accept it." The small space of the carriage made his voice sound harsh, Diana thought.

A voice from outside the coach—her mother's—made Diana sit back against the squabs; the earl's voice had also been quiet, and she had leaned forward, intent on his words. Almost, almost she thought he might tell something of himself—there was that strangely still quality about him that she remembered seeing before when he mentioned some memory or experience.

Her mother appeared at the carriage door, and smiled as Lord Brisbane helped her inside. "Thank you my lor—that is, Gavin." She gazed curiously at the two of them, and then looked surprised. "Is not Mr. Goldworthy attending?"

"He sends his apologies," Lord Brisbane said, and Diana thought she could hear a smile in his voice. "He will be a trifle late—a bit of business he needs to attend to first." She wondered what sort of business it was. She had seen him with the earl, talking with the estate's tenants, and then walking through the nearby village. No doubt it had something to do with Mr. Goldworthy's search for a suitable piece of property to buy.

"What a pity," Mrs. Carlyle said. "Such a pleasant gentleman, so cheerful. Well, I shall be glad to see him when he does arrive. Does he like music much, Gavin?"

The earl seemed willing to talk of his friend, certainly more so than he was willing to talk about himself, Diana noted. Mr. Goldworthy was a merchant, and had learned the law as well. Not a solicitor, but a barrister, and he had traveled the world as a youth. He had recently conceived a wish to set down roots, and was in fact looking for some small property to purchase. Lord Brisbane had invited him here to look about for a prospective home, and he had accepted.

Diana smiled to herself as she listened, inserting a comment here and there between her mother's questions and exclamations of interest. By the time they reached Lady Jardien's house, she had gathered more bits of information regarding the earl than he probably realized he had revealed. He had gone to India and to the Americas, and had even once skirted the mysterious islands of Japan on a Dutch ship. He had known illness and deprivation, and her heart went out to him—she well knew what that was like. He was ambitious, and worked hard wherever he had gone, even including manual labor.

He did not say any of this directly, but she could guess it from the references he made to various activities and the occasional stillness of his body when he spoke of such things.

No, Lord Brisbane, you do not say much, she thought, when the coach stopped and he helped her down from it. *No, you say very little, but I can guess.* She gazed at him for a moment, but at his questioning look, merely smiled, said, "Thank you for the dress," and stepped up to the door of Lady Jardien's house.

Chapter 9

Lady Jardien's drawing room glowed with many candles, and a warm fire burned in the fireplace not far from where the musicians played. Diana had always liked her hostess, for she was a shrewd and practical lady, although Diana knew that the lady did not, quite, approve of her. It had not mattered much before, but now, somehow, it did, perhaps because she felt so much like a fish out of water.

Diana stepped further into the room behind Lord Brisbane and her mother, as was proper, and looked about her at the flowers on the mantelpiece, at the way the draperies were tastefully pulled aside with gold bands. Lovely, and she wished she did not feel so unsettled so that she could enjoy the decorations.

Soon the earl and Mrs. Carlyle parted, and Diana came forward, and though she had been in Lady Jardien's drawing room before, and had met all the people in it, she felt, suddenly, as if she were a stranger.

All eyes had looked toward the door when the earl's name was announced, and all eyes were upon him, filled with curiosity. But then their gazes shifted, and widened, and the curiosity became rampant as Diana came out from behind him. She could see the attention grow, and she wanted to shrink behind him again.

It was too late, however; her mother had stepped ahead, and he had turned toward her and taken her hand, drawing her forward. Lord Brisbane gazed at her, and there was a challenge in his look; *coward* it said. A light irritation flashed through her and she lifted her chin in answer. She hated having people look at her, but at least she would pretend she did not care.

It was difficult: there was Johnny Ramsworth, who had teased her when she first came to Brisbane House, calling her a long Meg, and whom she had avoided ever since. He glanced at her, then glanced again, then was rooted to the spot as he stared. There was Mary Colesby, who had snubbed her at her coming-out party; her eyes widened upon catching sight of Diana, and a look of chagrin crossed her face. Diana winced. Mary Colesby's chagrin was no better than her snubs; Mary would not be her friend either way. And then there was Mr. Desmond Jardien, Lady Jardien's son, who fancied himself a rake and who had ignored Diana for as long as she could remember—until now. He looked up from talking to his fair companion, rested his eyes upon Diana, and a sudden light appeared in his eyes, and a slow smile formed on his lips.

An impatient sigh came from just the other side of her; Diana turned to see Lady Jardien gazing at her son disapprovingly. "The so-called Corsair. Idiot," she heard her mutter. "I would give half my hydrangeas if Lord Byron's works were never published." The lady turned her frank gaze to Diana. "Ignore him, Miss Carlyle. He will grow out of his infatuation with himself—I hope."

Immediately Diana felt a little better; Lady Jardien did not, it seemed, disapprove of her, but her son. She smiled. "And he is, after all, a few years younger than myself, I believe," Diana said.

An amused expression entered Lady Jardien's eyes. "Yes, he is, and I would be pleased if you would remind him of that fact." She looked Diana up and down. "Not that I think an alliance would be amiss between the two of you, but I think the boy's not ready for matrimony, not by a long road."

"I—I thank you, my lady," Diana said, surprised.

"Besides," her ladyship continued, "I believe you have a better prospect than my Desmond." She nodded at the earl, who had moved away to shake the hand of a neighbor. "And best wishes to you, too."

"Really, there is nothing—that is, we are not—he is not—" Diana took a breath, trying to keep her embarrassment under control. "Lady Jardien, I do not know what you have heard, but we are not even close to being—we will not marry."

Her ladyship stared at her for a moment, then shook her head. "Well, if he hasn't proposed, then I am surprised, for he looks at you as if he wanted to—well, never mind that! And if he has proposed, and you have refused, then you're more of a fool than I ever thought you were," she said bluntly. "For heaven's sake, girl, if he proposes, take him! No one could do much better here or even in London, I daresay." She gazed at Diana keenly. "Well, I won't say more to put you to a blush. But I'll tell you this: it won't do to keep living under his roof, even with your mother. The word has got out about the will, and if a marriage doesn't happen soon, people will wonder. Best to find yourself and your mother a cottage nearby if you don't mean to marry him."

Discomfort made Diana shift uneasily on her feet, but she shook her head. "Nothing can happen until a suitable amount of mourning has passed," she protested.

"True, but take care. If he keeps looking at you as he has so far, rumors will fly."

Diana only nodded politely, managing to keep her tongue between her teeth so she would not retort that there was nothing she could do about the way Lord Brisbane looked at her. But Lady Jardien seemed satisfied, and after patting her kindly on her arm, moved away to speak to another guest.

Only a few moments passed before Lady Jardien called everyone to attention, and introduced the first musician. It was Mary Colesby with her harp, and Diana sat down next to her mother and hoped the performance would not be long. There was a movement to the other side of her; it was Desmond, and she gave a mental groan. She did not want his attention, but his bow and glint of interest as he gazed at her told her that he was determined at least to speak to her.

"I hope she does not sing tonight," he whispered as he sat down next to her. "Can't stand her devilish caterwauling."

"That is unkind," Diana replied in as repelling tones as possible. "I am sure she practices daily." She glanced at him, almost smiling at his mode of dress: a combination of propriety and rebellion. No doubt he wished to emulate one of Byron's dashing heroes, but she saw the influence of his mother in the black coat, properly tied neckcloth, and knee breeches. However, his rebellion shouted forth in the form of his very red waistcoat, possibly put on at the last moment.

"I am sure she does practice, but it is of no use—she screeches at the high notes. There, you see?" He gazed at her for assent, but his gaze drifted lower to somewhere near the bodice of her dress.

Diana grimaced, and wished Miss Colesby would hurry so that she could have an excuse to rise and get away from Desmond. She kept her gaze straight ahead, as if the harp music enthralled all her senses. She noticed from the corner of hr eye that Mr. Jardien had leaned back in his chair and was still looking at her. She groaned mentally. Heavens, would the girl never stop?

It seemed like a lifetime before Miss Colesby's piece finished, and Diana's nerves were on edge by the time the last note died in the air. It was not just Desmond, but other gentlemen in the company. She was conscious of glances in her direction, where there had never been any before. She searched for Lord Brisbane, but he seemed always to be talking to one guest or another—the only man who did not seem to be looking at her! Not that she wished him to, of course. She clapped as Miss Colesby beamed and curtsied, then Diana hastily rose and walked away, ignoring Desmond's "I say, Miss Carlyle—" and her mother's questioning look. She hoped she was not being rude, but she felt as if a wall of eyes were upon her, and a suffocated feeling pressed upon her chest. Air . . . she needed air.

The drawing room opened out on one side to some stairs going down to a garden; the windowed doors were slightly open, for the room was very warm, and the night air was still and not as cold as usual. She did not look back, but stepped outside, and leaned against the railing of the stairs.

Taking in deep breaths, Diana closed her eyes. Her mind cleared, and she began to feel foolish, and then disgusted at herself. She was acting in a vaporish manner, very missish and stupid. And for what? All because people looked at her more than they had before. If she were normal, like other young ladies she knew, she would have enjoyed the attention instead of feeling as if the walls were closing in on her. It was why she preferred to stay on the estate, supervising the stables, riding, or reading a book, away from large groups of people and small spaces.

She was strong, however, and she could ride her horse faster than anyone—at least any lady she knew—and had no fear when driving any carriage or jumping her horse over any stile. Being in a room full of guests—she had been in such a situation before. This time should be no different.

But it was. She felt exposed—not the least because of the gown she wore. It was beautiful, it was fashionable, and perfectly proper, according to her mother. But it made her feel vulnerable, and she was not that. She was *not* that.

The dress made her feel unlike herself. How nonsensical! It was just some lengths of cloth sewn together. Danger, or insults, or challenges—those were legitimate reasons to feel one thing or another. Not some silly gown. She would go back into the drawing room again, and stare down anyone who dared look at her askance. She could do it—she was tall and could make herself imposing if she wished. The memory of Lord Brisbane's words about being grand came back to her, and she smiled. Yes, she would be grand and commanding if she could. Taking one more breath, she opened her eyes.

And saw before her Mr. Desmond Jardien. Diana gave a small groan, and then remembered her resolution. "Yes, what is it?" she said firmly. He was the same height as she—she could look him straight in the eyes.

For a moment Desmond looked uncertain. Then he smiled, saying, "You looked upset—I wondered if you were ill."

She made herself smile at him; he was being a good host, she supposed. "I had a headache, and the room was too warm, so I felt I needed some fresh air."

He took her hand. "Perhaps you wish to rest?"

"No, no, I am better, thank you." She tried to pull her hand away, but he held it still and brought it up to his lips.

"I am glad—I would not want you to be ill," he said, and moved closer with a quick step.

She shifted herself to one side, and he hit the stair railing and winced, but still did not release her hand.

"I think I should go back inside," she said, tugging at her hand.

"No, wait—" Desmond hesitated, and pulled her closer. "I couldn't believe it was you, Diana, when you first entered the room. You look like a queen, a goddess." He brought her hand to his lips again, and kissed it fervently, moving his lips onto her wrist and then her arm.

"Don't be silly—do let go of me!" She tugged again, her glove came off, and she turned to go into the drawing room again, feeling frantic. But he grabbed her arm again, and then her waist. He pulled her against him, and his face was suddenly very close to hers.

Anger mixed with fear made her push against him, then she stamped her foot, once, twice, finally hitting his foot. His grasp upon her loosened, and she was able to move away. But he still had hold of her arm, and when she looked at him, she saw sheer thwarted fury in his eyes. Fear rose again, and an echoing wrath, and her hands turned to fists.

With one huge swing, Diana's unprisoned arm came around, and her fist hit Mr. Desmond Jardien precisely on his nose.

"Arrgghh!" The young man doubled over, clutching his nose with both hands.

Diana turned and ran blindly, wanting just to get away, be anywhere but there by the stair railing and—oh, heavens, the son of her hostess. With a groan she ran faster—

Straight into something large and firm and which said, quite loudly. "Oof!" It seized her arms, and she struggled and tried to wrench away.

"Stop! Diana, stop." The voice was commanding—and familiar. She ceased her struggles and looked up. It was Lord Brisbane, his brows furrowed. "What the devil are you doing?" He moved his hands down her arms, and his frown deepened when he saw one of them had no glove. "Your hand—it is bleeding." He took out a handkerchief and dabbed at it.

"It . . . it is not my blood," she said, and tried to still herself. But she could feel herself shaking, whether from anger or fear, she was not sure.

"Not your blood?"

She swallowed, but her shaking continued. "I—oh, Gavin, I am afraid I bloodied Desmond's nose!" She glanced away from him, and noticed they were at the foot of the stairs leading out to the garden.

"Now why did you do that?" There was a hint of laughter in his voice, and she looked up at him.

"Don't laugh at me!" she cried, and tried to move away, but she stumbled. His hand came under her elbow and steadied her.

"Diana, sweet, I am not laughing at you." He took her by her arms again, then put onc hand under her chin, making her look at him. "You are shaking." His voice was soft, and made her trembling increase.

"I shall be well presently."

"Are you ill?"

"No—it is this stupid gown!" The words flew from her lips before she could stop them, and she realized how foolish they sounded.

His brows rose. "You are shaking as if you were standing in freezing weather. Since it is not that cold, I can only assume you are ill."

"No. Everyone was looking at me—the walls seemed to press on me, and I felt I could not breathe. And then *he* came out, and I thought he was concerned for my health, but he tried to kiss me, even though I told him he was being silly." Her words came spilling out in bursts. "I did not like it, and I stamped on his foot, and then I hit him on his nose—and oh, he is Lady Jardien's son, our hostess's son! She was kind to me tonight, but I cannot see how she will be, now that I have bloodied her son's nose!" Her shaking increased, and his arms came around her, moving her close to him. "I don't belong here, Gavin. I need to be outside. I seem not to be able to do anything right." Her words made no real sense, she knew, but it was all she could say. She pressed her cheek against his chest, closing her eyes and took another deep breath. His arms shifted away from her and she made a noise of protest; they came around her again and held her closer.

"Hush, now, my dear," he murmured. Slowly, her shaking ceased, and she realized he was stroking her back, a comforting sensation. "You need not go back in if you do not wish."

She released a long sigh. "In a little while," she said. "I am better. I don't know what has come over me—even Mama has said I have not been acting as I ought, and I am sorry for it." She looked up at him. "I don't usually act this way, truly. I have never hit anyone's nose before."

He grinned. "I would have, if someone was trying to maul me about. You are a formidable woman, indeed."

A reluctant chuckle burst from her. "But not a lady. You must see that. No lady would bloody anyone's nose."

His fingers came up under her chin. The light that managed to reach them from the windows above showed a laugh in his eyes. "I don't think I want a lady," he said, and his lips hovered over hers.

"Miss Carlyle! Lord Brisbane!"

The shocked voice of Lady Jardien shattered the comfort that had surrounded Diana, and she turned, startled.

If it had just been her hostess who had descended the stairs, perhaps she could have made some excuse. But Desmond was there, also, still holding his nose, and Mrs. Carlyle with Mr. Goldworthy beside her.

"Oh, Diana," her mother said, her voice mournful.

The pressure Diana had felt earlier returned, and she began to shake again. She shook her head. "It . . . it is not what you think," she said, not precisely sure what they were thinking, but feeling she had to say something.

"I certainly know what it looks like," Lady Jardien said sternly. "Indeed, I would like an explanation of what happened to my son." She shot a look at Mrs. Carlyle. "As for the rest, I suppose *that* should concern your mother more than it does me."

"Stubble it, Mother," Desmond growled. "It was nothing."

"Indeed," Lord Brisbane said smoothly. "It was an accident, and Miss Carlyle was just telling me she was afraid it was her fault. She was much shaken by the incident."

It was a weak explanation; even Diana knew it. Gavin had been about to kiss her, and no amount of conversation warranted him holding her so close to him. It was clear the rest of them thought so as well if their skeptical expressions and her mother's sad one were any indication. She looked at him; the light from the rooms above them and the shadows of the night sculpted his expression into stone, and he held his body very still. She let out a small moan.

He looked down at her, and for a moment indecision flashed across his face. A sigh slipped from him, and he put his arm around her shoulders.

"However, that was an old discussion; I am afraid you have interrupted us just as Miss Carlyle was about to give me her answer as to whether she would become my wife."

"Diana?" Her mother's voice lifted with hope.

"Well, well, my lad," Mr. Goldworthy said, chuckling. "It's about time, I say."

Diana looked at the earl, at his very still face, and how his chin lifted just a little, and she felt ill. She almost thought she heard a small *snap*—she felt as if a trap had been sprung. She shook her head, and put her hands over her face.

"I don't know," she said, her voice a whisper. "I don't know." She pushed suddenly away from him, and stumbled back. "I don't know," she said again, and turned and ran away.

Chapter 10

It was good to be back in a familiar place, Diana thought. One where she knew she was in command of her place and herself. She gazed around the dimness of the carriage house, breathing in the musty smells of dust, leather, and oil. She sighed.

Lady Jardien had been right. Rumors about the will had flown from one person to another, and that she and her mother lived in the same house as Lord Brisbane only made it worse. Even worse now that he had proposed, and she had not given him his answer, but run away.

Diana closed her eyes in shame—she had been cowardly, and had humiliated Lord Brisbane by running away. At least she had managed to make herself return to Lady Jardien's house, and had sat through the rest of the recitals. This time, Lord Brisbane sat beside her, and though she felt trapped sitting there between him and her mother, she had also felt less exposed. But she had declined—politely—an invitation to play the pianoforte; she was not sure her hands would be steady enough.

She smoothed her hand over the curricle in the carriage house—it soothed her to feel it. She had saved enough money to repair it, and selling off a young gelding—for which she had paid service on the horse's mother and had trained herself before her uncle had died—had given her a tidy profit. She had sent it off a month ago for repairs. Now it was back, in perfect condition for her to drive it.

Perhaps she would look about her for a cottage in which she

and her mother could live. There were a few abandoned cottages on the estate, within walking distance of the stables. Any one of them needed only a bit of repair and cleaning to make it comfortable to live in, she was sure. In fact, perhaps she should look at one of them, and see how much it might need in the way of repairs and renovations.

It would be a good chance to try out the curricle as well. The carriagewrights had found nothing wrong with it, except what damage the horses and the accident had done to it. She'd had one of her grooms travel to London, disguised as a prospective employee, investigate the matter as well, and he could not find anything amiss, either. She frowned, and went out to the stables, calling for a groom. Lord Brisbane had been right—it was not the curricle that had been the cause of her uncle's carriage accident.

The thought of the earl and the evening before gave her pause. She was very close to the edge of scandal, she knew. Going out in the curricle alone would cause more talk, perhaps, but it was not as if she had not gone out in it alone before. She had never gone far, just around and about the roads on the estate, never to the village. Some people had seen her driving the curricle before her uncle had passed away, and had thought her strange for doing it. A flare of rebellion burned in her. What difference could it make? Driving about in the curricle again would add little or nothing to the very large problem she already had.

Nate Staples came up with the horses, smiling shyly. "I've got the best harness, miss, and will put it on right enough."

"Very good." Diana nodded absently, then his words penetrated her thoughtful fog. "No, wait, not the best ones—I'd like to reserve those for racing or going at top speed, as my uncle used to. I prefer the old ones; I don't intend to go fast this time, only at a trot, just to feel the carriage's spring action." Nate looked indecisive, and she smiled. "Here, I'll hold the horses until you return."

"Aye, miss," he said, a doubtful look on his face as he left. Diana's smile turned wry. He knew better than to protest her orders, but some of the new stablehands were still unused to having a woman supervise the stables. She spoke to the horses gently, and stroked their noses, until Ned returned.

Ned was as good as his word, and harnessed the horses well and in good time. Diana climbed up into the curricle, and he handed her the reins.

"How is your cousin, by the by?" she asked.

Ned looked pleased. "Bob's better, miss. We were worried about 'is eyes, and the doctor was afeared of infection, because they'd blistered bad. But Bob's mam bought the poutices for it with the money you gave—and she thanks you, miss, and says she'll 'ave me bring back a bottle of her cordial for you next time I see her—and he's fair to recover."

Diana smiled. "I am glad. Do tell him we'll be pleased to see him back to work, and pleased to keep you, too, for there's more work to be done on building the stable addition, and Lord Brisbane's given me permission to buy more stock."

Ned's face split in a wide grin, and he bobbed his head respectfully. "I'm that glad, miss. It's fine cattle you 'ave, an' a blessin' to work with 'em." Diana gave a last smile, pulled down her hat's veil over her face, and touched her whip gently on the backs of her horses. She was off!

The various carriage craftsmen had done a fine job of repairing the curricle. They had oiled the axles and various joined parts of the coach; it ran with nary a squeak and bowled over the gravel road quickly and easily. She stayed on gravel for a bit, testing the springs over the bumps and ruts. The curricle bounced but did not jolt too much—yes, a very fine repair, as good as new. The carriage makers had said they had replaced the large, curving springs, and so they had, with superior ones as she had requested.

She looked ahead. A macadamed road was coming up soon; a mile on that, and she could go off to the west to one of the abandoned cottages on the estate.

Diana grinned as the curricle moved onto the paved road. Excellent! The carriage ran as smooth as silk as far as she was concerned. She decided to urge the horses on to a canter, and touched the whip to their backs again. The breeze from the faster pace brushed the veil over her face against her cheeks, and she laughed from sheer joy of the speed.

The laugh faded however, and she frowned. A sound, hoofbeats faster than that of her own horses, came from behind her. A single horseman, she believed, and she hoped that he would be sensible enough not to rush past the side of her horses and startle them. She would see him as soon as he came to the side of her coach—she did not want to look back and be distracted from her driving.

The sound of the single horseman came closer, and then it was to the side of her. She glanced down, irritated, at him, then her eyes widened. Lord Brisbane!

A dark look was on his face, and his lips had thinned to a straight, hard line. He glared at her, clearly angry.

"Stop this carriage at once!" he shouted above the thunder of hooves.

"Don't be silly!" she shouted back. "I can drive this curricle very well, as you can see."

"Damn it, Diana, stop! Are you insane, woman? I can very well see you can drive it—that's not the problem!"

A sudden fear struck her—had something happened at home? She pulled at the reins, slowing the horses to a stop. "What is it? Is it Mama? Is she hurt?"

"Get down!" He dismounted his horse and came toward her.

Reluctantly, she handed over the reins and descended from the carriage. They had come to the road leading to the old cottage; Lord Brisbane drew his horse and the carriage off the macadamed road and to the gravel one, and tied the reins to a stilepost nearby. She watched him—a muscle worked in his jaw, as if he were grinding his teeth. He then turned to her, his fists on his hips.

"What the devil were you doing taking out this curricle without telling me?"

Anger flared. "It's *my* curricle; I supposed I could go out in it now that it's repaired."

"Wrong." He strode to her. "Yours or not, those are *my* horses, are they not?" His eyes narrowed with anger, and she could feel her own hands curling into fists.

"Yes, but you have allowed me supervision over the stables; I believed I could do with the horses as I wished."

"Correct. *Allowed.* You are not to take out *my* horses to drive this carriage unless I give you permission to do so."

"How *dare* you!" she cried. "As if you did not know that I can handle any horse in your stable! Any of them! You *know* that. You know it!"

With a frustrated sound, the earl swept off his hat and hit the side of the curricle with it. "It's not your handling of the horses, you idiot, it's the curricle!" he shouted.

"There is nothing *wrong* with the curricle! I had it repaired, as you well know, and had a groom investigate the matter when he was in London. There was never anything wrong with the curricle from the outset!"

"But you did not see fit to inform me of it before you went out, did you? And I was fool enough to run after you." He stared at her angrily for a moment, then drew in a long breath and let it out again. "Very well," he said, in a calmer voice, just tinged with bitterness. "But there is still something *about* the curricle that caused your uncle's accident. You knew my concerns regarding it."

She did, and was sorry she did not inform him—it only made sense, for she and her mother were under his protection as, at the very least, guests, and at most, relatives living under his roof. It seemed she could not do anything right lately. Anger fled, and depression took its place. Diana closed her eyes, then looked at him straight in the eyes.

"I am sorry," she said stiffly. "However, you will not need to worry about me or my mother soon. I was going to inspect the cottage down this road." She nodded at the gravel road ahead. "It is unused, and I am certain if it is repaired, we may rent it from you, if you will allow it."

He stared at her in silence, then said, "You do not want to marry me."

She smiled wryly. "Well, I think it best. I had not thought of it before, but Lady Jardien is right: I cannot continue living under the same roof as you without causing scandal, even if my mother is there. Rumors are flying in earnest now."

"If we were to marry, the rumors would cease."

Diana cocked her head at him. "You have not really proposed to me—how can I accept or decline?"

A twinkle entered his eyes, and he abruptly knelt before her on one knee and put his hand over his heart. "My dear Miss Carlyle. Will you do me the very great honor of accepting my offer of marriage?"

He was in earnest now—he had to be, for they had been caught in a compromising position. He had said before he had wanted to marry her, but had said he could not propose at the time. Now he was proposing, and clearly because he had been forced into it. She did not know whether to laugh or cry. "You are dirtying your trousers, sir," she said instead, barely keeping her voice from shaking.

"For you, I will brave the displeasure of my valet," he said solemnly. "Besides, I have more in my wardrobe."

She gave an involuntary chuckle, then sobered. "Please do get up, Gavin."

"You must be in earnest; you seem only to use my Christian name when you are distressed." He rose, dusting off the leg of his trousers, then took her hand in his. "Well?" he said, gazing into her eyes.

"I . . . I cannot," she said, and the depression threatened to produce tears, but she swallowed and lifted her chin. "I don't see how you can marry an idiot."

"I retract everything I have said—I was angry and afraid for your safety."

She shook her head. "I don't think I am quite good enough to be a countess—or a wife."

He smiled. "Then we are a good match. I have not been certain since I gained the title that I am quite good enough to be an earl." He squeezed her hand, and it comforted her, but she could not allow herself to give in to it. "Besides," he said, "I believe I should be the judge of whether you would be a good enough wife."

"But you are not!" Diana gazed at him earnestly. "You did not wish to propose to me—you were forced into it. I cannot marry you when you do not wish it."

The look in his eyes became warm, and he gave her a brief kiss. "Believe me, I am becoming very much used to the idea. It helps, you know, to have fallen in love with you on first sight."

"But . . . but how do I know you have not attended to me because you want my dowry to run the estate?" It was something she had wondered about in the back of her mind, and she had to say it.

A flash of anger entered his eyes, but then he nodded. "A legitimate concern. I don't know why I did not think that might be your objection to my attentions." He smiled slightly. "I don't need your dowry, and in fact this estate produces less than what I already own. You may ask Mr. Goldworthy how much I am worth, if you will not take my word."

"But I am afraid!" she blurted. She did not mean to say it, but she realized it was the truth. He could not wish to marry her. She was not like other women, surely he could see that, especially after last night?

"Now that is a problem," he said. He turned and looked down the road toward the cottage, his face thoughtful. "Perhaps it would be best if you did live in the cottage for a while. I had not thought of the possible consequences of your continuing to live at Brisbane House, until after Lady Jardien's musicale." He gazed at her again. "Perhaps then you would be less afraid."

Diana let out a sigh of relief. "Yes, I think I might."

"It would not hurt to look at the cottage. I understand it is in good repair." He held out his hand. "Come, shall we go?"

She nodded, and turned to the curricle.

"No, not the curricle," he said. "I think it best if you rode my horse."

"But—"

"No," he said firmly. "I think you have not been out as long as your uncle had on the curricle before his horses went wild?"

"I have not; it has only been about twenty minutes. The accident occurred after thirty."

"Then I suggest you do as I say. I am not unreasonable," he said. "If the horses are calm past thirty minutes, then you may continue to drive the curricle. I shall walk beside you and lead the carriage horses."

"But you could be trampled if they become wild!"

He gave her carriage dress a significant look. "True. However, I believe I can move faster than you can. I do not believe your dress was made for running."

It was true, and his way was more practical; she could not argue with it. She let him help her onto his horse, and rode beside him as he led the carriage horses. But her stomach roiled at the thought of the danger to him, and she flinched at every snort and toss of the head that came from the horses he led.

Ten minutes passed, then twenty—their discourse was desultory, for Diana could not keep her mind on the subject of conversation. Lord Brisbane seemed at ease; he talked on this matter and that, and did not mind when she failed to reply. She began to smile; indeed, there were times when she did not reply, and he replied for her.

She relaxed a little as the time passed; the horses acted no differently than they normally would when drawing a carriage. But she was glad when they came near the cottage, nevertheless, and it was with a sigh of relief that she dismounted Lord Brisbane's horse at last.

The cottage was old, but the last tenants had clearly maintained it very well. They tethered the horses near the entrance, and as Diana and Lord Brisbane walked around the house, they could see nothing that needed repairs. There was even a small stable a little distance away.

"I wonder if we can go in?" Diana wondered. "Is it locked?"

Lord Brisbane felt in his pockets for a moment, then smiled. "It doesn't matter if it is; I believe I have the master key. Come, let us put the horses in the stable—if they are in luck, there will be some hay for them—and we can go in to see if the cottage will suit you."

They went to the stable; there was hay, a little dusty, but the horses nosed at it and began to munch on the clean hay below the surface. Diana sighed and felt a little easier. She was glad Lord Brisbane was not angry that she wished to live in the cottage with her mother. Indeed, she believed her mother would take more persuading than the earl. She gazed at him as they walked back to the cottage, and felt he was a good friend at the very least, and very tolerant of her fits and starts. Even when she did not like what he had to say, it still made sense to her, and he never assumed she could not understand his notions, nor was dismissive, but took the time to explain.

"Thank you," she said.

He looked a question at her.

"For understanding. For not being angry at me for—for acting as I did at the musicale. I know you must have been humiliated. I am sorry for that."

He smiled. "Well, at least you did not refuse outright. And I have been in worse situations."

"Such as?"

He laughed. "No, I will not air my embarrassing moments for you to enjoy. Not unless you tell me yours."

"Oh, I would not know which one to pick. I have a great many." She shot him a mischievous look. "You must tell me first, and then I will. I know that if I tell first, you will never get around to telling yours, for you have a very irritating way of going around the subject you don't wish to discuss until I forget about it completely."

"Mine are vulgar; to relate them would damage my consequence as earl beyond repair," he said solemnly, but his lips twitched upward.

"I promise you, I shall not tell a soul," Diana said.

"That is what all gossips say," he replied.

"I am not a gossip—" She gave him a sharp look. "And you are being provocative so that I will be put off the subject. Well, I will not, this time, so you may proceed to tell me."

Lord Brisbane sighed. "You know me so well. Are you sure you should not marry me immediately? I am convinced you would be very good for me."

She gave him a long look, and crossed her arms in front of her.

"Very well. Let me see . . ." He looked thoughtful for a minute, then nodded. "Ah, yes. When I was a youth, working on Mr. Goldworthy's ship, I was very much a lubber—that is, an awkward creature, hardly able to walk a ship's deck in a calm, much less haul rope. But like most halflings, I wished to prove myself, and would admit to no weakness."

Diana listened, all attention. At last she would learn something of him! They came around to the front of the house, and Lord Brisbane pushed the door latch. It opened easily, and he frowned.

"Odd. I hope the cottage was not furnished. It will be a bother if the contents of this house have been stolen."

"It was furnished—and look, it seems nothing has been disturbed." Diana gestured at the Holland-covered furniture. "It is a good thing we came here; we should look throughout to see if anything has been taken," Diana said. She glanced at him. "Meanwhile, you may go on with your story."

He smiled ruefully, then continued: "We'd just left the last kipping-ken—"

"What is that?" she asked. "A kipping-ken?"

"A lodging house," he replied. "A vulgar term, but I did warn you that all my embarrassing experiences were vulgar."

She chuckled. "Yes, but I shall not be shocked." They had passed through the small parlor, and Diana looked up the stairs nearby. "Shall we inspect the upstairs?" At his nod, she proceeded upward. "You must remember I have worked about the stables for a long time, and will not be shocked whatever you might say."

"We shall see!" he said, following after her.

The bedrooms were smaller than she was used to, but were very well lighted and airy, with large windows and the wallpaper was prettily patterned against a white background. She would not feel too confined here, Diana believed. She nodded her satisfaction. "I believe we should inspect the kitchens next," she said. They descended the stairs again. "You may proceed with your story, sir."

He hesitated, but she gave him a stern look at the foot of the stairs, and he continued. "I had felt queasy upon our departure from the inn, but was determined to be a man and ignore it. However, with my first step upon the gangplank of the ship, I felt a peculiar turning of my stomach. Before I could stop myself, I had given forth the contents of—" They had just come upon the entrance to the kitchen, and suspecting what might be next in his tale, Diana turned upon him.

"Lord Brisbane!" She eyed him in displeasure.

He looked not quite apologetic. "Are you shocked? I told you it would be vulgar."

"That is beyond vulgar, it is disgusting!" She stepped into the kitchen. An obnoxious odor came from the room—she wondered if the last tenants had left in a hurry and had left some meat to spoil. It would take a while to clean it and dispel the odor, but it could be done.

"But you said you would not be shocked. I wanted to see if it was true."

She looked at him and wrinkled her nose. "I am not shocked, I am—"

The expression on Lord Brisbane's face suddenly changed; he gazed past Diana, his lips pressed together. His body was rigid; it was as if he had turned to stone. *"Don't turn around,"* he said harshly.

But it was too late. She had turned and stared, and what was before her burned in her mind for that brief moment before Lord Brisbane seized her and pulled her hard against him. She pressed her fist tightly to her mouth, and clutched his coat with the other, turning her face to his chest.

"We must leave," he said. "Come—I believe Lord Jardien is the local magistrate and will be able to manage this."

She nodded, and took a breath to calm herself, and nearly choked, for the stench reminded her of what she had just seen.

Lord Brisbane pulled her away, hurrying her through the rooms and the cottage door to the fresh air outside.

Outside. Outside at last, Diana thought, thankful down to her bones for the unconfining air. She stumbled, fell to her knees, breathing in gulps, and a misty blackness seemed to creep in front of her. Abruptly she was pulled to her feet, then her back was thrust forcefully forward.

"Put your head between your knees," Lord Brisbane commanded. She complied, and the black mist receded. He continued to hold her by her waist, and finally her knees felt able to keep her steady.

"Let me up," she said. "I will not faint, I promise you." Slowly, he released her and almost stepped away, but she clutched his arm. "No," she whispered. "Don't leave me."

"I am here," he said gently, taking her in his arms. "You are safe."

She took in another breath, trying to calm herself, but a hysterical laugh broke out of her. "Of course, such—such things cannot hurt me. He—it is—Oh, dear God. Gavin, there is a dead man in that—that place!" She moaned, and her stomach rolled.

He moved a little, one arm still around her, and then pushed her forward, toward the stables. "Yes, so I noticed," he said dryly. "Come, we must hurry—Damn!" He turned her and held her until she finished retching into the grass.

"I am sorry," she said miserably. "At least I did not spill on your boots."

"Thank you," he replied, and a small twinkle briefly entered his eyes. "I am not sure if I would have had such presence of mind myself." He dabbed her mouth with his handkerchief, then pressed it into her hand. "Come, we must return home."

He strode to the stables, then led out the horses and the curricle. "I believe we can assume nothing will happen with the carriage horses. If they have not gone wild after all this time, then whatever made the ones your uncle had do so is not present here." He climbed into the curricle and held out his hand to her. "I will drive, and have someone fetch my horse later."

She clasped his hand and climbed up, not protesting. She only wanted to be away, as quickly as possible. "I do not think you will get anyone to come here to retrieve your horse, if they find out about the—it." She could not say the words.

Lord Brisbane grimaced. "Then I shall come back here myself. No doubt I will have to anyway." He snapped the whip above the horses' heads, and then went forward.

He drove them gradually faster, eventually into a canter, and the breeze blew over Diana's face. She closed her eyes, feeling the flow of air across her face, and it revived her. An image of the cottage came before her then, pretty, all light and airy—and then the abomination in the kitchen. She groaned.

"Gavin—I cannot live there. I cannot live in that cottage. Not with that—thing."

"I should hope not! You may stay with me as long as you wish." He glanced at her, and she almost wept at the kindness in his eyes.

She shook her head, then briefly pressed her palms against her forehead. "I do not know what to do! I thought I would be free at the cottage, away from people looking at me. But I cannot now. I would much rather marry you than live there," she said passionately.

"I am delighted to know that you would prefer to marry me than to live with a corpse." He nodded solemnly. "I have risen in your affection, I see."

A sudden bubble of laughter escaped her. "Oh, how can you joke at a time like this?"

His face turned grim. "My dear, if I were not joking now, I am sure I would be puking my guts as heartily as you did back there." A corner of his lips turned up, however. "On the other hand, I would not have to relate any of my embarrassing moments to you as I had started to do. You would experience it for yourself."

"How convenient it is that you were able to experience mine: now I will not have to relate any of my moments in return for yours," she retorted.

He gazed at her approvingly. "That's better," he said, and

she found she did feel very much recovered, and that he had meant to make her so. Gratitude warmed her; she realized it would have been a great loss to her indeed if she had never met him. He sighed and returned his eyes to the road in front of him. "A deuced good thing I invited Ned to visit. I'd thought I'd have him look into—other things, but it looks as if I'll need him for this one." He caught her curious gaze. "He is also a magistrate, and might be able to help Lord Jardien," he said.

It was with relief that Diana saw Brisbane House at last, and when the curricle stopped in front of it, she descended and began to hurry to the house. But Lord Brisbane leapt down and caught her hand.

"Wait, Diana." He hesitated, then looked into her eyes. "You know what we have found will cause a scandal."

She stared at him, the implications of the corpse in the cottage seeping into her. The image of the body flashed again into her mind, and this time she let herself see it, the way it was dressed, even to the watch fob her uncle had given him as a Christmas bonus last year.

"It is McKinney," she said, and felt ill again. She pressed her hand to her lips.

His hand tightened on hers. "How do you know?"

Diana raised her eyes to his and swallowed down bile. "He—it—he wore the same clothes as McKinney the last I saw him, and was still wearing the watch fob Uncle Charles had given him last year."

The earl emitted a curse she did not recognize. "There's our answer, then, to where he had gone." He grimaced. "Scandal indeed."

Panic rose in her—there would be more curious looks, and she did not know if she could stand it. "What must I do?" she whispered, barely able to speak.

Lord Brisbane looked away from her, gazing at the mansion before him. "You must truthfully answer whatever questions the magistrate asks you," he said. "And then . . . and then, I believe we should be married." He patted her hand, and his look was regretful. "I wish we could be married in happier circumstances, and . . . it is my hope that you will come someday to have some regard for me. But I do not know what else to do to keep the gossip and scandal at the lowest level possible."

Diana stared at him, the panic boiling within her. "Will I be safe?"

He took her hands in both of his and looked her firmly in the eyes. "Yes," he said. "To the best of my abilities, I will keep you safe, and let no one harm you, as long as I live."

She closed her eyes, and let out a breath, and felt the panic recede. She remembered how he had risked being trampled as he led the curricle horses, and how he had taken her in his arms in the cottage kitchen, protecting her from seeing more than she already had. He had been kind to her mother as well. She raised her chin, and looked at him.

"Yes," she said, and made her voice firm and clear. "Yes, I will marry you, Gavin."

He raised her hand to his lips. "Thank you," he said, and held her hand as they walked to the door of the house.

Chapter 11

Theirs would not be a hurried wedding—Mrs. Carlyle had been determined that banns be read for Lord Brisbane and Diana's marriage, and so they had been. But it would be small and private because they were still in a state of mourning; there was no way around it, and for that Diana was glad.

She sat in the drawing room, her hands on the keys of the pianoforte, but did not play. Instead, she looked out of the window at the blue summer sky. The panes formed small rectangles, the sun casting shadows on each edge—it looked like a cage. But then a quick movement caught her eye: swallows dove toward the house, outlined in each frame of window like quick sketches, then with a flick of their wings twisted away from the house and upward into the air. She envied them; she wished she could have wings so swift that a mere glance of a wingtip would send her away.

She had not wanted to wait to marry Lord Brisbane. The reading of the banns had given her time to think about it, and she would prefer to have it over with. Then life would go on. . . .

Not as usual, however. That could never be, no matter how she tried to make it so. She understood she could not, and understood that she *had* tried to pretend it could, ever since her uncle had died. The first part of her life had been filled with uncertainty and fear; the advent of her uncle had brought solidity and sureness, and when he was gone, she had fought to bring it back again. Or rather, pretended it had never left.

But finding McKinney in the cottage kitchen had shattered her illusions once and for all. She could pretend the first death was an accident, but when Lord Jardien had questioned her, and she had asked him a few tentative questions in return, it was clear that the second was no accident at all, for he said there had been a knife wound at the throat—

She shuddered, and it caused her fingers to press upon the keys of the pianoforte, making a discordant sound. An urge overcame her to drive her curricle, or ride her horse fast and furious across the fields, but she squashed it. This was her wedding day, and there was much to be done. Riding across the fields would be running away, and she had done enough of that.

The door opened, and her mother entered, looking distracted. She caught sight of Diana and shook her head. "What, are you still here? My dear, it wants but two hours before the wedding—you must dress, and hurry!"

"Yes, Mama," Diana said, and rose from the chair.

Her mother gazed at her keenly, however, came to her, and took her hand. "However, I think we can spare a few minutes to talk to each other. You are pale, love"—she put a hand on Diana's forehead—"but you are not feverish, so I can only assume you are anxious about the wedding."

Diana shook her head. "The wedding will soon be over."

"Is it Lord Brisbane?"

She stared at her mother and nodded slightly.

"He is a kind man, my dear, you need not worry about that. I have already told you what to expect tonight—"

Diana nodded.

"And do you have any more questions?"

A million questions ran through her mind, but Diana could not say even one of them, for none of them had anything to do with Lord Brisbane, and everything to do with herself. They were old questions she had put off asking for so long that she did not know how to put them into words. "No," she said at last.

Mrs. Carlyle squeezed her hand. "It has been a terrible time for all of us, love, and more terrible for you, I know. And . . ." She hesitated. "Sometimes there are things you cannot tell a mother; I remember there were things I could not tell mine, though I loved her dearly. But I believe Lord Brisbane loves you, and if you cannot tell me, you may tell him." Her brow creased as if in thought. "He is probably the most *listening* sort of man I have ever met." She laughed slightly. "That sounds odd, does it not? But I think it is true. You may tell him anything, and he would consider it carefully, and not tell anyone else if you asked him not to." Her mother smiled crookedly. "In that, you are most fortunate."

Diana remembered how her father had raged when he had lost all his money, and how he had left them so poor. Mama was right, of course; she was marrying a better man. Diana made herself smile. "I shall try not to be afraid, Mama."

"Good," Mrs. Carlyle said, smiling and squeezing her hand once more. "And of course, there is nothing to keep you from confiding in me as well from time to time. I do love you, my dear daughter, and though you are all of twenty-five, I would not like to think you have grown up so much that we cannot share our hearts from time to time."

Tears pricked at the edges of Diana's eyes, and she hugged her mother fiercely to hide them. "I am fortunate indeed," she said, "to have a friend and a mother in one person."

They parted, and Mrs. Carlyle hastily took a handkerchief from her sleeve and dabbed her eyes. "Oh, now look at what you have done! You have set me to weeping, and I have told myself I would not, not on your wedding day, for it should be a happy day, not one for tears." She laughed softly and shook her head. "I am a silly woman, to be sure!"

Diana took her hand and squeezed it. "No, not silly, but the best and wisest of mothers," she said, smiling.

"Oh, nonsense . . . and look at the time!" Mrs. Carlyle exclaimed. "Heavens, we shall never get to the church on time if we dawdle any longer. Come, my dear, hurry!"

She rose and stepped quickly out of the room, gesturing with her hand in a hurrying motion. Diana followed, and ascended the steps to her room.

The door opened to a flurry of maids and clothes, and Diana was swept up into it as if she had stepped into a snowstorm. She could hardly keep pace with all the petticoats, lace, necklaces, and anything else her mother and the maids had determined were essential. She felt tossed and shoved and moved this way and that until she was well nigh dizzy with it, and it was with complete bewilderment that she gazed at the lady in the mirror when the last maid stepped back with a confident nod.

There was no way she could look ethereal as she had always thought brides should appear. But the word "grand" came to her again as she gazed at the cream silk and lace that covered her.

Mostly covered her. Her eyes went to the lace that went from her chin to the crest of her bosom, and over her shoulders to the backs of her hands. Gossamerlike, transparent except for the sewn pearls that glimmered like bits of the moon in the curl of each lace pattern. It should have been modest, covering so much of her, if it had not shifted and shimmered with every breath, and brought attention to the very brief bodice.

The rest of the gown was very plain, a column of cream silk that hung from her bodice to the floor, with only small echoes of the bodice lace near the hem. But it served only to draw the eye upward, and Diana was not sure she wanted anyone's eye to be drawn there.

She said nothing, however, and only smiled and once again hugged her mother, who wept a few more tears. Diana kept her mind trained on the fact that she should be thankful the wedding would be very small, and aside from Vicar Southworthy, with only her mother and Mr. Goldworthy in attendance. She would not think of the wedding dinner afterward, when there would be more people. No, she would not think of it.

She was very successful not thinking of it, so much so that Diana felt a little numb as she was bundled into the coach for the short ride to the church. *The coach needs new springs,* she thought automatically as it bounced over a rut in the road, *I need to see they are replaced.* She realized what she was thinking and laughed a little hysterically that she would think of such things on her wedding day.

The coach stopped—too quickly, not quickly enough, she was not sure. The door opened, and she stumbled out and would have fallen, if it had not been for the supporting hand of Mr. Goldworthy under her elbow.

"Thank you," she said, and despised the way her voice shook. She lifted her chin and stared steadily at the doorway of the church, and the arching dimness within.

He patted her hand. "Aye, that's the spirit. But never fear; Gavin's a good lad, and steady. You've taken his heart, Miss Diana, I can see that clear enough, and he's not willing for you to return it." He nodded toward the church and chuckled. "Eh, I never thought I'd serve as best man to an earl, but here I am, and serving as father to the bride as well. Ned Goldworthy's gone up in the world, he has!" He gave her a wink, and Diana could not help laughing. "Aye, good! A bride should have a bit of color in her cheeks." He glanced at the church. "Well, into the parson's purse–net you go." Diana laughed at the thought of the church being stuffed with fish, put her hand on Mr. Goldworthy's arm, and ascended the steps.

It was an old church, part of a Norman abbey, made of gray stone. It was dim compared to the summer light outside, but the sun filtered through the stained glass windows and brightly colored the interior, nevertheless. Diana's eyes soon grew used to it, and she could see the people within at last.

Her mother was there, of course, and she was surprised to see Sir James Rackbury in one of the pews, for she thought he had decided to stay permanently in London. There was Vicar Southworthy ahead, looking less sour than he usually did, and in fact he gave her a short, grave smile as she came closer. And then there was Lord Brisbane . . . her bridegroom.

Diana took in a deep breath and let it out again. He wore black, and his neckcloth was snowy white, his embroidered waistcoat was the color of champagne, and he wore knee breeches of the palest fawn. With his hair in a windswept style, and not one strand out of place, he looked intimidatingly elegant. He was gazing at her, warmth and admiration in his eyes, and she felt a trembling go through her.

She was to marry him. Here. Now.

With a reassuring pat on her hand, Mr. Goldworthy bowed and moved away, and Diana stepped up next to the earl. She could not look at him, and looked down at her hands instead, as the vicar went through the ceremony. His voice came to her as if through a fog, and it took all her concentration to follow his words.

And then as if from a distance, she heard her mother's voice rise in protest, making Diana raise her head with a jerk to find Sir James had come up to the altar. A shock went through her. Impediment—Vicar Southworthy had just asked if there was any impediment to the marriage.

"What is the meaning of this?" the vicar said angrily.

"I say this marriage is being performed under false pretenses," Sir James replied. His slight smile was triumphant, and when he turned his gaze to Diana, sneering.

Diana glanced at Lord Brisbane, standing so very still. He said nothing, merely watched Sir James. For one moment, she thought there was a feral light in her bridegroom's eyes, as if he were poised to attack . . . but that was nonsense, for his face was smoothly urbane, as if he had not one concern in the world.

"I think you should explain yourself," the earl said, his voice calm, even pleasantly conversational. "You must have something very important to say; I see you are in such haste that you could not even dress for the occasion." His eyes flickered over Sir James's neckcloth and waistcoat. "A bit on the informal side, don't you think?"

"Damned mushroom," Sir James snarled. "You're no better than—"

"A mushroom!" Lord Brisbane looked pained. "I took great care to select this particular waistcoat at Weston's. He himself said I could carry off this sort of design. However, it is possible we were both mistaken." He shook his head woefully, and turned to Diana. "That's the impediment, my dear. Sir James must have seen that this waistcoat would never do for a wedding."

A hysterical giggle came to her lips—and died, for she looked at Gavin and remembered why he sometimes became frivolous and made jokes. Did he already know what Sir James's objection was? Understanding passed between them, and clear despair came into his eyes.

"This is no time for levity," Vicar Southworthy said, gazing at Lord Brisbane in disapproval. He turned to Sir James. "What is your objection?"

Sir James's smile returned. "This man who calls himself Gavin Sinclair is not the true Earl of Brisbane." He shot a pleased glance at Diana. "He is probably not even Gavin Sinclair."

"Nonsense!" Diana said firmly. "My uncle found him, he knew! He would not make a mistake like that." She would not believe it. She would *not.* The despair she had seen in Gavin's eyes had pierced her heart; surely he did not—he must be—She shook her head, then looked at Sir James's sneering face. Anger and humiliation boiled in her. How dare Sir James announce this, now, just as she was about to be wed! If whatever he knew were truly an impediment, why did he not mention it during the calling of the banns? She could not think it anything but maliciousness, a need to bring attention to himself, unless it had to do with a wager. But surely he would not cause such a scandal for a mere wager! It had to be malice and conceit.

"Your uncle is not as infallible as you think," Sir James said, and his self-satisfied voice grated on her ears. He jerked his chin at Gavin. "This man clawed his way up from the gutters—oh, he's well off now, I'm sure, by whatever hook or crook he used. But he's not a Sinclair, nor related—unless on the wrong side of the blanket—a nobody."

"I don't believe you!" Diana cried. "You are only throwing a stupid tantrum and causing trouble because you think you should have got the inheritance." She swallowed a lump in her throat and gazed at Gavin. Why did he not say something, anything to defend himself? He only stood, looking coolly down his nose at Sir James as if the man were an actor in a poor farce.

"You should have waited," Sir James said to her, his smile ironic. "But you wanted that title, didn't you?"

"Stop!"

Diana closed her mouth on her retort, and stared at the vicar. He was pale, and his hands shook, in anger or fear, she did not know. He gazed at Gavin, and then at Sir James.

"Sir James, I suggest you step down," he said, his voice clearly strained.

"But the impediment—"

"There is no impediment," Vicar Southworthy said quietly.

Lord Brisbane looked sharply at the vicar, and his lips pressed together in a white, rigid line.

"I have papers to show—" Sir James protested.

"There is no impediment," the vicar repeated, more loudly. He closed his eyes for a moment, then stared hard at Sir James. "There will be no further disturbance of this wedding ceremony; the marriage will proceed. If you continue to protest, I shall request you be bodily removed from this place."

The interior of the church fell into stillness, as the vicar and Sir James stared at each other in silence. Then Sir James turned, and stepped down.

"You'll regret this, Diana," he said, his manner suddenly smooth. "You'll not get the title or the money in the end."

"I care not," she said sharply. "I would marry him even if he were not the Earl of Brisbane, or even Gavin Sinclair." A movement at her side took her attention, and she looked up to see surprise on the earl's face. She lifted her chin, then turned to the vicar. "I thank you, Vicar Southworthy; you may proceed."

A slight chuckle came from beside her. "Yes, Vicar, I think

you had better, else our lady fire-eater will turn upon us, and then we shall both be in the suds."

The vicar merely nodded, his gaze avoiding the earl's. Diana looked from him to the earl and back again; a tension remained, despite Sir James's departure. Mr. Southworthy continued, drawing Diana's attention again to the ceremony.

But the energy of anger and indignation that had infused her suddenly left, now that the trouble was over, and she began to feel numb. Her voice answered the vicar, repeated the words, but she could not remember what she said, for the trembling went through her again, and she stiffened her spine and concentrated on banishing the shaking feeling that made her knees want to bend and fall to the floor. She would be strong. She *was* strong, and would not faint or act in a silly manner.

She heard the word "kiss" and looked up, startled, and felt Lord Brisbane's fingers under her chin, and his hand at her waist. Her breath came quickly as she looked into his eyes, for they held a deep warmth, as if a fire barely banked lived in them. And then his lips came over hers, softly, and she held on to him, for she felt her knees could not hold her up for all her determination that they must.

They parted, and he smiled at her, then turned away from the altar, still holding her. She was glad of his support; she could pretend that she could indeed walk, and that she was not shaking, and could even smile and return her mother's teary hug and kiss, and gravely accept Mr. Goldworthy's congratulations.

This time Gavin helped her up into the coach, and when the door closed upon them, he moved to sit beside her, even though there would be more room if he sat opposite. He took her hand in his and brought her hand to his lips, smiling.

"Well, that was an eventful ceremony. I am sorry it was upsetting for you; I wish I could have made it better."

Diana managed to return the smile. "I was not upset," she said and glanced nervously away.

"Liar," he said. "It was terrible for you. You were shaking like a leaf."

She glared at him. "No, I wasn't! I—" She caught the understanding glint in his eyes and looked down at her lap, her spark of anger gone. "Yes, I was shaking. I was afraid I was going to faint, and I worked very hard not to." She looked at him defiantly. "And I did not faint."

"You did extremely well, Lady Fire-eater. I thank you for your defense." He put his arm around her. "You are still trembling." He stroked her shoulder, and then his fingers came up to the back of her neck, kneading it gently. She sighed and closed her eyes, tipped back her head, and felt her spine unstiffen. Another, deeper, sigh released itself, and her hands fell open on her lap.

A chuckle made her open her eyes again. "I see you are feeling better."

She smiled. "Yes, thank you." She cocked her head at him. "Where did you learn to do that?"

"On my travels," he replied, and fell silent.

She made a disgusted snort. "Oh, you—! You never tell me anything. You shall, eventually, you know. I refuse to stay in the same house as a stranger for a husband." Husband. Her combined irritation and amusement fell from her and she stared at him. He was her husband, and they were married until death did them part. Forever. She swallowed, and looked down at her clasped hands in her lap.

He took her hand again, lightly stroking her palm with his thumb. "Look at me, Diana," he said. She raised her eyes to his, and he touched her cheek. "Don't be afraid. Whatever I am, you need not be afraid of me." He drew close and kissed her, gently, briefly. "Is that anything to be afraid of?"

"No," she said, still staring at him, and feeling a little disappointed at such a brief touch.

He kissed her again, more firmly. "Is that?" His hand held her waist and drew her closer.

"No." She found she was grasping tightly his other hand and her breath came a little faster.

"Or this?" he asked, and he pulled her very close and kissed her deeply.

She did not answer, and she did not want to, but held his hand tighter, her other one coming up to grab his coat's lapel. For all that the coach was dim and closed, she wanted to be closer to him, to burrow into him somehow. His lips left hers, but she could feel his mouth on her cheek, then her chin, then the touch of his lips through the lace on her shoulder.

The coach came to an abrupt halt, jolting them. They parted, and Diana stared at him, breathing quickly, watching how he stared in return, then shifted his gaze to her lips as if he wanted to kiss her again.

"I need to see that the coach springs are replaced," Diana said breathlessly.

His brows rose and his lips quirked up briefly. "How so?" he asked, his voice trembling slightly.

"So they won't jolt us the next time we ki—" She stopped and pressed her hands to her face, trying to suppress the blush that flared in her cheeks.

A shout of laughter broke from the earl. "Yes, definitely the springs must be replaced." He took her hand in his and gestured at the footman who had just stepped up to the coach and was opening the door. "Shall we go? Our guests await," he said.

Diana nodded, somehow feeling less anxious than she thought she would. The wedding dinner would be small, and the celebration afterward short, for they were still in mourning. She should go through that well if she concentrated on it, and then she could think of the next thing—

Her mind veered from it, and she gave herself a mental scolding as they ascended the steps to Brisbane House. The footman at the door grinned and opened the door for them, and she smiled and nodded in return. The butler's smile was just as happy as he bowed to them. She remembered the cheery faces of the maids who had dressed her for the wedding, and how the stableboy had whistled a song as he had taken the reins of the carriage horses, despite the black crepe that had been on every wall of the house a little more than two months ago.

They were happy for her; the wedding had brought joy to her home, and for at least a while they could celebrate.

Home. Her home. This was *her* home! She looked about the great hall with new eyes. She was the mistress of Brisbane House, no longer a hanger-on. How foolish she had been for not thinking of it! She remembered when she had first come here, how full of light and freshness it had been after the darkness of London, and how free she had felt from the dirt and the fear.

Joy flooded her, and filled her eyes with tears. She would not fear having to leave, this was forever her place, her home. She gazed at Gavin, her husband—yes, her husband—who, in marrying her, had given it to her. She squeezed his arm tightly, just as they came to the drawing room door.

"Gavin . . . I am home! This is *my* home!"

He grinned. "Yes, of course it is. You are now Lady Brisbane, mistress of Brisbane House. Did you not know it?"

She laughed out of sheer delight. "No, yes—I had not thought about it. But now I am, and oh, I may live in this wonderful bright place forever!" She reached up to touch his cheek. "Thank you," she said. "Thank you." Tentatively, she tiptoed and placed her lips on his. His breath seemed to catch when she had touched him, and he pulled her to him, and this time his kiss was deep and hungry.

A clearing of the throat made them part—heavens, they had kissed in front of the footmen! Diana's face grew warm and she shook her head, pressing a hand to her cheek. How could she have forgotten herself? A glance at one of the footmen showed a wide grin before the butler's stern gaze wiped it from his face.

But Diana's joy could not be erased. The door opened to the drawing room, and more happy faces greeted her: her mother, Mr. Goldworthy, the neighbors—Lord and Lady Jardien and their son, the Dunnings and the Maddens, among others. To be sure, there was curiosity on their faces, and she had overheard some of the maids say that some invited guests had declined to come because of the scandal of the recent finding in the cottage. But this once she did not let the curiosity and the intense attention to her dampen her spirits. Brisbane House, her sanctuary, was hers, and Gavin was the cause of this very great gift.

There was no dancing, of course, but there was music; her mother played, and another guest, and another. Even Miss Colesby had brought her harp, and this time Diana thought she played excellently with great talent. Gavin stayed by her side, leaving her only a few times to speak with guests or Mr. Goldworthy. She would look up from time to time and each time he was staring at her, and then would smile, and she discovered that she did not mind him looking at her so much at all.

Soon they moved to the dining room, and Diana ate with gusto, not caring that her appetite was not ladylike. The food was rich and sumptuous, with pheasant and mutton, and more removes than she could count. She laughed and talked, more than she could ever remember doing, and she did not even mind Desmond Jardien gazing at her with envious admiration.

The ladies and gentlemen parted after dinner, and her mother came to her, holding out her hands, then clasping Diana's tightly.

"Oh, my dear, it does my heart good to see you happy," she said, her own face lighted with joy. "I was afraid you did not like Gavin, or perhaps the thought of marriage . . ." She hesitated. "Because of mine, you see . . ."

She hugged her mother. "No, Mama, never blame yourself. I know you did the best you could, and I know there are marriages that are happy." She gave a smiling glance to Lady Jardien next to her. "I only need to see Lord and Lady Jardien together to know that."

"And if your marriage is half as happy as ours, then you will be a fortunate woman, Miss—" Lady Jardien chuckled. "No, it's not 'miss' anymore, is it, Lady Brisbane?"

Hearing the name and title applied to her was a shock—Diana had thought of herself as Miss Carlyle forever. She looked at Lady Jardien and wondered if she would be as happy with Gavin as the woman before her was with her husband.

She did not know, and she realized she had pushed aside the question whenever it had occurred to her.

She only nodded, however, to Lady Jardien, and then looked up to see the door opening and the gentlemen entering the room. Gavin's eyes sought her out and found her; he smiled and came toward her. A warmth rose in her heart; she recognized it as something that had occurred before in his presence, but she had pushed that aside, as well. *I cannot push aside any questions, not any more,* Diana thought. *I have made myself deliberately blind to so much—the people around me, and most of all, my own life. I can perceive clearly if I let myself. It is a weakness not to. And I* will *be strong.*

Gavin came to her side at last, after pausing to speak with this guest or that. He lifted her hand to his lips and gazed at her long and seriously. She looked at him in return and smiled. "I am glad I married you, Gavin," she said.

"Are you?" His brows rose, then he nodded. "I suppose it would be more comfortable living here than it would—"

She put her hand over his lips. "No. I know you were going to make a joke, and I know what you were going to say. Don't say it."

Quick anger passed over his face, then he gave her an apologetic look. "Stupid of me. I was distracted, and did not think of how my words might have affected you."

"Besides," Diana said, "I find I am glad not because I am Lady Brisbane, or because I am now mistress of this house." She cast him an uncertain look, wondering if she should say it, if he would wish to hear it, and if it were too bold of her to mention it. She took a deep breath. "I believe you are the best sort of man I could possibly hope to marry, and perhaps in time our . . . our regard for each other will be mutually satisfactory."

He grinned widely. "If I did not know better, I would think you were about to shake hands over a shipping partnership. No, I am sorry—" He took her hand, keeping her from moving from him, and bent close to her ear, whispering. "I dare not admit it aloud, but I believe I am as unsettled as a cat regarding the state of matrimony, and must make jokes to cover it up. There, I have admitted a shameful, unmanly sin: cowardice. You must not come to such hasty conclusions about me without knowing my vices, or surely your regard for me will not be . . . satisfactory."

She looked at him askance, watching his expression for any hint of insincerity. But there was no laughing glint in his eyes, and there was a stillness behind his smile. She nodded thoughtfully. "And yet," she said, "when I ask about your travels or your life, you say very little about them, if anything."

"My travels are the least of your concerns," he said in a light voice. But his expression was the same, and he moved away from her to converse with Lord Jardien.

She watched him from time to time as she talked with various guests. He was congenial and from time to time she heard him laugh at a joke, or make a flippant remark. He was right that she did not know him, and she was right that he would not reveal much of himself. She did not know how she could change that, but she could try. Most certainly, she would find out what was behind the altercation in the church.

The sunlight dimmed, and candles were lit, but the guests did not seem eager to stay. They gave the newly wed pair sly looks, and though Diana tried her best to ignore them, she could not help blushing. Her mother and Mr. Goldworthy were more discreet; they hid their smiles behind yawns and claims of fatigue. The servants, clearing the glasses, remained after the guests left, but their yawns were not feigned, and they hurried through their duties.

And then, at last, the bride and groom were alone. Diana sat in a chair and gazed at Gavin standing near the fireplace, how the firelight moved the night's shadows over his face, hiding and revealing. He leaned against one end of the mantelpiece, and twirled the stem of a brandy glass between his fingers. The brandy left in it swirled and dipped, then slid down the side of the glass in a golden film. He gazed at it for a moment, then quickly drank it down.

"Shall we go, Diana?" he said.

"Yes," she said, rose from her chair, and held out her hand to him. He stared at her hand for a moment, then at her face, then set down the glass on the mantelpiece and clasped her hand.

He led the way up the stairs, and brought her to her new room. She touched the door, but did not go in—another change, she thought. Gazing at him, she tiptoed and kissed him, and felt his arms come around her. But it was a brief kiss, and he looked intently at her when they parted, as if trying to see into her soul.

"Is this what you want, Diana?" he said. "This marriage?"

She watched him silently for a moment, then slowly nodded. "I believe it is. There is not a great deal for a woman like myself to do in the world, after all. I was not sure I would like to be married to anyone, but it is not as if I could truly make a living as a groom or a stableboy. And marriage, I suppose, is a sort of occupation." She smiled slightly. "Besides, it is not as if we can do anything about it now that we are wed but make the best of it." She looked at him steadily. "And I am glad it is you I married, even though I do not know a great deal about you, as you said."

"You are a fool, my dear," he said, but his voice was soft, and his fingers caressed her cheek.

"And yet, you have said you wanted to marry me."

"I am a fool, as well."

"Then we are well matched, are we not?" she said, and moved away. She curtsied, and opened the door. "I give you good night, sir," she said, and went into her room.

Chapter 12

Diana leaned against the closed door, wondering if she was indeed a fool, but it was of no use to speculate about the foolishness or wisdom of marrying Lord Brisbane. It was done, and she would deal with whatever came her way. She would not pretend this or that thing did not exist, but face it. She let out a long sigh, then nodded to the maid, who stood ready to help her change for the night.

Her nightgown was new, made of sheer cotton lawn, and embroidered with eyelets on the bodice. She had never worn anything like it, usually sleeping in an old shift. Sitting on the edge of her bed, she smoothed the fabric over her knees, then waved the maid away with a smile when the girl yawned once too often. The door closed behind her, and Diana was alone.

She looked around her room. The few lit candles and the fire in the hearth showed a pretty room, decorated in a light color, not discernible in the dimness. She had never been in this room before—she supposed it belonged to the last Lady Brisbane. She was now the countess, and—she glanced at the connecting door—and she would see her husband soon.

Her feet grew cold, and she moved into her bed, tucking them under the covers. The clock on the mantelpiece ticked away the minutes, but the door between her room and Gavin's did not open. Would he come into her room? She had understood that this was usually the way of it from what her mother had told her.

But another hour passed, and the door still did not open. Diana gnawed on her lower lip. Perhaps Gavin wished her to be comfortable in her room first; perhaps he would come to her tomorrow night. She could pretend that this was her usual room, and that she would sleep as usual. Her eyes scanned the walls of her room again. It seemed cold and unfriendly despite what she could see of its decoration.

She stared at the connecting door. No. Did she not say she would not pretend any longer? She was married, and it was best if she dealt with whatever came with it without delay. Moving her feet to the floor, she slid off the bed, and almost stumbled. She was shaking again. Muttering a curse she had heard a stableboy use, she clenched her hands into fists and lifted her chin. If Gavin would not come to her, she would go to him.

The door opened easily when she turned the doorknob, making no sound. She stepped in and looked cautiously about; the room had only a brace of candles lit, near where Gavin sat with his back to her, brandy glass in hand. He swirled the liquid in the glass, staring at it, then sipped it, then swirled it again.

The words Diana had thought she would say stuck in her throat; she could only stare at him, mute. She looked at his bed—it was very large—and thought she should at least get into it. Slowly she went to it, her feet making no sound on the soft and heavy carpet. She was glad; she did not wish to disturb him if he wanted only to drink and stare into the fire.

The bed creaked when she sat on it, however, and he stood abruptly and turned to her.

"What are you doing here?"

Diana swallowed, then lifted her chin. "You did not come to me, so I came to you."

He set down his glass with a sharp click on the side table, then strode to the bed. She could not see his face; the firelight behind him made him seem a tall, looming shadow. He stood there, silent, his fists on his waist. "I want no sacrificial lamb, Diana."

"I am not—you see I came here willingly."

"Really?" He walked to the bed, then pushed her down to

the pillows. He moved upon her, his lips hovering over hers. "You are shaking, my dear."

"If I am, it is because I do not know what to expect of you," she retorted, anger flaring. "You have made sure of it." She was glad of her anger; it banished her trembling.

"You could have stayed in your room."

She could feel his breath upon her lips, and his heart beating against her own wildly thumping one. "If you must know," she said angrily, "I did not want to be alone. I was afraid."

A sigh slipped from him, and he moved off of her. "I will summon a maid to stay with you."

"No." She clutched his arm. "I wish to be here, with you."

"Why?"

"Ohh!" She thumped the bed with her fist. "Must I always be the one to reveal myself? It is not fair! I will tell you nothing more of myself if you do not tell me of you. I *will* stay here, and *you* will stay here. If I must, I will hold you down with all my might—and you will have to fight me, for I am very strong, stronger than you might think." Her words spilled from her lips, stumbling over each other with mixed anger, frustration, and chagrin.

"Now that is an interesting prospect," Gavin replied. "I have never been held down by a woman before. I wonder if I shall like it? How would you do it?" He held out his hands. "Perhaps you should try."

"Ohhh!" Diana cried in frustration, and covered her face with her hands. "I wish you would not—oh, you are odious!"

"What, are you not going to hold me down?" A large sigh came from him. "I was beginning to look forward to it."

There was silence for a moment, while Diana thought of how she might wreak vengeance upon his head, and then she moved her fingers apart and looked at him. He was lying on his side, watching her, a wide grin on his face.

"You are a horrible man," she said. "I do not know why I consented to marry you."

"Because it was better than . . ." He paused as if thinking over a difficult problem. "Than being alone by yourself in a strange room."

"You are also very silly."

He laughed. "Come, then." He pushed aside the bedcovers, and she slid in, and he pulled them up again under her chin. His hand went to the belt of his robe, and she closed her eyes, feeling the trembling come over her again. The bedcovers rustled, the bed shifted and dipped, and then was still. Diana opened her eyes again—he was lying as he was before, except she could see he had no shirt on. She made herself look at him, at his bare chest and then at his face. "I won't do anything you will not like," he said gently. He stroked her cheek, and slipped his arm beneath her head, drawing her closer.

Diana stiffened then relaxed. He was only holding her, that was all, and it was like a hug, only lying down. It was, in fact, very comfortable. She let herself put her head upon his chest, rubbing her cheek against it, and heard him draw in a long breath and let it out again. She waited, but he did nothing more except stroke her arm and then her waist.

She began to feel warm and a little drowsy, and she turned a little, snuggling into him. Another sigh came from him.

"Diana," he said softly, "you are a mystery. So strong and brave, but very afraid. Afraid even of people looking at you. And yet you look the wildest stallion in the eye without the slightest qualm. I wonder what makes you so."

Her mind drifted over her life, touched upon her resolution to face what questions she avoided, and flinched. She opened her eyes—she must have almost fallen asleep. "If I tell you, you must tell me about your life." She did not know what made her say it; perhaps it was because she felt so comfortable.

There was silence, then: "Very well."

She was fully awake now. "Do you promise?"

A pause. "Yes, I promise."

"I do not like people looking at me because . . . because I am afraid they will see the bad thing about me." There, she said it. The trembling shook her again. But he held her close and rocked her a little, and it subsided.

"I have not seen anything bad, Diana," he said. His voice was gentle and comforting. "Did I not say I fell in love with you the moment I saw you? I did not see anything wrong then, and I do not now."

"But you were joking."

"No, I was not."

She lifted her head and looked at him. "You were not?"

He bent down and kissed her. "I was not," he said again.

A sigh escaped her. "I am glad."

The fire in the hearth crackled in the room's silence while the tolling of a distant clock came from somewhere in the house. "What is the bad thing you think you have?" he said at last.

His arms were still around her, and his hand was still stroking her waist, circling down to her hip and then to her ribs. How soothing it felt! "I don't know," she said. "But I had it when I was a girl, before my uncle came to take my mother and me away."

"How do you know?"

Perhaps it would not be so terrible to tell him, Diana thought. Her mother said he was a listening sort of man. "It is a long story," she said.

"Tell me." He held her closer, and she could not help letting out a deep sigh.

"It was just before my uncle came for us. My father was dead, and we had little money, so Mama and I moved to smaller rooms. Mama was very good with the needle, so she went every day to a dressmaker's shop to work, while I stayed behind and kept up our room, for we could afford no servants . . ."

The memories came back, too clearly, as if they had been preserved in some cold, dark corner of her mind. They had had little food, and Diana's mother had carefully parceled it out, but Diana could remember how her stomach had growled.

"But I grew used to it," she said. "One does, I think." She felt Gavin press a light kiss on her hair, and she sighed again.

She took pride in helping her mother, and made sure their room in the boarding house was clean and well-swept. She even took out the chamber pot, going down the stairs to empty it. But there was never enough money, and their clothes grew threadbare. Diana had wished she could somehow earn money, but could not think of a way to do it.

But a man had approached her, one of the boarders—she had seen him before, watching her as she passed him from time to time, and he would smile, as if he liked her. He had offered her money if she would do something for him, and she was at first glad she could find a way to help her mother. She had even asked for the money first, and he had agreed with another smile.

"And then he took off my clothes and looked and looked at me, and . . ." Diana faltered. Gavin's grip upon her had tightened, and his hand had stopped stroking her.

"You need not tell me," he said, his voice a whisper.

"Are you angry?"

"Not at you," he said. "Does your mother know?"

"Yes, for I told her, and showed her the money. She was so angry, Gavin, and threw the coins away, then held me and kissed me as if I were a baby instead of a big girl. She did not let me go for a long time, weeping. She did not go to the dressmaker's shop the next day, but wrote a letter to my uncle, and for more than a week we did not go out of the room, for that man who—that man would come to our door at all manner of times, and say hateful things through it." She closed her eyes, and tried to slow her breathing, which came in gasps. "I could not go out, Gavin! Mama had locked the door, for she was afraid he would come in, and we could not even go out to buy food. She grew ill, and I was so afraid, but she would not let me go out to find a doctor. So we stayed, locked in, and sometimes I would tell myself stories, and pretend I was not inside, but outside, with nobody about but me. I pretended I would run, far away and fast, so no one could catch me. I did not feel so hungry that way."

Diana felt herself shaking again, and despised herself for not being strong enough to stop it. Gavin must despise her, too, for succumbing to the fear, for it had happened so long ago. Perhaps now he, too, could see what it was about her that was bad and caused that man to look and look at her as if she had something forbidden and evil in her. She rolled away from Gavin, but he only pulled her to him again, her back against his chest.

"Stay with me, Diana." He put another kiss upon her hair, and held her tight—if he kissed her, he must not despise her very much, she thought. His hand rubbed her waist, and then her back and shoulders, and the shaking dissipated. He kissed her cheek, a brief touch, and she felt her body loosen and relax. "Your uncle came for you then, am I right?"

She sighed again. "Yes, and the door opened wide, and he took us away, and I have never seen so bright a house as Brisbane House, or a place as free and green and clean as this area of Somerset. It was heaven to me. I could go out-of-doors whenever I wanted, and ran and ran, just as I had pretended in that dark room in London. I learned how to ride horses, and it was better than any pretending, for it was as if I could fly, anywhere."

"And the man—what of him?"

Diana tensed, but Gavin's fingers were rubbing her neck, and she could not stay tense for long. "I remember Uncle Charles told me he had got rid of him."

"Ah, well," he said in a conversational tone. "Since your uncle was an efficient and thorough man, I imagine he must have got rid of that damn bloody"—he rattled off a number of unfamiliar words—"quite well."

"You *are* angry," Diana said.

"Only because your uncle has robbed me of the chance to get rid of that"—more unfamiliar words—"myself."

She rolled over onto her back. "Would you have?"

"Yes," he said, kissing her gently. "Except I would have tortured him first."

"Really? How?"

He grinned suddenly. "You are a bloodthirsty wench. I would have strung him up through his"—he paused—"his ankles."

Diana shuddered, then thought about how agonized and ill with weeping and hunger her mother had been so long ago. "Very appropriate," she said firmly. She released a long breath, and with it a dark, hard knot inside of her also loosened. She gazed at him smiling at her, and touched his face; he took her hand and kissed her fingers.

"What a pity Brisbane House does not have a dungeon," he said, his grin growing wider.

"Why is that?"

"Because I would have had him chained up so that you could have thrown hot irons at him. Think how satisfying that would have been. Do you think your mother would have liked to have participated, as well?"

Diana laughed, for the image of her gentle and delicate mother savagely flinging hot irons at the villain was absurd. But she said, "I think she would have enjoyed it immensely," and realized perhaps her mother would have.

"I see I have married into a family of very fierce women," he said, and kissed her again.

"Do you mind?" she said, a little breathlessly.

"No," he said. "I adore fierce women." And kissed her again, gently, but she opened her mouth to him as he had asked her that time in the maze and the kiss turned deep.

It was a gloriously rich kiss, full and slow, and she could only move languidly, her arms sliding up around his neck and around his back. She felt his hands move down her shoulders to her waist, then to her hips, pulling her up hard against him.

Then, abruptly, he moved away from her. He gazed at her, an intense heat in his eyes, but he only stroked her cheek. "I think perhaps you might not be ready for this."

At first she was bewildered, not sure what he meant, then

remembered what her mother had told her regarding the marriage bed. "I do not know, either," she said honestly. "But I shall not know if we do not try."

He kissed her again, gently. "If you wish me to stop at any time, then tell me and I shall." His smile was wry. "It'll be damned difficult, but I shall stop. I won't even look at you if you would prefer I do not."

She thought about it for a moment, then shook her head. "I will have to try not to be so afraid . . . and you have said you have not seen anything bad about me—yet."

He chuckled. "I shall never see anything bad about you."

"Then I think I shall not mind it much if you look at me."

"Good," he said, and kissed her again, and began unbuttoning her gown. He slipped his hand inside the bodice and then stopped. "What is this?"

She gazed at him uncertainly. The fire and candlelight illuminated surprise, not anger or disgust, and she let out a deep breath. "It is my bindings." He looked at her questioningly. "When I don't put them on, I receive too many looks, and so I have taken to putting them on most of the time."

"Even when you sleep?" He looked incredulous. "They must be damned uncomfortable."

"Not when I sleep." She bit her lip, embarrassed. "Tonight I was afraid . . ."

"My dear, you need not be. I did say I would stop if you did not like what I do."

She thought about this for a moment. She had resolved not to be cowardly, and so she would not. "I will take them off, then," she said.

She sat up, and pulled down the top of her nightgown, blushing, for Gavin slowly sat up as well, watching her, the bedcovers dropping down about his hips. The candlelight burnished the lean, hard planes of his chest and the muscles of his arms, but he did not at all seem self-conscious about his bareness. She supposed such things were allowed between a husband and wife. She tugged at the knot at one side, then grimaced. "I am afraid I tied it too tightly."

She thought he uttered a small groan, but he said, "Let me try." His fingers fumbled with the knot, and his hands seemed oddly unsteady. "Devil take it," he muttered, and moved off the bed. She quickly averted her eyes, but not before the firelight caught the long lean stretch of thigh and buttock. A glint caught her eyes, and she gasped.

A dagger. It was small and neat, and she gazed at him, wondering why he carried such a weapon. She watched him as he pulled at the knot, and quickly slit the fabric behind it. The two ends fell apart, and he tossed the knot aside, then tucked the knife somewhere to the side of the bed.

His eyes met hers, almost a challenge, and her questions died on her lips. She took the ends of the bindings in her hands instead, and began to unwind it from around her. A glance at his face made her hands shake; he was watching with a very odd expression, one she did not know how to interpret.

Finally she was done, and forced her hands to her sides, though they curled up into fists. She would *not* be a coward, and if Gavin despised her or was repulsed by her, then she would make herself bear it. She would even bind herself up again, and not mind being uncomfortable.

"Dear God in Heaven," he whispered.

She could not stand it. "I am sorry," she said, and hid her face in her hands. "I am sorry if I disgust you."

"Disgust me?"

Was there a laugh in his voice? She brought her hands down, fists once again, and looked at him. "Don't laugh at me," she said angrily. "And . . . and you should not take God's name in vain." It was a ridiculous protest, considering the amount of vulgar cursing she had heard from him already, but she could think of nothing else to say.

This time he did laugh. "Madam, that was no curse, but a prayer of the most heartfelt thanksgiving." His arms came around her and pulled her down to the bed, kissing her hotly. "I have been blessed," he said, with each word trailing kisses from her throat to the tip of one breast. "Not only have I managed to marry the lady with whom I have fallen desperately in love, but she has the most magnificently endowed figure I could have ever imagined." He kissed her lips again, and kissed another line from throat to her other breast. "Thank you, thank you, thank you," he said between each kiss.

She began to giggle, because the kisses tickled, and then she began to laugh because she felt suddenly free—and she was, of course, because she had not her bindings on, but she felt free inside, as if some binding on her heart was also gone. She could not stop giggling, for his hands went all over her and his fingers sliding over her breasts and belly and thighs tickled terribly.

Her laughter ceased, however, when he pulled her hand down upon him, and she looked at him wide-eyed. She bit her lip, wondering if it would be proper if she looked. Well, she had allowed him to look at her; she certainly should be allowed to look at him! Carefully she glanced downward.

"Oh, thank goodness," she said, breathing a sigh of relief.

"I do not think that was a curse," Gavin said, breathing deeply himself.

"No, it was not," Diana said. "You see, I have seen how horses go about breeding, and I was afraid yours would be as large as a stallion's. I am very thankful it is not, for I believe I would have a difficult time of it if it were."

A choking sound came from him, and he suddenly buried his face between her breasts, his shoulders shaking. She pushed at him, and he rolled over, roaring with laughter.

"That's a devilish thing to say to one's bridegroom," he said, gasping.

"Why? It is only the truth. I should not at all wish to be split in two, which I might well be if it were that large. It would hurt horribly, I imagine." She leaned over him, slapping his chest with her hand. "What is so funny?"

"You, sweet one," he said, and pulled her down to him, kissing her soundly. He sobered suddenly. "It might hurt, nevertheless."

She wet her lips, feeling nervous. "I have been told so."

"Only briefly," he said, and she began to move to the side, but he grasped her hips tightly. "Stay as you are." He closed his eyes and pressed himself up against her. His movement made her feel warm and languid, and then hot as his fingers ran along her waist to her breasts. "Yes," he murmured. "Yes."

A strange sizzle coursed through her body, forcing her to moan and move upon him, making her breathe in gasps.

"God, Diana, this is heaven." His voice was a harsh whisper, and he shifted under her and then a hard pressure moved between her thighs. Her eyes widened and a small protesting sound came from her throat as it moved into her, a stretching ache. "Sorry . . ." He took in a deep breath. "I will stop if you wish it—but please say you do *not* wish it."

"I do not wish you to stop," she said, and gingerly settled herself down upon him.

"Thank God," he said. He groaned, and surged upward.

Diana bit her lip, for it ached again, and then the ache faded as Gavin moved in her again and touched her where they joined. Fire burned there, and she clutched him tightly, and then a bubbling, a bursting, up through her belly and her breasts, forced a cry and a deep moan from her throat.

Rolling her under him, he pressed deep into her, again and again, his mouth upon hers, breathing her breath. She twisted under him, for the bursting came once more, making her clutch him tightly as his breath rasped harshly in his throat with one last thrust.

He sank down upon her, a groan leaving him. She sighed, feeling boneless and sluggish, and closed her eyes, only opening them again when he shifted their positions to their sides and kissed her mouth, cheek, and neck. He gazed at her, the wonder in his eyes making her feel light. Diana smiled.

"How beautiful you are," he said.

She shook her head and glanced away, not able to say anything and feeling suddenly shy.

He lifted her chin with his hand, making her look at him. He kissed her, then said, "I have been around the world, and have seen many women. But I have never seen one made of gold as you are." He threaded his fingers through her hair and kissed a strand of it. "Golden hair, golden skin." His hand curled under her breast. "Beautiful," he said, and put his hands around her waist, then smoothed them over her hips. "Magnificent."

She looked into his eyes, and the fire that had earlier coursed through her body seemed to linger in her heart. He gazed and gazed at her, as if he could not get enough of looking at her, and she found she did not mind it at all, and perhaps had not minded it for a long time. She reached up and kissed him, and his breath grew ragged.

"God, how I love you," he said, pulling her close again. "Say you love me, Diana, even if you don't mean it."

She held his face between her hands, and gazed long into his eyes. "I do love you, Gavin, and I mean it," she said, and knew, with the shattering of the walls around her heart, that it was true.

He looked at her, startled, shaking his head slightly.

"I do," she said. "I was too afraid to think it, but I am not afraid now."

He gave a slight, incredulous laugh, and held her tightly, seeming unable to speak. He kissed her instead again, and the kisses became heated once more, and once more they loved until they could not move any longer, then finally, finally slept.

Chapter 13

Gavin Sinclair, Earl of Brisbane, gazed at his sleeping wife and regretted that he had been forced to marry her.

He watched her even breathing, how her full and beautifully rounded breasts rose and fell, and grinned, remembering the night before. He could not regret that part of it. What he had told her was true: when she had turned and looked at him that day in the woods, rain-soaked and sobbing, he had fallen instantly in love with her. At first he had thought it was sheer lust; her wet clothes had clung to her, outlining a lush and voluptuous figure, and he had wanted her instantly. His fastidiousness had kept him from seeking whores in different ports, but it did not mean he had not any desire for women, and the desire did accumulate after a while.

But then she had turned and gazed at him with her curiously light eyes, wet with tears of grief, and her full lips had pressed tightly together in an attempt to control her emotions. Her spine had stiffened as if she had heard the summoning of a military drum . . . and he had, at that moment, fallen in love with her, body and soul.

He had resisted the idea, of course, especially when he had discovered who she was. But he had been forced into the role of earl, and as such, was responsible for those who lived upon his property and to those related to him. He grimaced. He supposed he could have had Diana and her mother leave Brisbane House, but the conditions of the late earl's will made it clear that they would struggle with the amount of money the bequest gave them.

And the thought of not seeing her every day . . . even though he knew it was wise if he did not see her, he could not bring himself to suggest she go. It was a bad choice; once he had touched her, he could not keep his hands from her, and when she did not keep him from kissing her, he only wanted more.

Last night she said she loved him. He ran a finger along her cheek, wondering if it was true. He grimaced. He had been mad with lust and love combined, and had lost control of himself, wanting to hear the words from her.

And she had said them. If he had not asked, she might not have mentioned it. She was wary, like a wild fox, and watched him—and others, for that matter—carefully. She had cause to be wary. He gazed at her sleeping face and remembered the fear on it last night. At least that monster had not raped her; Gavin had seen the evidence of her virginity on the sheets this morning, though he had not been sure when he had entered her last night. But the man's terrorizing of her and her mother had left its mark, and Diana was like a wild creature, fearing confinement of any sort, and yet hiding herself for fear of being trapped or found wanting.

His mind went over the recent deaths on his estates. A monster then, a monster now. Yes, she had much to be wary about.

But his wife was not totally helpless, thank God. She was, oddly, a practical woman, a woman who commanded respect. He had watched her fearlessly break a stallion, neatly dodging hooves and teeth, ordering grooms and stableboys about in her firm, husky voice. She brooked no disobedience, her stern gaze making even the most recalcitrant apologize on the instant, and her smiles of thanks to those who obeyed her were sweet. It was why he had her continue supervising the stables; it kept her occupied, and he doubted he could do as well as she. She had great power and strength in her character, though she seemed not to know it, and tried over-hard to have the strength she thought she did not have.

He knew the feeling well. He had been servant and slave, prisoner and drudge, and had escaped to claw his way out of poverty to eventually owning a ship of his own. He controlled more than a few business concerns, and he had in his hands the mortgages of more than a few prominent peers. Now he was a peer himself, and he found he liked it very well even though he was not used to it. And now that he had it, he would prefer not to have anyone take it from his control.

It was better than vengeance, the reason he had decided to accept the late Lord Brisbane's offer of work. The inheritance came to him as a surprise, and it was one more clue as to why he might have been abducted and bundled off to sea when he was a youth, and showed him that Charles Carlyle had not been the one to do it, despite the vague memory of the Carlyle name at the time. He suspected that the person behind his abduction and the deaths of Lord Brisbane and the head groom were one and the same. How convenient it was that his own interests and that of the estate had dovetailed so neatly. Further, it seemed Vicar Southworthy knew something about his, Gavin's, claim to the earldom, if his reaction at Sir James's objection to his marriage was any indication. He would have to speak to him, soon.

And Sir James. He, really, had the best reason to wish the late Lord Brisbane out of the way, as well as Gavin. He was also older than Gavin by a decade, and would have been old enough to plan and carry out an abduction. He frowned. And yet, the man had no real financial reason to commit murder; Gavin had investigated his finances, and there was no evidence then or now that the man needed money. Sir James had indeed been very successful at the gaming tables, and did not seem to be the type to care for owning property in the country; he had more than enough to buy himself a tidy bit of land if he had wished. It did not quite fit.

And then, Diana. He had not wanted to marry her this soon, before he was completely certain of his own position. Ironic, that, for before he knew who she was, he had been quite determined that she would be his wife, and he usually got what he wanted, sooner or later.

He gazed at his wife, her face smooth and innocent in sleep, and wondered if she really was innocent. His gut clenched at the thought. Of all the people in Brisbane House, she had the best opportunity to plan and execute an accident for her uncle. She knew the stables well, and commanded the grooms and the stableboys. She was expert at driving the curricle—he had seen it himself. Of course she would make sure that the horses would not rear and buck when she was driving it.

No, she could not have done it. Everything she did showed a strong loyalty and affection for her uncle. Besides, if it were indeed true that Charles Carlyle had saved her and her mother, then she owed her life to him.

If it were true. Gavin almost groaned aloud. He must keep all possibilities in his mind, even if it meant his wife was a murderess. He had to realize his love for her could be clouding his mind, now, even as he gazed at her sleepily opening eyes, and returned her slow, sleepy smile. He had known that she was the other half of him the first time he had gazed into her eyes. But if she were indeed the other half of him, then she was just as capable of killing a man as he. It was surprising how easy it was to kill.

He had much work to do, many questions to ask. But now, now Diana held out her arms to him, and he could not help sinking into her softness and strength, and driving her to cries of passion and release as he buried himself in her gift of heat and oblivion.

Gavin rolled away at last, and began to rise from the bed, but Diana caught his arm. He turned to her, and saw she had paled.

"What is that? On your back?"

He hesitated, wondering how he would tell her—and if he would at all. "Old wounds," he said, knowing his answer would not suffice. He shrugged, as if they were inconsequential.

"And severe," she said, gazing at him sternly as if he were a recalcitrant stableboy. "You will tell me how you got them. I said I would tell you of my life if you told me of yours last night, and as you see, I have not forgotten it. And this time"—her lips turned up for a moment—"I will hold you down until you do."

"Breakfast first, and then I will tell you," he said beginning to move away from her in the hopes that he could distract her. "After all our activity—"

His breath left him suddenly as Diana leaped and pushed him down to the pillows, her hair flying about her fiercely determined face. She sat on him, her hands on his shoulders holding him down as she stared at him with icy blue eyes.

"You *shall* tell me," she said in a low voice. *"Now."* An almost savage smile formed on her face, and she bent toward him until her lips almost touched his. "I will not be put off, not any longer." She pressed her mouth hard against his, her hair coming down around him like feathers against his flesh, her breasts pressing into his chest. He groaned, desiring her again, and grasped her hips.

But she twisted away, still holding his shoulders. "No. You will tell me first," she said, though her face flushed and her eyes grew heavy with want.

He gazed at her, her chin thrust forward stubbornly, and her eyes staring with determination into his, and began to laugh. A formidable woman, indeed. "Witch," he said, and put his hand behind her head to take a kiss. "Very well."

She grinned her triumph, but was careful not to shift all of her body away from him, and settled her chin on her hands that were clasped on his chest. He gazed at her for a moment, thinking of how he might tell her about the wounds he had received. He sighed. Where else but the beginning? It could not hurt, he thought, to tell her how he had gotten them, if he was prudent about it.

"When I was about sixteen, I awoke one day to find myself bound and gagged upon Mr. Goldworthy's ship, my stomach churning with each pitch of the waves, my head pounding with pain, and my back burning as if I had been seared with a dozen brands."

He saw her face pale, and her throat move in a swallow. "Oh heavens," she whispered. "Not . . . not . . ."

"Hush, love," he said, smoothing back a strand of hair that had fallen across her face. "Do you want to hear this?" She nodded, and he continued. "I did not know why I was there, or why I had been treated so," he said. "Indeed, when Ned Goldworthy found me, I thought he had been the one who had done it."

But he had not, and the man who had become his friend had been as horrified as any good man might. The merchant had cleaned him and cared for him, giving him whatever remedies he had at hand to heal his wounds and rid him of the ensuing fever. At last Gavin had become well, but they could not turn back. Mr. Goldworthy's ship was bound to Spain with supplies, and had to be there soon. Eventually, he came back to England, but it was the long way about, for Bonaparte had lined his forces against England at Boulogne at the time, and it was a tricky thing to get past the French tyrant's eye with a goods-laden ship.

Gavin paused, looping a strand of Diana's hair around his finger, remembering those days. He had found it at once exciting and terrifying, and was often half groggy trying to suppress the occasional seasickness he'd get. But throughout it all, he had had one thought, and that was to return to England and have his revenge against whoever it was that had beaten him almost senseless. No, not almost senseless . . .

"Surely, that is not it?" Diana's voice pierced his thoughts, and he gazed at her, wondering how much more he should tell her.

"That is all," he said at last.

"You must know who did this to you!" Her eyes showed horror and grief for the youth he had been.

"No, I do not know," he blurted. "I don't remember." He mentally cursed himself; he did not mean to tell her that much. But he had told no one except for Ned Goldworthy; now that he had begun, it threatened to burst from him, all of it.

She frowned. "Surely you must remember such a horrible thing! I can remember far beyond the age of fifteen—indeed, I believe my earliest memories were perhaps three years of age."

"No, I do not," he said again, and shrugged. "The blow to my head, the fever—I do not know which one robbed me of my memory of it." He gazed at her horrified face and his anger rose again, hard and cold. "You see, you should not have married me." His anger wanted to push her away from him. "I have no memory of being Gavin Sinclair before the age of fifteen—I am certainly the nobody Sir James claimed I am," he said bitterly.

"Oh, Gavin!" she cried, and kissed him, holding him tight. She looked up at him again, her lips pressed tightly together for a moment. "I think we should build a dungeon. Then when we find who did this to you, we shall chain him up and fling hot irons at him."

He laughed, and kissed her again, her form against him an unfamiliar comfort. It was odd how he had searched for comfort and ease, and now that he had it, he felt somehow that he could not quite settle into it. He was used to hard work and sacrifice, not a soft bed and a soft woman.

A rumbling came from beside him, and he grinned to see Diana blush and press her hand over her stomach.

"Yes, I agree, it is past time for our breakfast," he said, and easily moved from beneath her. He rose and pulled the bell rope, giving a side glance at Diana as he did so. She was watching him, discontent flickering over her face, as if he were some strange new animal and as if she were puzzling over what to do with him. He smiled slightly. It would be interesting to see what she would conclude. "Come now, you will need to dress yourself before our breakfast arrives; I dislike the idea of anyone else seeing as much of you as I do now." He sighed to see how her blush spread to her breasts as she pulled on her discarded nightgown, and sybaritic images of food and womanly flesh flickered through his mind.

He made himself turn away and draw on his robe. Later, he

thought, smiling widely. He had his riches and his comforts, and even a title now, and he would not give them up.

His smile faded. Indeed, once he had hold of a thing, he never could let go. He would find out who had abducted him, and somehow retrieve his memories.

He watched his wife open the connecting door and go through to her own room. Yes, it was unfortunate that he had married Diana. For whoever had abducted him had no doubt killed the last Lord Brisbane, and if it was because of the inheritance, then Gavin Sinclair would be the next to die.

And his wife, should she be carrying his child. Yes, he should not have married her. It put her in that much more danger.

The ride to Vicar Southworthy's house was not long, which was fortunate, for Gavin felt uncomfortable leaving Diana behind at Brisbane House, even though there were servants a-plenty around her. But he did not want to tell her fully of his fears, for she would certainly begin to question him, or worse, other people, and he did not want the killer's attention brought upon her. It was a fine line he walked, whether to tell her all, or only enough to keep her safe. Discretion being the better part of valor, it was no doubt wise to say as little as possible.

He knew that he could easily be killed himself; the murderer could hide behind a tree or tall bush, and shoot him. But that did not seem to be the man's style. It was indirect, always, whether it was abduction or causing some accident or other. Except for his own abduction, it seemed to center around horses or races of some kind; the late Lord Brisbane had told him that, at least. At present, he would make sure to be in no race, and if someone planned to abduct him again and falsify an "accident" around it, he had a small pistol in his coat pocket, already primed. He had, also, his dagger in its sheath, tucked neatly in his boot. His instincts told him he would not need it once he was at the vicar's house, but one could never be sure.

He smiled grimly. Few gentlemen would think to carry a dagger; it was fortunate, therefore, that he had not thought himself a gentleman for a very long time. An unexpected weapon was always an asset.

The road curved around a hillock, and the vicar's house appeared, a large, neat building of gray stone, the property around it clearly well-maintained. The living was a generous one, and Gavin saw no need to change it at the moment until such time Mr. Southworthy deemed it necessary to marry and have a family. So far, the man seemed not interested in matrimony, if the local gossip was correct; he was devoted to his parish, and worked harder than most clergymen Gavin had known.

He dismounted and tied the reins of his horse to a post, then knocked on the door. A maid opened it and curtsied, gazing with awe at him when he announced who he was. His smile turned wry after he nodded at her and she turned away to tell the vicar. She obviously thought him very grand indeed, when even as much as five years ago, she would not have thought twice about him, nor would any other servant. A title was all that separated the Earl of Brisbane from plain Mr. Gavin Sinclair, but it made all the difference in the world, it seemed.

He did not expect it when Vicar Southworthy came to meet him personally; he had thought he would send another servant to direct him to his parlor. Perhaps earls and such were accorded such distinction. But the vicar, indeed, entered next.

Mr. Southworthy's steady gaze might have made Gavin think the man's mind was untroubled, but his pale face and tightly pressed lips as the vicar gave his stiff bow told him differently. It would not do to put the man at a formal distance; the earl had found that a certain informality often disarmed a man of his mental defenses and one could procure more information far easier than if one maintained formality. He held out his hand, therefore, and the vicar hesitantly took it, then shook it firmly.

"If you will come this way," Mr. Southworthy said. "I have ordered the maid to bring refreshment into the parlor."

"My pleasure," Gavin replied, and followed him through a door.

The room was austere, with few decorations, but pleasant enough, and the furniture was comfortable. They sat, and the vicar poured the tea when it came, but when Gavin opened his mouth to speak, Mr. Southworthy held up his hand.

"Please . . . I know why you have come here." The man put his cup on the table, rattling the saucer, then stood, gazing defensively at Gavin, his chin raised.

"Do you?" Gavin said, watching him carefully. A tight expectant knot formed in the pit of his belly, but he kept his face bland.

"The church—Sir James's outburst—" The vicar swallowed, and misery entered his eyes. "You must not think I would allow any doubt to be cast on your inheritance, for of course you are indeed the heir, as you well know."

He wanted to release a sigh of relief, but he did not; it was important not to let Southworthy know more than he should. Gavin merely nodded and gave the man all his attention.

The vicar began to pace, his steps agitated. "I cannot keep it a secret—the shame—I have remembered it all these years, and thought there was nothing to be done, and then you returned, the heir, and I knew it was only a matter of time."

"I am listening," Gavin said, and made his voice gentle.

The vicar threw him a grateful look and returned to his chair, briefly pressing his palms to his eyes. He rested his elbows on his knees, clasping his hands, and sighed. "I remember, when I was a boy, and lived with my father in London, there was a noise in the night, and I woke up, wondering what it was. I crept down the stairs, and frightened by steps coming toward me, I hid in the cellar." He grimaced and glanced at the earl. "I knew well my father's temper and did not want to risk it."

He sighed. "A lantern shone, and curses and a cry, and there was my father with a boy not much older than myself. I did not know who he was, but thought he looked somewhat familiar." He swallowed and bitterness crept across his face. "My father then began beating him, demanding papers—marriage lines, letters, whatever it was that he could not find when he went searching. But the boy would say nothing—he just stared at him."

The vicar covered his face again with trembling hands, then gave a deep sigh and pressed them against his knees. "I did not know why my father wanted these things, or why he treated the boy so, but I was too cowardly to stop him."

A glimmer of memory stirred . . . Gavin could not quite bring it forth, but the vicar's words formed an image in his mind, strangely familiar, and his back stiffened, as if in readiness for a blow.

"I hid and did nothing until it was done, until the boy, unconscious, was taken away. Then I crept out, and returned to my bed and did not sleep at all until the dawn."

Questions built up behind Gavin's lips, pushing to be asked, but he clenched his teeth tightly together. His mother, his father—no, he would not ask about them, not yet.

The vicar's face turned wretched. "I watched and listened and learned—quietly, out of the way of my father, for I knew how easily his violence could turn on me and my mother. And I did nothing, still nothing."

Gavin nodded, even sympathetically, for he knew that it would bring forth more information. He was quite right; the vicar's face grew more miserable than ever at his understanding gaze. Guilt pricked the earl. There would have been nothing a boy of that age could do against his father . . . but he could not stop the man now from revealing his shame, for it would also mean he might not find what he needed to know, and that could be a matter of life and death.

"I was helpless!" the vicar cried. "But at least I could find out what my father was after, and in good time reveal it." He sighed again and shook his head. "My father was mad; he was mad with greed and wanted to be the Earl of Brisbane. Your father had already been lost at sea, and you were beginning to take on the reins of business. Sir James's father was dead as well, recently, and thank God it was from illness and not from my father's hand.

"But my father had decided to take fate into his own hands and make sure of his succession; he came masked into your house, bound your mother to her bed, tying her mouth so that no one would hear her screams. I do not know why he could not find the marriage lines, or why he thought you would know, but he could not, and took you from your house."

"I had them rolled and tucked in my belt," Gavin said softly. It was the only thing of his family he had had when he woke up on Mr. Goldworthy's ship, that and a small portrait of his mother in his jacket pocket.

"My father thought he would rid himself of you and Sir James—accidents, you know—and then finally the earl." Mr. Southworthy looked down at his hands, nodding absently. "I suppose my father thought you dead from the beating—I certainly thought so, for you would not wake. He took you away, and I did not see you again until the day the will was read." He gazed at Gavin steadily. "I recognized you immediately. Your face is the same as that boy's. Weathered and leaner, but the same. I thought you might say something then, but you did not, then I realized of course you would not recognize me, and my father never mentioned his own name in your presence, at least I did not hear him say it in the cellar."

"What happened to your father?" Gavin asked gently.

"He died of an apoplexy only a few months after that, and before he could do more harm, thank God," the vicar said harshly. "And released my mother and myself from the daily fear under which we lived."

"And your mother?"

The vicar's face softened, and he sighed. "She lives with me here. Her mind has aged faster than her body, no doubt from the mental hardship of living with my father. She does not like to come out of her room, but will come out from time to time."

"I would like to meet her," Gavin said.

The vicar shot him a surprised look, then nodded, and left the parlor.

Gavin sighed, and his shoulders ached with the sudden release of tension. So, it was the elder Mr. Southworthy who had abducted him, and left him for dead. And he had planned accidents for the prospective heirs of the Brisbane estate. It made sense; killing the earl and then his heirs would have brought more notice upon their accidents than the other way about. At least he now had the answer to that.

He took another sip of tea, then chewed contemplatively upon a biscuit, gazing at the hearth before him. And he had, at last, the answer for which he had been looking for years: he was truly Gavin Sinclair, and the heir to the Brisbane estate.

When he had come back to England and searched for his identity, for his family, he had come back to the Sinclair house. His parents' marriage lines and the portrait was all that he had as evidence. Mrs. Sinclair had died of lung fever while he was gone at sea, so she could not identify him. The servants they had had were gone as well, and he could not remember any of them. There was his portrait as a very little boy in the house he had lived in. The miniature he had had in his pocket matched the lady in that portrait; therefore she had to be Mrs. Sinclair. But he had not remembered her, nor the tall man who stood next to her, and for all the little boy in the large portrait in the Sinclair house had had the same coloring, he had stared at him with no recognition at all. All he could feel looking at the painted family had been a distant sadness, as if he mourned the demise of a seldom-seen acquaintance.

There had been nothing to do but sell the house and keep what family belongings he thought he might like—the large portrait, some pieces of jewelry, which he had put into storage under Mr. Goldworthy's advice. His friend had also helped him contact his father's business associates, but there was little recognition in their eyes; they had had little to do with halflings and his father had apparently kept his business affairs strictly separate from his family life. But he claimed what savings and income there was, and under Mr. Goldworthy's instruction, invested it, then sailed off to sea.

But always there had been that doubt, and he had felt like an impostor, for small inklings of images would come to him in the night, only to disappear from his memory again when he woke. It was as if his life before the abduction had been wiped clean, a blank.

He had determined to make a life for himself, build himself anew, and so he did. He had been captured by pirates, had been sold as a slave, escaped, and had more adventures than most men might or would want to have. He had gained a fortune, lost one, and gained another one, and now had a title and property. Gavin smiled to himself wryly. If he had wished to remake his life, he had done so with a vengeance.

Vengeance. Ah, yes. There was that, too, driving him to make a success of himself, so that he would be in a good position to pursue it. He raised his head and gazed around the vicar's austere parlor. He could, if he wished, do just that, right now. He could strip Southworthy of his living as a vicar, and the man would be as homeless as he, Gavin, had been. Shifting uncomfortably in his seat, he took another sip of tea. And yet, somehow the wish for vengeance had lost the fire it once had. He grimaced. He was becoming too comfortable in his new life. Comfort could rob a man of the sharpness needed for survival.

The door opened, and the vicar entered, his arms supporting a very elderly woman. Or no, perhaps not that elderly. Her hair was white, but her face was not as lined as Gavin supposed a very old woman's might be. She walked slowly, with a slight limp, and he watched as Southworthy helped her to a comfortable-looking chair, and put a cup of tea in her hands.

"Be careful, Mother, the tea is very warm, so you must sip it and not drink it in a gulp," the vicar said gently.

Mrs. Southworthy smiled at him and sipped her tea obediently. "You are a good boy, Lionel," she said, then turned to Gavin and started, her face growing frightened, and almost spilled her drink. The vicar quickly took it from her, and she leaned toward him. "Who is that man, Lionel? Will he beat me?"

"No, no, Mother, he is the Earl of Brisbane," the vicar said hastily, sending an apologetic glance at Gavin. "He will not touch a hair on your head, I promise you."

Mrs. Southworthy breathed a sigh of relief. "You are a good boy, Lionel," she said again, and nibbled the biscuit he put in her hand.

"You may call me Gavin," the earl said, making his voice gentle. "I will not hurt you, but have come to call upon you and have tea. I like tea and biscuits, do not you?"

The woman's face brightened. "Yes, I like many kinds of biscuits, and Cook makes all the kinds I like." The vicar shot a surprised and grateful look at him, his shoulders losing their stiffness.

Gavin stayed for another quarter of an hour, conversing on simple topics which Mrs. Southworthy might understand. He stood, finally, and the vicar rose as well. He gazed at the earl, and his posture stiffened once again.

"I will understand it if you wish me to resign my position," he said firmly. "I would not blame you. The shame of it—" His mouth closed tightly for a moment. "I could have said something before this, but I did not." He sighed, and smiled wryly. "It is a relief to reveal it at last. At least I have that."

Gavin stared at him for a long moment. "There was nothing a boy could do," he said. "Not with a mother to protect."

Vicar Southworthy gazed at him and mutely shook his head. The earl held out his hand, and Southworthy took it. The man's hand trembled for a moment, then clasped the earl's firmly.

"Thank you, my lord," he said. "Thank you."

The Earl of Brisbane merely nodded, then turned away. As he untied his horse, he glanced through the parlor window to see the vicar patting his mother's hand, and helping her up again. Next quarter-day, he thought, the vicar would get an increase in his living. At the very least, his mother needed a new dress.

A sudden sound of hoofbeats caught his ear, and a flash of blue caught his eye.

Diana! Gavin gazed grimly at the retreating figure galloping away on her horse. What the devil was she doing here? Listening, possibly, though he never thought her the type to eavesdrop. He quickly mounted his horse and spurred it to a gallop. He wondered how much she had heard, and what she would make of it. Well, he would be sure to find out.

Chapter 14

Diana rode as swiftly away from the vicar's house as she could, but she was certain Gavin had seen her. She had stayed too long, listening to the conversation between Mr. Southworthy and the earl. She cast a quick glance behind her—yes, Gavin was following her.

She let out an exasperated breath. He had seen her, therefore it was useless to ride off, thinking he would not catch up with her. He would, of course, if not here, then at home. She slowed her horse to a canter, then a trot, then at last to a stop, and watched him as he rode up to her.

He sat silent on his horse for a moment, as if waiting for her to give some sort of excuse for eavesdropping. But she refused to be the first to speak, and merely gazed at him.

"Well, madam?" he asked.

She raised her brows. "Well?"

"You were eavesdropping, were you not?"

"And if I were?"

An annoyed expression flashed upon his face. "You need not listen at doors; if you need to know anything, I shall tell you."

"Oh, really?" Diana retorted. "I seem to remember I had to hold you down this morning before you would tell me about the scars on your back. I cannot hold you down every time I ask a question."

He grinned suddenly. "You could try. And think how well it worked. I told you, did I not?"

She remembered how she had done it, and her face grew

hot. She had been . . . uninhibited the night before, and that morning; it was not fair of him to remind her and put her to the blush. Eyeing him sternly, she said, "Nevertheless, it is not something I can do all the time. It would not be proper. If you will not tell me any other way—and do not deny that you don't put me off, because you do!—then I am left with eavesdropping."

His face grew annoyed again. "I shall tell you when I see fit."

Her hands clutched her reins in anger, and her horse moved uneasily. "I shall be the judge of that. If it concerns your safety, mine, or that of our people, then I should know, and I *shall* find out, one way or another. You might as well tell me everything from the start."

A shuttered look entered his eyes. It was as if he had closed himself off from her, and she felt suddenly alone. Her anger flared again, however: she would not again live in ignorance of what was going on around her. For all that she had loved her uncle as if he had been her own father, she had learned his way of keeping people in ignorance was not necessarily to their benefit. She would not allow it to happen to her again.

"Very well," she said. "You need not tell me. I can do very well on my own." She smiled ironically. "You forget, I have discerned things before, quite accurately. I can do so again."

"Oh?" His voice was skeptical, deliberately so, she believed, because she could see the uneasiness in his eyes. Her anger faded, and she almost smiled. One way or another, she would get her way, because it was the *right* way.

"Indeed." She turned her horse toward Brisbane House, and he turned his alongside hers. "I will not deny I overheard what Mr. Southworthy said, poor man." She paused, thinking of what had been revealed. She had known the vicar lived with his mother, but she had only glimpsed her occasionally, for the woman was very reclusive. Gavin had been very gentle with her, and indeed with Mr. Southworthy. Any other man might have exacted some revenge on the spot, she thought. She suppressed a smile. Her husband was more softhearted than he would probably admit.

"And from it," she continued, "I can conclude that it was probably not Mr. Southworthy or his father who caused my uncle's accident or . . . McKinney's death."

"It may still be our vicar," Gavin said, and his eyes watched her, as if watching for a way to catch her out on her reasoning. "He is still in line for the inheritance. Perhaps he killed McKinney because the groom knew how he had done it."

"No, I think it would most likely be Sir James," she said. "I had thought he tried to disturb our wedding so that he could bring attention to himself—he has done something like that in the past, after all—but it is probably because he does not like the idea that a marriage would mean more trouble for him. I might be breeding, after all."

Gavin gave her a sharp look, and she grinned.

"No, I have no idea if I am, for it has been too short a time. Even *I* know that."

A small smile turned up his lips for a moment, then he sobered. "But you could be, and that puts you in more danger than ever, Diana." He gazed at her, his eyes frustrated. "It was for that reason I did not want to marry you. Unmarried, you would have been no impediment to his succession. You would have been safe."

A sharp shock of fear went through her—she had known it, of course, but to hear Gavin say it made it more real than she had wanted it to be. She swallowed, then lifted her chin. "There is nothing we can do about that now . . . except, I suppose, have Sir James arrested."

Gavin shook his head. "No, there is no evidence; just his presence at your uncle's accident, and his presence at other races that went awry."

"But he must have won a great deal of money at each one," Diana said. "That would be evidence, would it not?"

He shook his head again. "No, for so did others. Anyone might have done it."

Diana thought over the matter, her hands growing tight on

the reins. Her horse stopped and when she loosened the reins began to crop grass. "Well, then, we shall have to trap him," she said slowly. "Yes, perhaps have another race, and see if he does anything." She looked at Gavin. "I could do it. I could be in the race, and then you could—"

"No!" The fury in his voice made his horse shy and it took a moment before he had it under control. "That is the most stupid idea I have ever heard. If I am not mistaken, your uncle tried the same thing, and I would not be surprised if McKinney was involved in the plan as well, which no doubt was precisely why he was killed. He must have found out who it was."

"Ah!" Diana said, and smiled smugly, for she had at last made her husband reveal his thoughts upon the matter.

"Damn!" he said, as realization dawned on his face. He pressed his lips together in frustration. "You are an impossible woman, Diana!"

She grinned. "No, no," she said. "Formidable. You said so, yourself." She quickly shook her reins and her horse came to attention. "And I think my idea is a very good one." She dug her heels into her horse, and it sprang into a gallop.

A curse sounded behind her, and she laughed, for this time she was not the one at the disadvantage. She rode her horse into the stables, and after she handed the horse to the stableboy, she ran into the house, surprising Mr. Goldworthy in conversation with her mother.

She stopped, greeted them politely, and noted her mother's flushed cheeks and sparkling eyes. A glance at Mr. Goldworthy showed his usual cheerful countenance, but whenever he looked at her mother, his gaze softened. The thought occurred to Diana that perhaps her mother liked Mr. Goldworthy very much indeed; she felt odd about it, for she had never thought her mother might have an affection for a man after her father died . . . except for her Uncle Charles. Past images, words, thoughts clicked in Diana's mind, and her eyes widened. Could it be that—

"Diana!" Gavin's voice—a roar, more than a shout. Mr. Goldworthy's brows rose, and Mama's face grew worried.

"Excuse me, sir, and, Mama, but I think I must run," Diana said, chuckling. She picked up her skirts and ran up the stairs to her room, closing the door and locking it.

There! She leaned against the door, hearing his footsteps pound up the stairs, and grinned. She would not let him in—it served him right to be frustrated, for he had frustrated her ever since she had met him, making her work for every bit of information she could get out of him. Well, she could be as stubborn as he.

The doorknob shook as he tried the door, and then the door itself shook when he pounded at it. "Damn it, Diana, you had better not start such a crazy scheme, or you shall be sorry for it, I promise you!"

She merely laughed, which caused more curses. Ah, vengeance was sweet!

Suddenly there was silence, and then the opening and closing of the door to Gavin's bedroom—oh, no, the connecting door! She had never had one before, and had forgotten she had one now. Diana ran to it, and put her shoulder against it, but it was too late. The door was already open, and she was flung away from it from the force of Gavin's push.

He strode to her and caught her as she stumbled, his face stormy. "Forget it," he said, his voice harsh. "Forget that plan, because you will not be involved in it. I did not marry you and save your reputation just to see you killed."

"If I plan carefully, I shall not be killed," she said breathlessly. "It can work if we only do that." She had suggested it flippantly at first, but she began to see it might work now that she thought more about it.

He held her tightly to him, and seized her chin with his hand. He said nothing for a moment, his gaze drilling into her. "You will not. I will not allow it. I do not let go of anything I have in my possession, and you are mine now, Diana. Never forget it." He pressed his mouth hard upon hers, and she clutched his coat, opening her lips. Her heart beat fiercely, savagely, and a breathless, uncontrollable laugh escaped her when his lips went to her throat beneath the hastily opened riding habit. His anger did not frighten her, and she understood that it never had. He had never frightened her, no matter what he did, but she had discovered a wild exhilaration lived in her, and rose to the surface whenever he was near.

"I am only yours when *I* wish it, Gavin," she said, her breath coming in gasps. "You may possess me by law, but nobody will tell me what to do. Nobody possesses me."

He gazed at her with angry, slitted eyes. "You forget. I have been nobody for a long time."

He kissed her again, and she wanted him, and his hands moved over her as quickly as did hers on him. Their clothes fell unheeded on the floor, making a bed for them. His entry was hot and hard, and she moaned and seized his face, kissing him wildly. His movements upon her were insistent, as if he wanted her to give in to him, to say she would not put herself in danger. But she only voiced the melting urgency that rose in her belly and the flash of almost unbearable heat, and said nothing in reply to his harsh groan of completion.

There was stillness except for their breathing, and slowly Gavin rose to his elbows above her and stared at her. She smiled gently, and kissed him again, slowly, sensually. A long sigh came from him, wafting over her lips. Again she kissed him, in case he should want to speak, and he began to touch her again.

He rolled to his side, and then lifted her in his arms, taking her to her bed. This time they loved slowly, his touch gentle and light, and he was long in finishing so that it became slow, pleasurable torture for her.

Perhaps in some way he believed she had given in, Diana thought, as she snuggled into his chest and listened to his even breathing, slowing into sleep. But she would not, for despite his insistence that she not be involved in the racing plan, she could tell from one moment of hesitation on his face when they were out in the fields that he thought the plan itself might have some merit.

Indeed, she would not be surprised if he tried it himself. It would be just the sort of thing he would do, she believed, for he had clearly been a man of risk and had endured hardship in his life. So she had managed to get out of Mr. Goldworthy, bit by bit, during their dinners and during evening gatherings in the drawing room.

But Gavin was the earl, and he should not be the one to risk his life. If he died, and nothing could be proven, then the title and lands would go to Sir James, if she were not already with child. But if she died, it would spare Gavin's life for that much longer, and give him time to find some evidence against Sir James. She moved herself closer to Gavin, as if the press of his flesh against her could make her feel more secure.

She would not die, of course. She would plan it carefully—perhaps with the new groom, Nate Staples. When Gavin let it about that he would be racing against someone else, then Nate would tell her, and she would make sure it was she who would race, not Gavin. She sighed and closed her eyes. Her husband was very stubborn, but he would find she was more so than he.

Gavin woke slowly, opened his eyes, and gazed about the unfamiliar room. A warm softness moved against him—Diana. This was Diana's room. He smiled, remembering their wild loving, very glad he had married her. His mind turned to her words about racing, however, and he frowned. She would not race in that curricle, of course, but her plan did have merit. It was better than waiting for Sir James to make a move. The man still skulked about the village, and had a room at a nearby inn. It was a good thing the wedding had been small, with only Mrs. Carlyle and Ned Goldworthy in attendance. Everyone had made sure that news of Sir James's interruption did not leave the church walls, so there was no further scandal than there already had been, with McKinney's death and the hasty wedding.

If he had a race—perhaps with Lord Jardien, who was known to be an excellent whip—then it would bring Sir James out to wager. He had heard that Sir James could never resist a wager.

Yes, and having Lord Jardien as his opponent would be perfect. The man was the local magistrate, and Gavin had told him all his concerns, and Mr. Goldworthy had told him everything he had found out in London as well. They had only strong suspicions, but firm evidence would ensure that Sir James would be eliminated entirely.

Yes, he should do this immediately—the sooner the better. Gavin moved slowly and reluctantly away from his sleeping wife. He would make sure not to tell her, and would let the stable servants know that whoever would let her know would lose his job. If she found out, it would be too late.

He picked up his clothes that had fallen to the floor and grimaced. Not the way to treat clothes made by Weston himself. His valet would have a small fit, but there was no helping it. Gavin glanced at Diana, still sleeping soundly, and grinned. Really, there was no helping it at all.

The race was easily arranged. Lord Jardien was dubious, but Mr. Goldworthy had thought it would work, especially since they were going to watch Sir James closely. The head groom, Joe Baggins, nodded thoughtfully over their plan, and added a few suggestions of his own. And they all agreed they would not tell Lady Brisbane. Lady Jardien would call upon her and engage her in conversation so that Diana would be occupied, and if she found out about the race, it would be too late for her to involve herself in it.

And yet as Gavin watched his wife eat her supper that evening, he could not help feeling uneasy. She had said nothing more about the racing plan she had thought of, and when he reminded her that she would not pursue it, she had shrugged a shoulder, clearly irritated, and said, "Oh, that!" as if it had been a silly idea she wanted to forget.

Her manner was no different than usual. She smiled at something Mr. Goldworthy said, and then listened intently to some words from her mother. She ate heartily of her meal, her appetite neither more nor less than it usually was. He tapped his fingers on the tabletop as he sipped his wine. Something about her bothered him, however.

She looked up at him at that moment, and smiled at him—there! There was a bland look in her eyes as she smiled, as if she were concealing something. Was she? It could very well be that she was planning to have her own race . . . but no, she could not, for he would know of it. He had ordered the servants to tell him if she were planning any such thing, and they had reported nothing.

Did she plan to interfere with him? He took another sip of wine. Even if she suspected he was racing, she could not know the date or the time of it, not yet, for it had not been announced, only that it would occur. Wagers were being made at little meetings among a few gentlemen at dinners or routs, quickly silenced as ladies passed by—wagered racing was not something talked of in front of the ladies.

No, she could not know, at least not the specifics. He pushed his plate away, and gestured to a footman to take it. Yet, he would not put it past her to find out, one way or another. He wondered if having Lady Jardien call upon her would be enough. His gaze moved to Mrs. Carlyle, and he inserted an innocuous comment into the conversation, for she looked at him questioningly. Perhaps he would ask Mrs. Carlyle to help keep Diana occupied. If he told her it was for her daughter's safety, she would certainly try.

Truth to tell, it would be simpler to tie up Diana and be done with it, but he was sure she would find some way of escape. Further, Mrs. Carlyle would also find out about it, and though she was a delicate and gentle lady, he had little doubt she could be moved to ferocity when it came to her daughter's welfare. He would prefer to spend his energies apprehending Sir James than to waste them on arguing. Better that he enlist Mrs. Carlyle's aid than bring her displeasure upon him.

The company at last rose from the table, and because their number was small, Mrs. Carlyle suggested they remove themselves to the drawing room after refreshing themselves. Gavin repressed a grin as Ned Goldworthy agreed with alacrity; his friend was very taken with Mrs. Carlyle, and after her mourning was over might just begin to court her. He suspected that she had been very much in love with the late Lord Brisbane if not actually his lover; her grief had been that of a wife, not a sister-in-law. Whatever the case, she had been very discreet; he doubted even Diana was aware of it.

A good attribute, especially since he would have to depend on her discretion soon. He went up to his room, and could hear Diana move about in hers, and almost went to her to warn her not to interfere with him again. But it would not be wise; best to pretend the assumption she would be a meek wife even though he knew she would not be. She would think him satisfied with her demeanor, and so she would not be as much on her guard.

Gavin grinned. No, she would never be a meek wife, and though it was troublesome, he preferred her as she was, wild and strong, and even, at certain times—his grin grew wider—savage. He would never be bored with her, and would never tire of looking at her and conversing with her. She had the veneer and discipline of a gentlewoman over the heart of a lioness, and he found the combination irresistible.

He exited his room at the same time Diana did hers, and she put her hand upon his arm. She was silent beside him, and cast him a look, clearly speculative. He kept himself from smiling. Yes, she was planning something, most possibly concerning the race, and he would be certain to thwart her. It was for her own safety; he could not do otherwise.

They parted once they entered the drawing room, and Gavin made sure he moved toward Mrs. Carlyle before Diana could. He saw his wife shrug slightly, then smile and begin to talk to Mr. Goldworthy.

"Mrs. Carlyle," he said, then hesitated, as if uncertain. She looked at him questioningly. "Madam, I was wondering if you could help me."

She smiled. "But of course, Gavin."

"I think—and I hope I do not offend—that we can say Diana is . . . headstrong?"

Mrs. Carlyle laughed. "Yes, I think we can definitely say that. She has been so since an infant, and more so after we left London." She shook her head. "After all the constraints under which we lived there, I could not find it in my heart to restrain her any more than necessary, and I am afraid she is sometimes not as ladylike as she could be." A shadow flitted over her face, and she sighed.

"She told me," he said simply.

She looked at him, her face paling. "I was not sure . . . I thought she might confide in you."

"You had a difficult time of it. It must have been terrifying for you."

Tears formed in the lady's eyes, but she swallowed and lifted her chin, a gesture very like Diana's. "She was very brave, though I know she was frightened. I was very ill—not an excuse, I know—"

He took her hand and pressed it. "Madam, you did all you could, and kept her safe until your brother-in-law arrived."

She swallowed again. "Not safe enough."

"Enough," he said. "She was, and is, without doubt the most flawlessly beautiful woman I have ever met."

Mrs. Carlyle gazed for a long moment at him, as if thinking over his words, then sighed. "Safe enough, then. I am glad." She gazed at him and nodded wisely. "I knew you would understand. I told her you were the most listening sort of man I have ever met."

Surprise made him raise his brows. He had not thought of himself in those terms, but he supposed he was. He had to be in his line of work, to gather the information he needed to accomplish his goals.

"Why, thank you, ma'am," he said, and grinned. "I am very flattered."

"You are welcome," Mrs. Carlyle said, smiling slightly. "I am glad Diana married you. She needs someone to listen to her."

He nodded, and reflected that perhaps this was true. In that way, Diana was like himself, reluctant to reveal herself, so as to keep herself invulnerable. But he said, "Alas, if only she would listen to *me.*"

"How so?" she asked.

He hesitated, gauging his words carefully. "I have, with Lord Jardien and Mr. Goldworthy, been investigating the unfortunate death upon this property."

Her eyes widened, and she shuddered. "So Mr. Goldworthy has told me."

Gavin mentally hoped that it was all his garrulous friend had told her. "But your daughter believes she can help in this matter. Perhaps she can," he said, keeping his voice reasonable. "However, I would prefer she be safe and stay away from whatever activities in which we may involve ourselves." He smiled at her. "I love her, you know. I would not want her to come to any harm."

Mrs. Carlyle visibly melted, and she clasped his hand tightly. "Of course, Gavin! I will do whatever I can to help you, especially if it concerns her safety."

He sighed, as if with relief. "Thank you. I knew I could depend on you. If you could, tomorrow, keep her occupied around the noon hour, I would be most grateful. Lady Jardien will call upon you before then, I believe, as her husband has instructed her."

She nodded. "Very good," she said. "We can have a luncheon, and I will be sure that Diana will not leave. She cannot, especially in front of Lady Jardien, for she dare not be so rude after the near-scandal at the musicale."

"An excellent scheme," Gavin replied. He smiled, rising, and bowed slightly. "I thank you." There, he thought. For all that Diana was headstrong, she clearly loved her mother, and would not want to displease her or disgrace herself in front of her or Lady Jardien. Indeed, he had seen more than a few times Mrs. Carlyle's stern but loving eye stop Diana before she spoke words she would regret or before she took foolhardy action.

And yet, as he looked at his wife's cheerful face and caught again another bland smile, he could not help thinking he should make sure she was better watched. He would put one of the grooms to the duty, if she ventured near the stables. If she proved troublesome, he would have no hesitation tying her to a hay bale if he had to. Better that than risk her life in a carriage accident.

Chapter 15

Gavin did not linger in her bed the next morning as he had in days past, Diana noted. He sometimes liked to caress her as she slept, so that at the moment of waking she was ready for him. So he had done this time, but he moved from her after they were done, sooner than before, and his movements as he prepared himself for the day were preoccupied.

It was today, then, she thought. He would have the race today. Or, if not, she would not be amiss to watch the stables anyway. If there was any more activity than before, that would tell her, to be sure.

"I am going for my morning ride, Gavin. Would you like to accompany me?" she called to the other room. She rang for her maid, and opened her wardrobe, thinking perhaps she should order another riding dress. Black, of course, for she was still in mourning, but her old one was beginning to fray at the sleeves.

"I am afraid I cannot—I have business to conduct with Mr. Goldworthy," he replied. He was at the threshold of their connecting door, gazing at her in his lazy way. She knew well by now that his habitual expression was deceptive, and she could not always depend on discerning his intent from it. "However, I would be pleased if you had one of the undergrooms or stableboys accompany you on your ride."

"Of course," she said. "I know Sir James is still about, and am not so foolish to risk my life should he decide to wager it for anything." She shrugged, and could not help glancing at her husband to see what his reaction would be.

He nodded, seeming to accept her words, and she suppressed a smile. In a way, it was good that they had not known each other long; he could not always guess from her expression or from her ways what she might do, and in this case, it was very convenient. She did not want him to guess.

"I suppose I shall ask . . . Will Smith," she said. Poor Will was probably the least intelligent boy in the stables; he would no doubt be easy to convince that her actions would be in Gavin's best interests.

"No, I will request that Nate Staples accompany you," Gavin said firmly.

Diana hesitated—Nate would be more difficult to convince. No matter, he was new to the stables and valued his position. She could convince him. "Oh, very well!" she made herself say in a pettish voice and turned away to hide her smile.

She felt his arms come around her from behind. "My love, I know you want to help trap Sir James, but I cannot allow it." He pushed her hair away from the nape of her neck and kissed her there. "I would willingly die to keep you from harm."

But it is not your place to do so, Diana thought. *You are the Earl of Brisbane. You have a name and a heritage to maintain.* But she did not say it, for she knew he would not listen. Instead, she turned in his arms, gazing steadily into his eyes. She moved her hands beneath his robe, sliding them across his chest, around to his back and below, and watched his eyes grow hot.

"I know," she said, and kissed him. "But I prefer you very much alive."

"Witch," he murmured, his hand cradling her head as he deepened their kiss.

A knock made them part, and Diana grinned to hear a muttered curse from her husband as he went to his own room when she called in the maid. It was his own fault; he had taught her how to tease and seduce, and it served him right that she turn the tables on him.

She dressed and had a brief breakfast, and then went to the stables, watching the grooms and the stableboys carefully.

They went about their business as usual, talking of ordinary things. But there was an undercurrent of excitement, and it confirmed her notion that this indeed was the day. Her stomach grew leaden—today was the day Gavin might die, if she did not stop him from racing. Fierce determination made her hands ball into fists. She would not let it happen. The image of her uncle's carriage accident came to her, except Gavin's bloodied face was there instead. Her heart twisted in pain, almost making her gasp. No, she would not let it happen. She loved him, more than her own life, she knew that now. He had said he had loved her on first sight; even though she had thought she had not in return, she knew it was because she had been blind. He was her other half; their natures were alike as the twin get of a wolf: fierce and hot and cunning. She would never tire of loving him, arguing with him, or even—she smiled abruptly—holding him down until he told her what she wanted to know.

She gestured to Nate Staples, telling him that he was to accompany her, and he grinned as he obediently saddled her horse, then brought another for his use.

They had ridden into the fields and over a stile, when Diana slowed her horse and turned to the stableboy. "Nate . . . the race Lord Brisbane is to have is today, is it not?"

The youth hesitated. "I can't say, my lady."

She smiled at him. "But of course it is. Have I not supervised the stables since my uncle's time? Naturally I would know of these things." She glanced at the sun above. "I imagine it will happen"—she chose a probable time—"around noon." It would give plenty of time for the staff to ready the curricle for a race, and it was approximately the same time her uncle had had his.

The stableboy's alarmed expression confirmed it.

"Noon, then," she said. She gazed at Nate, and there was no need to make her expression grave, for the danger Gavin was risking almost made her choke. But she made herself continue. "Nate . . . can I trust you?"

The youth nodded firmly. "Yes, my lady."

"His lordship is in very great danger," she said, and allowed the trembling she felt to come into her voice.

" 'E can 'andle the coach, my lady, I've seen 'im—" He stopped abruptly, realizing what he had revealed.

She smiled kindly at him. "Don't worry, Nate. I know all about it." She did know now, of course. The stableboy looked relieved. "Of course I know he is a good whip, even a superior one. I am not afraid of that," she said.

"But . . ." she hesitated. "You will not tell anyone of this, will you?"

The youth shook his head.

"Good." She gazed at him and let out a little sob—real, for the thought of Gavin coming to harm frightened her as nothing else did. "I will tell you then: there is a man who is trying to kill my husband."

"Cor!" Nate's eyes widened.

"It's true," she said urgently. "He will strike during the race, or possibly before it. We cannot let it happen." She held out her hand to him, then let it drop in a helpless manner she would normally despise. "I need your help, Nate. We must save Lord Brisbane." She looked at him earnestly. "We must keep him from driving in the race."

Nate looked dubious. " 'Is lordship said as 'ow you might put a stick in 'is spokes—"

Diana put a wounded expression on her face.

"—Not to 'urt 'im, my lady!" he said, looking alarmed. "Just that you wouldn't like 'im to drive yer curricle."

"It isn't that, Nate, it *isn't*." She hesitated, thinking of how much she should reveal. "You remember what happened to McKinney, don't you?"

He shuddered. "Aye, my lady."

"The same man means to kill his lordship. Indeed, he killed my uncle, too. You *must* see I cannot have it happen."

"No, my lady."

"Then you must help me. Indeed, you may even help me catch the villain."

The stableboy stared at her indecisively for a few minutes,

and Diana itched to shake him to make him do as she wished. He nodded firmly. "Aye, I'll 'elp you."

"Thank you, Nate." She smiled, relieved, at him. "I am very grateful. I shall make sure you are well-rewarded."

They continued to ride their horses at a walk, and Diana told him of her plans, and was pleased to see the youth enter into them with enthusiasm. He was thin, but he was sturdy, and she was sure that between the two of them, they could keep Gavin safe.

The earl walked to the carriage house, careful to look about him to see that Diana was not following him. He had seen her go out with the stableboy as escort, but he would not put it past her to trick the youth and escape to cause him mischief. He greeted the grooms as he passed them, then saw an unfamiliar face.

"You—what's your name?" he called out.

The youth glanced at him, surprised. He looked familiar, but Gavin could not place him . . . ah, he had a resemblance to Nate Staples, except he had brown hair instead of yellow, and his eyes were red-rimmed, as if he lacked sleep.

"Bob Staples, my lord," he said. "I worked 'ere summat, but me blinkers got bad when the old lord—" He stopped, his face growing worried. "Beggin' yer pardon, yer lordship. I wisht I coulda been 'ere to do my duty, but I did send me cousin Nate, and he's a trusty lad, and I thought it'd do no 'arm."

Gavin nodded. "You did well, and if it was some illness, I would not have wanted you to pass it along to any of my other servants."

The youth scratched his head, clearly puzzled. "Warn't sick, yer lordship—got summat in me eyes when I was cleaning the harness after the race. 'Twas like fire, like the time me mum's pepper got in me face."

Gavin had begun to turn toward the carriage house again, but Bob's words stopped him. It was a little thing . . . of course there might be some new material used to clean harnesses and such that could be caustic in some way. But he had never heard of it, and oil would not hurt anyone's eyes.

"What were you using to clean them?" he asked.

The youth looked anxious. "Neatsfoot oil, yer lordship. McKinney always said to use it."

"Nothing else?"

"No, yer lordship."

Gavin stared hard at him until the stableboy almost wilted where he stood. "Which of the parts were you cleaning?" he asked finally.

"I dunno—I was cleaning all of them—'twas a long time ago." Bob Staples paused, looking almost ill. "Did I do wrong?" he asked in a whisper.

"No," Gavin replied. "No, you did not." He fished in his pocket for a shilling and tossed it to him. "Indeed, I think you may have helped me a great deal."

The youth caught the coin and breathed a large sigh of relief. "I'm that glad, yer lordship," he said, and hurried away.

Gavin strode to the carriage house, then gazed at the curricle. It was a sleek machine, shiny after its repair. He had driven this one before from time to time, for Diana had grudgingly agreed that he was competent enough to handle it. He smiled slightly. She was very possessive of it, and he could not blame her; anyone would be, who owned such a carriage.

The curricle was faultless, and had been, even when the late Lord Brisbane had driven it. Something had been done to the harness, or some part of it, and it had affected the horses in such a way that they had gone mad with pain. But how had it been done, so that it occurred later, and not as soon as the equipment had been put on the horses?

He sighed, and the sound echoed in the quiet around him. He supposed he would find out, soon. He had ordered the head groom to keep a good eye on Sir James, but keep his distance, and not do anything until the race was off. Whatever the substance that had been put on the harness, it had not taken effect until about thirty minutes had gone by in the race. He had calculated about where in the course it would be; he would slow the horses about that time, and as soon as there were any signs of discomfort in them, he would leap from the carriage and—he hoped—his fall would be cushioned by the haystacks he had ordered put along the way.

Well, it was nearing time to prepare for the race. He would—

A shove, and the floor of the carriage house came up to slam the air from his lungs. A weight sat upon his back, making it even more difficult to catch his breath again.

"I am sorry, my love," came Diana's voice. "But I cannot let you drive my curricle."

He struggled under her, cursing, then felt cloth come over his mouth, muffling him. His head jerked back as it was tied behind his head. He twisted his body, but another weight came down upon his legs.

"That's right, Nate," Diana said. "Hold him down, will you?" Gavin could feel a rope come around his ankles, tying them tightly together.

"I don't like it, yer ladyship," Nate said. " 'Tis his lordship, after all."

"It's to save his *life,* Nate!" she replied. "He'll be grateful to you in the end, depend upon it."

Curses sputtered against the cloth between Gavin's teeth, and he twisted under them again. God help him, the woman must be a sorceress. How she had convinced the stableboy against his express wishes—He would not let her get away with this—

"Right you are, yer ladyship," Nate said, his voice sounding dubious nevertheless. " 'Is 'ands next?"

"Very good!" Diana said approvingly. "I know he will be difficult about it, but we must be firm!"

Gavin clenched his hands and tried to move his arms away from his sides, fighting the rope that looped around one then another wrist, but it did no good; his wife had apparently planned the whole attack very carefully. His wrists were drawn tightly behind his back, and at last the weight on him came off.

He managed to turn on his side, and glared at Diana. Her face was flushed with the effort of tying him up, but her eyes were triumphant.

"I am sorry, Gavin," she said again, and her expression became regretful. "But I cannot let you risk your life. You are the Earl of Brisbane. If you die, and nothing can be proved against—against the villain, then he will inherit the title. You owe it to your heritage to live." She bent and kissed his cheek. "And I would surely die of grief if you were no longer with me. I do not think I could bear it."

He could see tears form in her eyes, and he groaned. *Don't do this, Diana, dear God, don't do this.*

She turned to Nate Staples. "Now, we must hide him. We cannot risk the chance that the villain will find him helpless here and kill him."

Gavin struggled and did all he could to thwart them, but a combination of dragging and rolling put him into a storage closet near the harness rack. The door closed, and he was in complete darkness.

Almost—the closet was roughly made, and there were chinks between the wooden boards. He could see Diana and the stableboy through one large hole as she passed the rack.

"There, we have done it," she said. "Now, I shall take his lordship's place in the race."

"But you said—" Nate protested.

She eyed him sternly. "The race is a matter of honor, and must continue. Besides, we cannot catch the villain if it does not go on—if the horses do not react as I believe they will during the race, then we have nothing with which to accuse the villain."

Nate shook his head. "I can't think 'tis right, yer ladyship."

"It will be, Nate, you shall see." With a confident smile, she patted his arm and walked out of the carriage house, the stableboy following reluctantly behind her.

Gavin groaned again. Damn the woman! He had to get out of here as quickly as possible, before she ventured out on the curricle. He twisted his hands to his side and brought his knees to his chin, trying to reach a finger to his boot. He had slipped in his dagger in its sheath, his usual precaution, and he was once again glad his experiences had taught him not to be a complete gentleman.

His fingers could not quite reach it. He tipped back his head, taking a deep breath and resting a moment. Perhaps he could get his arms around to the front of him somehow.

He hunched his body down, twisting his wrists in their bonds until they were wet with sweat or blood . . . and the bonds loosened a little. He took another deep breath.

And held it. A movement through the crack between the boards caught his eye, and he peered through it.

Sir James. Gavin slowly, quietly, let out his breath and stayed very, very still.

The man looked about him and stepped toward the harness. He patted his pocket, then reached in, drawing out what looked like a vial. Another search in his pocket brought out a yellow strip, which he briefly rubbed between his fingers—beeswax, Gavin thought. Sir James unstopped the vial, shaking something out of it onto the strip.

He lifted his head suddenly. Gavin held his breath, careful to make no noise or sound. Sir James relaxed, and turned to the harness on the rack. His hand hovered above the leather pieces, then pounced on one of them.

The crupper. Of course. Gavin watched as the man smoothed the beeswax on the inner, cushioned side of the crupper's loop, then put it down again. Quickly he stoppered the vial and put it and the remaining wax into his pocket, looked about him again, then left, quickly, his steps a mere whisper.

Gavin closed his eyes, resting his head against the side of the closet. It made sense. No one would think to look at the crupper; it was always cleaned after every use, and presumed to be ready whenever it was needed. The crupper would be looped under the horse's tail, and the beeswax would hold firm until the heat of exercise melted the wax, releasing whatever caustic substance was under it.

That was why the horses acted no differently than usual before the race or at the very beginning. It would take a good thirty minutes of exercise on a cool spring day to soften the wax enough for the substance—pepper or the oil extract of it—to come to the surface, causing acute pain, even blistering under the horse's tail. The horse would go wild with pain, become uncontrollable, no matter the skill or the strength of the driver.

But this was not spring, but summer, and the race would occur at noon. It would not be thirty minutes into the race, but sooner, and the stacks of hay along the road would do no one—Diana—any good.

Gavin desperately twisted his hands and pulled at the rope behind him. The bonds loosened again, a little. He glimpsed the grooms talking and laughing as they entered the carriage house, taking the harness off the rack and pulling the curricle from its stall a little, the better to attach the equipment. He tried to call out, but the muffled sounds were drowned under the rumble of wheels, the noise of conversation, and the clop of horses' hooves. His feet could not kick hard enough at the closet's wooden boards to make enough sound to be heard over it all. The grooms were fast and efficient: it was a matter of minutes before they had the horses hitched and led them and the curricle out of the carriage house.

Again he pulled, and the bonds loosened much more, enough so that he could move his arms down his sides, slowly, much too slowly. At last his hands were before him. His fingers touched inside his boot and slipped upon the hilt of the dagger—they were no doubt slick with blood, for his wrists stung and his palms felt wet.

He seized the dagger, and cut the rope around his ankles, and then between his hands. He stood, and almost stumbled, for his legs sizzled from being cramped, but he took firm hold of the cloth around his mouth, and ripped it off.

The door of the storage closet flew open with a bang, startling an undergroom. Rage and fear boiled within the earl at the thought of the danger Diana was bringing upon herself, but he forced himself to summon cool strategy as well.

Gavin caught the gaze of the groom before him and stared at him grimly. "Tell Lord Jardien to arrest Sir James."

"What—my lord—" stammered the groom. "His lordship has already gone on the race—"

Lord Brisbane let out a foul curse. "Then tell Mr. Goldworthy, damn your eyes! And get me a horse. A fast one. Now!"

Chapter 16

Diana ignored the stunned expression on the head groom's face, and tried not to look at Mr. Goldworthy as she tooled the curricle out into the stableyard and down the road to the entrance gates where the race was to begin. Lord Jardien was waiting there in a fine curricle of his own, a pair of fresh grays moving restlessly in front. Groups of sportsmen and spectators lined the road as she neared the gate, and she could feel every eye on her.

Some faces were angry, some were speculative, some amused, and some gazed at her as if she were some freak in a raree show. A familiar shaking threatened to take her, but she forcefully banished it, raising her head high. She could not afford to be anxious about how they looked at her, for her horses would sense her anxiety, and that was dangerous in this already dangerous situation. She could not care about scandal—and what she was doing was scandalous in the extreme, for no lady raced in public—for her husband's life was at stake. If they did not flush out Sir James this time, he would be free to strike again, and no doubt more directly than he had been.

"What's the meaning of this?" Lord Jardien demanded. "I was to race with your husband, not you!" Murmurs of agreement rose around them.

Diana stiffened her back, and raised her chin. She glimpsed Mr. Goldworthy hurrying up to them, a worried look in his eyes. "My husband is indisposed," she said, and stared Lord Jardien hard in the eyes. "I am taking his place. As my neighbors know, I am more than capable of handling this carriage and these horses, possibly"—she cast a roguish grin at the spectators around her—"possibly better than Lord Brisbane." She would prefer not to sacrifice Gavin's dignity in this manner, but if it meant the race would go on, and evidence found against Sir James, she would do it. Some gentlemen chuckled; she saw some money change hands, and took heart from their good humor.

"Lass, you shouldn't do this." Mr. Goldworthy stood at the side of the curricle, his usually cheerful face worried. "Gavin's got a temper on him, and he won't like this once he finds out." A puzzled look came over his face. "Eh, but I can't understand what's to do with him. The lad was in good frame this morning."

"You need not worry," Diana said cheerfully. "He is quite safe."

A look of dawning horror and suspicion came over Mr. Goldworthy's face. "Eh, never say you—"

"It was necessary to keep him safe," Diana said, bending down to him and speaking in a low voice. "He is the earl. If anything happens to him, then the title will go to that . . . that *villain.* It is wrong for him to have it, you know it is. If anything happens to me, Gavin may marry again, but he will still be earl. He must be." She jerked her head at Lord Jardien. "Tell him."

Mr. Goldworthy nodded reluctantly and went to Lord Jardien, and Diana watched as her neighbor leaned down and discussed the matter with him.

Lord Jardien rose and gazed, frustrated, at her. "We could race tomorrow, when Lord Brisbane is not indisposed."

Diana laughed. "I am not so ignorant, my lord. I will not let you win by default." Murmurs of agreement rose around her.

"Let her drive!" cried a voice from the crowd.

"Yes, let her race!" cried another, and yet another. More money changed hands, and she gazed at Lord Jardien triumphantly.

His gaze grew more angry, then he nodded sharply. "Very well!" he said, and moved his carriage to the gate. Diana sighed with relief and did likewise.

Silence descended upon the groups of men around them, and only the sounds of the restless stamping of horses' hooves, the jangle of harness links, and the hard beating of her heart reached Diana's ears. Mr. Goldworthy strode in front of them, a large white handkerchief in his hand. He looked at his watch, and Diana glanced at the one pinned to her bosom. Twenty minutes—she would be safe, and not even wait until thirty—and she would stop the horses and leave her carriage. She was no fool and did not intend to be killed. She pulled her veil over her face; the road was dry, and the dust kicked up from the race would be thick. Her heart beat harder, anticipating the swift beat of hooves on the road in just a few seconds.

The handkerchief dropped from Mr. Goldworthy's hand. Diana slackened the reins, gently touched her whip to the horses' backs, and grinned as they leaped into a gallop.

Lord Jardien's carriage was beside her, and she restrained the urge to race ahead of him—she could do it, for her horses were fresh and strong and they could outrun his easily. But she needed to pace them, and make sure that she timed her arrival exactly at the haystacks Nate had said her husband had set up at the side of the road.

She wished this were a real race, and that she could enjoy it more, for the sun was hot on her veiled face, and a cool breeze wafted over her forehead, cooling the perspiration that beaded there. But she could feel the bands of tension in her arms and her shoulders, and the dryness in her mouth at the thought that in a few moments, she might—if she were not alert and careful—she might just die.

A quick look at her watch—only five minutes! It seemed like hours had gone by, though she knew it could not be so. She glanced at Lord Jardien. His face was a study of concentration, but a short glance from him in return showed he was still angry. No matter; she would deal with that later.

One horse in front of her tossed its head restlessly, and she frowned. No, it could not be so soon, it was only past five minutes. Her hands pricked with sweat under her leather gloves. She must be in control. She could not let nerves overcome her.

A shout behind her almost made Diana turn her head, but she kept her eyes ahead of her. She could not let herself be distracted. But a glance to the side of her showed that Lord Jardien's carriage had fallen behind. What was he thinking of? Surely he knew he must keep up with her?

But a thunder of hooves—not from two horses abreast, but a single horse—came up faster behind her, and at last she glanced slightly behind.

Gavin! Anger flared, and she touched the whip once more on her horses' backs. How had he released himself? She had been sure that no one would hear him, not with all the noise of preparation going on around him. An image of the dagger he had used on her bindings the night of their wedding came before her, and she ground her teeth in frustration. He must have had it hidden somewhere on his person.

He came up to the side of the carriage at last. "Stop, Diana!" he shouted.

"No! It is not yet time!" She glanced at him—he rode Lightning! How dare he! She gently flicked the whip again, and the horses went a little faster.

"Stop, damn you, woman!" he shouted again. "It *is* time—the stuff is on the crupper—the summer heat—stop, now!"

But it was too late. A high scream came from the horse in front of her, and the reins almost pulled her arm from its socket. She pulled hard on the reins, ignoring the pain, but the second horse caught the fear from the other and would not heed her strength. The curricle went faster.

"Drop the reins, Diana! Now!"

She could not—she had to keep the horses in control. A flash of memory: her uncle's accident, the horses, the gunshot. They would die if she did not keep control.

"Drop them, and jump to me. God, Diana, do it now!"

She glanced to her side—Gavin's face, the familiar lazy expression fled, an agonized look on it instead, his hand extended to her. *I would willingly die to keep you from harm.* He had said that, this morning. She gazed at Gavin again—his eyes stared into hers. He would die if she died, for they were one soul. His heart told her this, his heart that shone in his despairing eyes, here, now.

Now. She dropped the reins and grasped his hand, and he pulled her off the carriage. Her hip hit a corner of it, painfully, then slapped the side of his saddle as his arm came around her waist. A crash and frightened neighs sounded in the distance, and Diana groaned, pressing her face into his shoulder. Lightning came to a halt and shied, almost making her drop from Gavin's grasp.

"Stop it!" came her and Gavin's voice at the same time, and the horse settled down, almost sheepishly. He released her, and she slipped to the grass, and he, also, dismounted.

"Gavin, I—" she began, but his mouth stopped her. His lips were hard on hers, his fingers digging into her shoulders. Just as abruptly he parted from her, glaring into her eyes.

"You idiot. You stupid little idiot."

"I am not, I planned it carefully—" She could not look at him, and she looked away. But her eyes caught sight of his hands, and she gasped, and felt her heart twist painfully. "Oh, Gavin—your hands—your wrists—they are bleeding! It must have been the ropes—Oh, I am so sorry!" She seized his hand and kissed it, smoothing away his shirt cuff from his wrists so that it would not stick to the raw flesh there.

"You could have been *killed*." His hand seized her chin and forced it up. The despair she had seen in his eyes moments ago appeared again, and he kissed her once more, more gently. "You will never do this again, for by God, I'll whip you within an inch of your life if you do," he whispered against her lips.

"No, you won't," she said, and kissed him in return. "You told me just this morning you would willingly die before you let me come to harm, and I know you are not a liar."

A laugh burst from him, and he pulled her to him tightly.

"You are a witch, Diana. A sorceress. And you know me too damned well."

She rubbed her cheek on his chest, then the thunder of hooves made her jerk up her head. It was the head groom, Joe Baggins, and beside him, Nate Staples, who looked very sheepish.

"The carriage has crashed farther down the road," Gavin said. "I have heard no further sounds from the horses—I hope they may be. unharmed."

"Yes, my lord," Joe replied, and turned to Nate. "You, boy, ride back to the stables and direct the men down the road to me." Nate nodded and rode off, while Joe continued down the road.

The conversation between the men made the full force of what had happened hit Diana like a storm. She swallowed, but the trembling would not go away, and a small moan escaped her.

"We must go back," she said, and her voice shook. "Sir James . . . and then the poor horses—"

"We will go home," Gavin said, and stroked her back soothingly. "Ned and Lord Jardien will have caught Sir James by this time. I told Ned to hold him, and to search his pockets. It was very clever, actually. I saw Sir James put a caustic substance—possibly pepper oil or the like—on a piece of soft wax and seal it to the inside of the crupper." His voice grew grim. "But unlike your uncle's race in the springtime, it is summer now, and the melting occurred faster."

Diana shuddered again, then sighed as his stroking continued. "But the poor horses . . . I should attend to them."

"No," he said, and led her to the gelding. "The servants shall do it. You have trained them well; I have every confidence in them." His voice became gentle. "You need not go through that again. Once is enough." He mounted, then held out his hand to her. She gazed into his eyes, and a sudden release of tension made her unwilling to resist his command. She felt suddenly bone weary, and her shoulder ached, and all she really wanted was to go home. "Come, my love," he said.

She grasped his hand, and hoisted herself up behind him, then put her arms around his waist. She sighed and closed her eyes, and rested her cheek on his back. "I do love you, Gavin," she said. "I was so very wrong when I thought you were just a fribble, a silly dandy concerned with nothing but his clothes. You are not like that at all."

"I am glad you now think otherwise, for you are quite right," he said, and kicked the horse gradually from a walk, to a trot, and then to a canter. "I am concerned about my boots as well as my clothes. I think those ropes scratched them, and they have lost their shine." He extended one foot away from the side of the horse, and peered down at it. "Yes, I do believe I see a large scratch. Alas! My valet will have an apoplexy, and then what shall I do? My consequence as the Earl of Brisbane will suffer, I am sure of it, if my valet expires of an apoplexy. Think of the scandal!"

Diana laughed, then sobered. "It shall not matter, for we are sunk in scandal already. Oh, Gavin, I know I have only made it worse by racing in public. But I could not bear the thought of you risking your life, dying like my uncle did. I would willingly have died to prevent it." The horse slowed, then stopped, and she looked up to see that they were home at last.

Shouting and the sounds of struggle caught her attention, and Diana could see Sir James in Lord Jardien's and Mr. Goldworthy's grasp. Sir James's hands were tied, and his eyes were filled with fear and anger, but she felt no pity for him; he had killed her uncle, had no doubt killed McKinney, and had tried to kill Gavin. He deserved no pity.

Fury shook her, and she dismounted, barely noticing that Gavin had dismounted and handed the reins of the horse to the stableboy. But a hand on her arm slowed her steps toward Sir James, so that they approached the man together.

"No, Diana. The law will deal with him. I daresay justice will be quite swift and quite deadly." His voice was easy and conversational, but his gaze upon Sir James was icy, and the man paled.

"A wager . . . I only wished to win. . . . I had to win. . . ." Sir James said, his voice a whine.

A low growl came from Mr. Goldworthy, and Lord Jardien looked at the prisoner with disbelief.

The earl's lip curled in disgust. "You wagered poorly, and lost this time. You lost even more upon McKinney's death. I imagine whatever money you won will do you no good from now on."

Diana looked up at Gavin, and his expression softened and warmed when he turned his eyes to her. "Come, my love, it is finished here." He took her hand.

She knew he was right, but residual anger made her pull away. "He killed my uncle—"

"And if the law does not adequately deal with him, then I shall make sure we do," Gavin said calmly, and took her hand again.

"Oh, really?" Diana gazed at him skeptically, but she let him lead her away toward the house.

"But of course." His lips twitched upward. "I shall build a dungeon and we shall spirit him away from his too-lenient jailors. Then we will chain him in a very dark cell and fling hot irons at him."

An unwilling spurt of laughter escaped her. "I shall enjoy that," she said, then sobered as she looked once more at Sir James. "There has been so much death and destruction, Gavin."

He took her hands and smiled at her. Her breath caught at the heat and love in his eyes as he raised her hands to his lips.

"My love, try not to dwell on it. There are better things to think of now that Sir James is caught and will be dealt with." He opened the door, and stepped in.

Diana let him take her into the house, for she ached and was tired, and had no energy left to argue. Her mother was there in the hall, looking at once anxious and relieved and seemed about to speak, but Gavin held up his hand to her and shook his head, smiling. She looked at both of them, smiled widely, and a distinct giggle came from her as she left to go into the drawing room. Diana blushed, but let him take her up the stairs to their chambers. "Other things? Such as?" she said, her voice unsteady.

"Scandal," he replied. "I think we should cause more of it."

She choked, barely restraining her laughter. He pushed open the door of her room, and pulled the bell rope. "Oh?" she managed to say. "How so?"

A maid appeared, gazing at them round-eyed, and Gavin bent to whisper something in her ear. She blushed hotly, then grinned, and ran out of the room.

"First, we shall bathe—together," he said, and began unbuttoning her riding habit. Diana thought of the prospect and her breath came quickly. He kissed her, long and slowly, then parted from her to pull down one shoulder of her dress. "And then I shall lay you on my bed. I will rub the aches away from your shoulders and back. Then . . ." Mischief gleamed in his eyes. "What if I turned you over and took a bowl of sliced strawberries and cream and placed the strawberries all over your—"

"Gavin!" she cried, scandalized. "*Strawberries?* For heaven's sake! I cannot help thinking it would be horribly messy, and what would the servants think?"

"I imagine it would be very messy," he replied, grinning and apparently contemplating the idea with decided pleasure. "We can always take another bath afterward, but not before I—"

"You are a terrible tease!" Diana exclaimed, putting her hand over his mouth, for some servants had entered with some bath implements, and the maid had returned with jugs of hot water.

He took her hand and kissed it. "But I told you I wanted to create more scandal, did I not?" he said, and kissed her again. Diana sighed. She could not help herself. She returned his kiss with all the love she had in her heart, completely heedless of the departing servants, and certain she would want to cause scandal with Gavin for the rest of her life.